Canalside Tale

John H. Grandits

<<<>>>

Canalside Tale

No Frills
<<<>>>
Buffalo
Buffalo, NY

No Frills Buffalo Press
119 Dorchester Buffalo, New York 14213
For more information visit
Nofrillsbuffalo.com

To my wonderful Irish-American mother. And to all my immigrant forebears who struggled to make their place in this land.

I

Blinking open his crusty eyes, he was anxious to embrace his woman as she helped him with his boots. Yet, as he shook off the last traces of sleep, he looked down to see a persistent wharf rat tugging at his laces, no doubt attracted to the stench of the whiskey that had spilled onto his feet the night before. Letting out a ferocious oath, he leapt up and sent the squealing vermin sailing off into a dark corner of the alley.

By now he was shaking with rage, not so much the result of his encounter with one of the countless furry denizens of Canal Street, but by the shame of finding himself in such a humiliating and helpless position. Men like Danny "Brick Fist" Doyle, first sergeant of the city police department, never allowed themselves to be left vulnerable. After dusting to off the stinking grit left by his cobblestone mattress, he kicked aside the mounds of rubbish and barreled his way through the back door.

The scent of perfume filling the hallway reminded him of the shaky condition of his stomach, and the continuing price of his nighttime misadventure. After making his way to a room at the far end, he spotted the middle-aged proprietress of Egan's Boarding House, otherwise known as Big Tits Kate's, calmly fixing her morning tea.

"Who the fuck shanghaied me! I'll crush 'em!" Just then, he remembered to check his money clip, which appeared to be intact.

"Keep your knickers on, Danny; you don't look too worse for wear."

"Where's Cat, she did this!"

"Cat? I wasn't gonna waste her on you last night! No, it was Rolly Molly. After you passed out fumblin' with your sheath, she tried to move ya on, but you stumbled off half-cocked," she chuckled, "and flipped over the porch railing. She checked; you were fine." With that, she grabbed his chin and turned his face before giving a nod of approval, "Yeah, no scars, you're still a handsome lad, with your wavy black hair and bluebonnet eyes."

Brushing her hand aside, he bellowed, "You left me out there, ya crazy whore!"

"Oh, where were we gonna put ya, in one of the beds? You'd be owin' me a lot more than your usual four bits! Besides, it was a pretty night." She wasn't joking and he knew it. Kate's hard but still beautiful face reflected a practicality that governed her life. Rather than being relegated to sweatshops or scullery duties after the death of her butcher husband, she chose a more lucrative, albeit less savory path. Her unbendable resolve and business skills produced a more than comfortable lifestyle that included the education of her only son at a prestigious medical school in Boston.

"Just this one time, sister, and don't you forget it!"

"You're a hard-nosed slugger, Danny, but our little money arrangement works well and I'll always cut ya slack."

"As long as that's the case, I'll keep the heat off your pretty *arse*, Katie Eagan!"

"Bunk! My fat arse couldn't make me a nickel anymore. But enough about my bottom. That young copper who's beginnin' to work the neighborhood was lookin' for ya. He told Dandy Jack that your captain wants to see ya later on."

"Well, if the truth be told, I wouldn't mind humpin' that bottom of yours, but alas, I got my duties," he leered, before flashing a surprisingly bright smile.

Rolling her eyes, she shooed him off, "And your envelope is under the bar in the front parlor."

After arriving at the rickety porch that served as the entrance to "Big Tits," Danny lost little time in ripping open the packet so as to confirm its contents. Satisfied that Kate was true to her word, he headed down the raised wooden walkway that fronted Buffalo's most notorious thoroughfare, Canal Street. The street played host to a slew of bordellos, dance halls and saloons, and given its dissolute reputation, it was no place for the naïve or defenseless; nonetheless, many a hapless victim met his demise at the hands of the ever-present cut-throats who prowled the cesspool of dives, looking for bumpkins and strangers. With most of the buildings butting-up against the Erie Canal, it was no wonder rumors persisted that the murderous thieves would dispatch their prey's weighted-down remains via trap doors and chutes spilling-out into the adjacent waters.

For those unfortunates condemned to make their homes within the crammed precinct, the conditions were desperate. Unskilled immigrant day-laborers and their families oftentimes shared one room in buildings so poorly constructed that their walls were constantly being braced up to prevent collapse. Given its vice, crime and squalor, it was no wonder that the city's respectable citizens, whether they be Victorian blue-bloods or the working class masses, enthusiastically embraced the term, "Infected District," when referring to the area.

As Sergeant Doyle made his way down the block, the irritating yet largely benign odor of the bordello had been replaced by a pestilent air that hung over the area like a moldy blanket. Likewise, he couldn't escape the visual blight that filled the landscape. Whether slumped against gaslights or spilling from the walkway into the fetid gutters, a host of broken revelers were showing the effects of the previous night. Ignoring the fact of his own transgressions, Doyle was quick to use his boot to rouse the slumbering drunks. "Get up ya stinkin' sots! Earn some money to feed that nest a' brats ya bred!" Catching sight of some nearby panhandlers, he expressed his disapproval in a similar fashion. Aware of Danny's fierce reputation, they lost little time in abandoning the scene.

Turning down the ill-named Maiden Lane, he spotted the Star Theater, home to some of the "Buffalo Gals," immortalized years earlier by the famous minstrel, E.P. Christy. He was tempted to stop for a quick snort, but his better judgment prevailed. He knew that in light of the wide berth the Captain had given him, any request for his presence was to be taken seriously.

Despite his penchant for accepting "gifts," he considered himself a topflight lawman, and as first sergeant detective, he was often assigned to the District when the department command needed his unique skills. The hulking copper grew up tough, and nothing had changed in the intervening years. Certainly, those who ran afoul of Brick Fist Doyle were deeply regretting their actions long before he ran them off to the pokey. Although he assailed the District's dissolute nature, and often brought a swift punishment to its wayward visitors, he was not immune to succumbing to its sinful charms. He ignored any sense of contradiction and instead took pride in being the man everyone knew—and feared.

Satisfied with his efforts at street cleaning, he made his way to the Commercial Street Bridge that spanned the canal. Looking down, he cast his eyes on a sea of barges and packet boats slowly rocking on a waterway filled with an effluence of sewage, and a flotilla of empty bottles. The vessels were packed so tight, that a person could easily skip from boat to boat, without so much as getting his pant cuff wet.

As he approached a newsstand at the far end of the bridge, he slowed down to observe a scene unfolding next to a blacksmith's shop; however, his focus was broken by the sweet sound of a female voice.

"Are you a good natured gentleman?" she purred, using a sexual come-on common at the time.

Boiling at the interruption, he spit out in a whisper, "Ya don't know me, do ya, sister!" Glaring at the overly-rouged teenage girl, he continued, "Get back to the farm, little girl. The next time I see ya, I'll have your tart arse in jail!" Not needing to confirm the girl's compliance, he returned his attention to the situation up the street. A cartman, no doubt on his way to the warehouses down the hill, left his wagon at the curb before walking over to the smithy. By this time in the morning, a steady stream of laborers, clerks and tradesmen were rushing about the street, tending to their business; however, amid the chaos, his detective's eye fixed on a little drama that was beginning to play out. After casting a shifty glance in either direction, a bystander parked himself next to the cart while he read the morning paper. A greasy porkpie hat could not conceal the tufts of wiry red hair that established the bystander's identity. Emmon Foley was one of three flame-haired brothers who'd been practicing their felonious craft since their Tinker family arrived on America's shores. The clan had worked their way up the criminal hierarchy of Canal Street to where they were now foot soldiers for Finbar "Fingers" Carnahan, the crime lord of the District.

As with any expert in one's field, Sergeant Doyle was able to recognize the masterful yet nuanced skills of his criminal counterpart. While Foley's left hand held up the paper, the other worked deftly behind the temporary shield. Seeing all he needed, Danny slapped his derby tight and ran towards the now startled perpetrator. Realizing he'd been spotted, Foley began to feverishly hurl a trove of small tools and coins into the back of the wagon.

"Don't move a muscle, Emmy!" Doyle bellowed as he grabbed the ill-fated thief by the nape of the neck. By now, the cart-man had heard the ruckus and rushed out to the street. Catching on to what had happened, he was ripe for a fight, yet Danny would have none of it. After emptying out the remaining contents of Foley's jacket, he pointed to the young worker, "You got your stuff so be off with ya, lad, and keep your eyes about ya from now on!"

As the cart-man began pulling his trailer down the road, the unrepentant culprit made a vain attempt to push off Brick Fist's grip. "

"Ah, be nice now," the detective cracked as he shoved his prisoner into the adjacent alley.

Despite being mocked for his unfortunate resemblance to the ape-like Irish caricatures depicted in the "Know-Nothing" press, Emmon Foley had standing among the city's criminal element, due to his talents with a knife; a fact not lost on Doyle as he stood in the ready. Still, Emmon was no match for his older brother, "Doc," the ferocious ringleader of the family business. Given his criminal pedigree, Emmon affected a defiant pose as he faced the lawman; but he lost his nerve and was quick to duck when Brick Fist made a move for his pocket.

Pulling out his tobacco and calmly rolling a cigarette, Danny observed, "With the sun's beautiful rays shinin' on this shithole, there ain't no need for violence. Do ya want a smoke?"

"Fuck you, Doyle!" the thief hissed through the hole in his teeth.

"Emmy, why ya pushin' me to beat you, when we can just talk?"

With that, Foley cleared his throat and spit just to the side of Danny's boot.

"Lucky for you ya got a good aim, *boyo*!" the detective glared; but returning to his more amiable demeanor, he went on, "Since the cat's got your tongue, I'll go on. So, why in the name of all the saints, would you be carrying-on with this shit, after ya made your way up to workin' for Fingers? I don't think he'd like it, ya know." Doyle prided himself on being in the know, thinking that it separated himself from the rest of the hacks on the force. As such, if Danny learned one thing over the course of the years, it was that criminals were predictable and that if something was different or out of sorts, something was up. The fact that Foley was acting on his own was odd, and it piqued Danny's interest.

"Fingers likes us just fine. He doesn't make us suck his cock like your boss makes you."

In an instant Danny cracked Foley with a force that caused his head to snap back. "Sweet Jesus, Emmy, see what ya made me do," he barked as the criminal stumbled against the wall. "Well, I guess you don't wanna talk. Still, I ain't gonna bust up your face or drag ya up to jail; but I am gonna go over my rules, which you should know by now! You can roll all the uptown dandies and bigwigs ya want, so long as ya don't hurt 'em and I don't see ya. But ya don't fuck with the workers or the other fine citizens who live here. Otherwise, you'll make me mad, and you know me when I'm mad. Hell, I bet that thievin' Bishop couldn't even absolve me after I've gone off. So, do I make myself clear?" He paused, before leaning closer and yelling, "I can't hear ya, Mister Foley!" Unwilling to tempt the fates, Foley finally managed a barely audible grunt.

After gesturing that the man was free to go, Danny pushed him out to the street with a kick in the pants. As he watched the emancipated gangster scurry towards the docks, he felt torn. He hated the Foleys and he would have loved letting off some steam at Emmy's expense before hauling him off; however, he knew Fingers would have him out in hours. More importantly, although he didn't know what it was, he believed that something must be up, and he was going to keep his ear to the ground until he found out. Anything to do with the crime boss Carnahan whetted Doyle's appetite.

The specter of Finbar "Fingers" Carnahan loomed large over the District. His fingers, ergo the nickname, were everywhere: gin mills, whorehouses, gambling joints, dance halls and protection; which was particularly galling to Danny, given his pride in his fearsome reputation. Cementing Fingers' criminal grip was the fact that he made his presence known in political circles, where a wide range of office holders owed him favors. Naturally, these favors, secured through his financial generosity and other means, brought him incalculable benefits.

Carnahan grew up in the District under the most squalid of circumstances, the son of a scullery maid who cleaned the saloons. Shuttled among the back rooms of various taverns, his young eyes witnessed all manner of criminality; however, he was an extremely precocious child, who caught the eye of the local pastor. At the priest's behest, a group of well-to-do Catholic benefactors paid for his education. As such, he ultimately found himself a student at the city's premier parochial elementary and secondary schools. This was followed by four years at a Catholic university, up the road in Niagara Falls; however, the Civil War ended his subsequent study of the law. His experiences in the great conflict had the effect of confirming to him that blood and violence were fundamental aspects of life. Upon returning home, the former Major was impatient in his role as a book keeper, and was desperate to achieve all the comforts denied him as a child. After accumulating a tidy sum skimming off from his employer, a man who made a fortune profiteering during the war, he bought his first saloon, a dive he rechristened "The Last Laugh." Soon, the combination of his intelligence, leadership and vicious determination served to parlay his initial investment into a vast criminal enterprise. In the process, he broke every conceivable law and moral precept, convinced that society's rules were merely there to inhibit his ability to gain success. His "business" success translated into a substantial fortune. Yet despite his wealth, he insisted on living in the District, having converted the top floor of a warehouse across from the central wharf into a luxury apartment and headquarters.

Over the years, Fingers had made a number of generous offers to recruit Danny; but despite his willingness to receive "gifts" from the likes of gamblers and madams, the detective resisted Carnahan's overtures. Something restrained him from taking that step; for even though his actions were often at odds with his position, Brick Fist stubbornly clung to his role as a lawman.

II

As Sergeant Doyle worked his way up Commercial Street, a variety of legitimate businesses began to replace the District's dives and bordellos. An air of manic energy reigned over the streetscape as hordes of workers rushed about, engaged in the daily commerce of the great inland port.

Dodging piles of slop left by the trolley horses and other beasts of burden, the detective finally arrived at the Police Headquarters on the corner of Terrace Street. Its location, at the cusp of the "Infected District," was not by accident, for besides being the Department's command center, it was, by far, its busiest precinct. Until recently, it was the Western Hotel, for decades one of the premier lodgings in the city. Just beneath its roof line, one could still make out a faded and peeling mural trumpeting its position as "the last grand hotel on the way west." Its brooding stone walls held the lawbreakers rounded up the night before. For those lucky enough to have family and means, release would come before the day's end. For those unfortunate others, it would be a short trip to the county jail.

Its once grand lobby now housed a booking station where officers sat at their desks furiously scribbling down their arrest reports. The main staircase led to the second floor offices of the department command; whereas the top two floors housed officers' lockers and "rooms" for a new type of guest. The basement was one of the last stops for those poor souls who had met their ends within the network of adjoining streets; and for a good number condemned to anonymity, the next stop would be the potters' field on Limestone Hill.

As Danny wound his way through the thicket of desks, he was met by the deafening silence and cold stares of his fellow officers. It was no secret that most of his colleagues had little use for him. The reasons for this attitude were their disgust over his debauched nature and loose ethics, and jealousy over his crime fighting successes. Danny's privileged position within the force only added fuel to the fire. Although others, if not most, crossed ethical lines, his "indiscretions" were the ones that stood out, and whatever goodwill had previously existed between him and his brother coppers, had largely eroded.

Just as Doyle was about to climb the stairs, a stage whisper pierced the air, "Watch the rail boys, his palm's still greasy." The agitator made no attempt to hide his identity. Sporting a crisply pressed uniform and sparkling buttons, he leaned back in his chair while staring straight into Danny's eyes.

"Ah, Spit n' Polish Perry! Tell me, ya still buggerin' your wife's nephew?"

As Spit n' Polish sprung to his feet, the desk lieutenant was quick to intervene, "Park your arse, Perry and cool your cannons, Doyle." Pulling the detective off to the side, he cautioned, "Danny, isn't it time that ya finally cleaned it up!"

"And isn't it time, Lieutenant Broderick, that your wife n' kids deserve better than that rat-trap on Fulton Street."

"It's from my honest wages, Danny."

"Maybe ya forgot what it's like sittin' here on your high n' mighty, but I deserve more for what I do, tendin' to that trash out there; and so do you!"

"And what about God, Danny?"

"Oh, Jesus," he sarcastically laughed, "beggin' your pardon, Lieutenant." Turning serious he continued, "You're my 'ol pal, Billy, but when are ya gonna give the boot to that plaster master that keeps ya on your knees?"

Shaking his head in exasperation, the lieutenant conceded, "Okay, old friend, ya better be gettin' up to the Captain, he's been expectin' you."

After giving Broderick a playful poke to the jaw, Doyle headed up the stairway, but feeling the other coppers' looks penetrating through the back of his jacket, he turned and cracked a smirk before continuing on.

He quickly arrived at his destination, which was marked by the lean caption, "Captain Collins," stenciled onto the opaque glass of the door. After softly knocking, as if to mimic the old man's quiet demeanor, he waited for the familiar response, "come and sit down, son." As he swung open the door, he was greeted by the musty smell of an old room, and muted light coming from a half-shaded window. In fact, everything about the Captain was muted, be it the spare furniture of his office or his spare frame, itself. Patrick Collins was a portrait of mediocrity, having made no waves and having dutifully towed the line for those business and political powers to whom he owed his rise through the ranks. Having spent little time on the streets, he looked fundamentally at ease as he sat at his desk reading reports and jotting down notes. Although the odd pair shared a mutual loathing, they managed to co-exist, since their professional relationship had proven to be beneficial to both.

Rising from his spartan wooden chair, Collins walked over to the file cabinet and returned with a pitcher of water and two glasses. "Nice and warm, the way I like it; good for the kidneys that way. May I pour you some?" The dingy condition of the glasses blunted any desire on Danny's part to quench a growing thirst inspired by last night's bout with whiskey. "No thanks, sir."

"It might help with the hot-coppers."

"I'm fine," Doyle shot back, unable to hide an edge.

A thick crop of white hair served to accentuate the thin outline of Collins' face, and as his stone gray eyes peered over his pince-nez spectacles, he evoked the image of a headmaster examining one of his charges over some infraction

"Well, whatever the case, how are things in the District, Daniel?" In an attempt to appeal to his uptown patrons, the Captain had trained himself to perfect his diction; however, regardless of his best efforts, he couldn't quite jettison the brogue he brought over as a child from Cork. "As you know, we needed your special talents. Things were getting out of hand down there."

"I talked to most of the owners and bouncers; along with cracking some heads and hauling in some of the usual scum." As was the case with his boss, Danny had learned to affect a more refined manner of speech; yet, for him it was solely a matter of pride, especially when dealing with the command or others he wished to impress.

"Good! I see the cages upstairs have more guests; but none of the owners, of course," he asked as a look of concern crossed his face. After all, a monthly stipend from the saloonkeepers' association helped secure a comfortable and fashionable lifestyle for him and his wife.

"Don't worry, they all understand," Doyle replied as he fought to hide his disdain in having to calm the Captain's fears. He always considered his "gifts" hard earned and deserved, the result of putting his balls on the line on a daily basis. On the other hand, this social-climbing little mouse, who hid behind a mask of professional integrity, reaped substantial rewards while playing with numbers behind his desk.

"Well, I'm not going to put you back in the First, just yet. So keep it up, you know what I want."

Barely able to acknowledge Collins' superior status, Danny just nodded.

"Which brings me to the next matter; I know you have a special relationship with Mister Prescott, so listen up. He has come to me with some pressing concerns about his factory and I'm damn sure going to address them! Unionists, or whatever they want to call themselves! God damned anarchists, that's what they are; wanting to destroy all that's good in this country! Well, not on my watch! I'm working on a plan to put a quick end to this rabble rousing. Lazy sots! Why don't these shirkers quit their bellyaching and work harder so they can pull themselves up; not to uptown, mind you, where through my tireless efforts I plan to live someday, but at least to the point where they can earn some respectability and get out of their miserable hovels. So be aware and keep your eyes and ears open."

"Is that all, Captain?"

"Oh, no, there's more, Daniel. Mister Cleveland's Democratic friends are making noise about running him for mayor next year; promising a new broom to sweep things out."

"Ah, "Big Steve", he's not a bad fella. I remember he defended one of the Fenians back in sixty-six. As for being mayor, he likes the good times too much; German beer; and especially chasing those fancy, uptown rich girls."

"No matter; you just remember, boyo, that my friends are your friends, and I expect you to ante up for the Republicans when I call you in next week."

"So, is that what you called me in for, Captain?" While having a little fun, Doyle knew there was the inevitable more.

"No, most importantly, I have a special assignment for you, Daniel. Here, I want you to take a look at this letter I received yesterday."

Taking a moment to peruse its contents, Doyle struck a thoughtful pose before answering, "I see…"

"You understand my concern, of course. I'm sure you'll approach this in your usual way and in a manner that is appropriate."

"I'll handle it."

"Good, and oh yes, I want you to begin taking young Costello under your wing. He's been doing fine working the neighborhood, but he can use your expertise."

Besides figuring Costello had some family or political connections, Doyle had his limits in dealing with Collins. "You know I don't take to apprentices, or anyone for that matter; they cramp my getting the job done."

"That's an order, and before you go: I still have a soft spot for you, Daniel, but you test my generosity. Look at you, looking like you just rolled out of bed, needing a shave and all. We've gone over this before."

Finally, Brick Fist had had enough. "Listen, I think we both know the value of my role and I trust you're still happy."

"Just the same—"

"I've got to be getting to business," he snapped as he struck out the door.

Finished with his hated nemesis, he was almost happy to be wading through the piercing looks of his police colleagues. Upon reaching the street, he felt a joyous release at once more being on his familiar turf.

Looking out towards the Central Wharf, his eyes were met by a vista of American commercial might. An army of laborers, tradesmen, wagons and carts scrambled among a mass of buildings that tended to the hungry demands of the shipping colossus that was Buffalo. Within the animated cluster of streets, every warehouse, or for that matter, every available empty space was crammed with tier upon tier of barrels, crates and bales. In addition, a steady flow of locomotives belched and groaned as they pulled their massive cargos and laid down a billowy stream of steam along the horizon. Hovering over this commercial landscape was a forest of stacks, masts and riggings that belonged to the ships that crowded the harbor. Completing this industrial tableau were the soaring elevators that held a sea of prairie grain and gave the city its title as, "Miller to the World." Early in the century, as the terminus of "Clinton's ditch," it had been the starting off point for the pioneer masses as they headed west in search of a new life. Since then, it had become the eastern transit point for the fruits of their descendants' labor.

No doubt, Buffalo's location on the Eastern Shore of the Great Lakes played a prominent role in securing its place on the commercial map. As a hub for lake shipping, railroads and canal transport, it became a vital link between the resource-rich American Heartland and the great cities of the East. Over the last decades, Buffalo's boomtown status attracted waves of immigrants and all manner of strivers, who saw the opportunity to improve their lives. Their subsequent industry and labor helped fuel the area's economic engine.

The scene never ceased to amaze Doyle. It also served to remind him of the fortunes that the city generated and the money that was owed him as one of its protectors. Of the few things in life that held his interest, money was at the forefront, since he long ago vowed that he would never be found lacking in it again.

Reluctantly, he realized that he had little time to savor the spectacle. As such, he walked a short distance to where Terrace met Main, the site of Liberty Pole Square, a memorial to the country's legacy of freedom. Rising one hundred and fifty feet into the air, the pole was Buffalo's earliest and most notable landmark. Since its construction some sixty years earlier, it had become the city's main gathering place for celebrating Independence Day and other civic events. On those occasions, it drew large masses of the urban poor who lived and worked in the surrounding area; and who, despite their pitiful stations in life, showed great love and enthusiasm for a nation that oftentimes was less than embracing of them.

As he waited for the trolley that would take him to his uptown destination, he spied a pair of scruffy ragamuffins emerge from the locksmith's shanty perched against the Mercantile Building. They were lugging overflowing buckets of ash, no doubt coming from the stove used to warm the little shed during the daybreak hours. Neither child could have been more than seven or eight years old, and given their shared golden locks and pug noses, they had to be brothers.

Showing uncommon strength for children that small, they managed to load the ungainly cargo onto the rear of a dogcart. After the big brother unhitched an aged, mangy mastiff and led it to the public fountain in the Square, the younger tyke plopped himself on the bumper of the wagon and began to play with a whirligig that he pulled from his pants pocket. Soon, he was a mass of giggles as he spun a whirling button on strings suspended between his hands; however, within an instant, his happy face took on a crimson hue before collapsing into an anguished cry.

As traffic flowed uninterrupted and without concern, Doyle found himself heading to the little one's side. The reason for the pitiful outburst became obvious as the whimpering child was now on his knees, poking his tiny hand into a nearby storm drain, searching for the runaway button.

When Danny scooped him up by the seat of his patchwork pants, he ran into a swirl of kicking feet that just missed his chest. "Watch it ya little bugg... uh, okay, it's okay, little friend. I'm afraid it's gone for good, but we'll fix it."

By now, the older brother returned with the newly animated beast at his side. Looking on suspiciously, he watched as Danny lowered the sobbing child onto his knee.

Wasting no time, the detective pulled out his pocketknife and cut off a button from his coat. In quick succession, he unraveled the string, restrung the button and soon had it whirling like a dervish. Before giving him back the toy and letting him down, he pulled out a handkerchief and began cleaning the boy's grimy hands. "And don't go stickin' your mitts down there again. You'll catch the ten plagues!"

This was met by a preoccupied nod and beaming smile as the little street urchin resumed his play; however, as the older boy ordered him back to work, Danny intervened. "Whadyah gonna make today?"

"Two bits and what's it ta ya," the big brother quipped.

"Cause I'm a copper. So, who's it for?"

"Me ma n' me baby sisters; me *da's* dead," the little one replied.

With that, Brick Fist slipped them each a greenback before declaring, "Now, I want ya to take your wares down to the soap-man and then bring the money to your ma before takin' the day off to play."

Although looking confused, the children quickly nodded before rehitching the patient canine to the cart. As Danny watched them coax the beast down the street, he felt a familiar knot grip his stomach. Shaking it off, he redirected his path to the wooden walkway across the street. No sooner had he advanced a few steps than he spotted a woman moving at a brisk pace from the direction of the Spaulding Exchange, an ancient edifice that still housed a host of offices catering to the business of the harbor.

She wore a tan walking skirt, a white, high-collared blouse and a tight-fitting bodice jacket; an ensemble that did little to hide her curvy figure. Along with a luxurious crown of auburn hair swept up into a French bun and topped with a stylish riding hat, it all combined to create a most fashionable and striking picture. Nonetheless, her appearance captured a practical side as well: wearing a long, western-style duster, no doubt in response to the pervasive soot that filled the air, and toting a well-worn carpet bag stuffed with all manner of papers and notebooks.

She carried herself with dignity and a fluidity of movement. The latter reflected both her innate grace and her childhood, tomboy athleticism. As the beautiful and educated daughter of the most successful saloonkeeper in the Irish First Ward, Keena Shea was beyond Doyle's grasp. Certainly, in light of his reputation, no decent woman would have him, as if he cared. Still, Keena was different and he couldn't escape the urges she inspired within him.

Danny was a frequent, if at times less than welcome visitor to her father's tavern, "Horgan's Hilt." It was a neighborhood institution and Keena was central to it. Upon the early death of her mother, she took charge of her younger siblings, and after completing her college studies, she refused to be relegated to the usual role of schoolmarm, and instead chose to assume the role of her father's principal assistant, managing all the financial affairs of the business. Spirited and popular with the multitude making up her Irish, First Ward neighborhood, she was also a loyal daughter of the church; but not to the point where it interfered with her lust for life.

With her working in the little office behind the bar, she and Doyle often had the chance to talk; yet despite their contrasting stations in life, she was always kind and engaging, with the exception of her light-hearted exasperations in the face of his overbearing pronouncements.

It was now apparent that she was heading his way. Although unwilling to admit it, he was excited at the prospect.

"I saw that, Sergeant Doyle; you big softie!"

"Ah, for Christ's sake, he was a public nuisance! I had to shut the little snapper up. Otherwise, I'd have to run 'em in."

"Always the profane one, aren't you, Danny," she softly chuckled as she shook her head.

"You can't be profane if there's nothing up there to be profane about, gal."

"Well, getting back to the matter at hand, it was a lovely gesture, Danny. And to show you how impressed I am, I'll play the tailor and sew you a new button the next time you're down at the bar."

"Thanks, but let's not make a big to-do about it."

"But it well should be a big to-do! Little ones like that shouldn't be out slaving. Their families should get proper wages, so they don't have to be working like that, but be in school!"

"Ah, so that's where you're coming from, the Spaulding Building; up there to see those trouble-making radicals of the K of L?"

"That's right! I do a lot of work for the Knights of Labor. They fight for working people and for other injustices; like the condition of those pathetic children!" She roared as a scarlet blush swept across her cheeks.

"Those unionists want their cut just like everybody else. They just use good people like you. I learned a long time ago that there's people with money and there's people with shi... er... nothing, and you better go for the money. It's just the way it is, Keena."

"Tings must change," she insisted, slipping back into an Irish accent as she grew more animated. "And tings will change when people unite and fight for what's right! Unions are the only way for workers to stand up to the bosses who exploit and abuse 'em. The movement's beginnin' to grow around the country, and we're gonna make it work here!"

"Listen, Keena, I know what you're feeling." "There's a hard order to life; something you never experienced. It's a tough world, but people like me have to keep it from getting worse and going into chaos; and while I'm getting it done, someday I'll have the money."

"So I've observed, Sergeant. And by the way, don't go shoveling that malarkey about me being some garden flower, I helped raise three sisters and worked all my life."

"Go ahead and condemn me but if it weren't for the likes of me, you couldn't make it to the end of the street before one of your fine working men would be dragging your pretty... er... before he'd be dragging you into an alley."

"Gentlemen don't talk like that, Mister Doyle."

"Gentlemen! You mean like that lily-livered boyfriend of yours?"

"Mister Riley is a fine man and I won't be having you knock him down!"

"Okay, Okay, Keena, I'll be respectful," he leered with an arched eyebrow.

"Your pretty-boy looks don't work with me, Detective Doyle; so don't even try."

"As if I'd want to try, with all those radical ideas of yours. I suppose you're one of those women pushing for the vote, too."

"Quit trying to pick my scab, Danny. You know quite well that I support Susan B. Anthony and the women's suffrage movement. I could go on but I'd only be wasting my breath on the likes of you."

"Sufferin' indeed! for all us men! And what does a big man like Blinky Shea think of all this, after spendin' so much money on your fancy education."

"My father doesn't have a say in my opinions, but just for your information, he respects my positions."

"Ah, what's the world coming to," he sighed as he cracked a smile.

"Modern times, Danny. It's Eighteen-eighty if you haven't noticed. And speaking of time, I better get my... I better get back to the tavern. I've got a lot of bookwork to do."

"And I better get back to work keepin' a lid on things so that you can save the world."

"Oh, come on. I think I'm beginning to see through you, Mister Brick Fist. There still may be a heart under all that bluster. So, I believe it's my duty to drive the truth through that thick Irish skull of yours. In the meantime, *slán*, Sergeant."

"And goodbye to you, Miss Shea; and don't go telling your ol' man to water down the whiskey."

"Up yours, Doyle!"

"That's a fine Catholic girl for ya!" he laughed in response.

Despite their sometimes contentious discussions, he couldn't help but revel in her vital spirit. And as he watched her march down the street with a confident air, he couldn't help but wonder what her hair would look like as it spilled from her well-constructed bun onto her naked shoulders. After reminding himself of the absurdity of such thoughts, he spun around and headed back towards the trolley stop.

As the coachman pulled his team to a stop, Danny hopped on board without so much as making eye contact. For Doyle, it was a source of pride not to show his badge, knowing that the driver, regardless of who he was, knew him by his reputation.

Since it was an unseasonably warm autumn day, he decided to hold onto the headboard rail of the driver's platform and observe the goings-on. Leaving the harborside in its wake, the streetcar slowly carried him up Main Street, the city's principal artery. It was the preferred address to all manner of businesses that flourished within the climate of Buffalo's booming economy. A host of companies, including many of the great names of American commerce and banking, occupied a landscape of mammoth stone buildings that reflected financial power. Main Street and its immediate environs was also home to many of the city's premier restaurants, theaters and stores. For those who could afford it, Downtown was a Mecca for indulging their tastes in dining, fashion and entertainment. As such, the city, as evidenced by the unfolding scene, was a moneymaking colossus fed by the multitudes rushing about.

Whenever he took this trip, Doyle could virtually feel the economic vibrancy that surrounded him; and he could certainly see it. Whether it be watching as a valet carried the luggage of a rich visitor through the doors of the grand Iroquois Hotel; seeing a driver help a gilded dowager into the Delmonico for an early lunch; or witnessing a bevy of scraping assistants tend to the needs of a business executive leaving the towering, six-story headquarters of the German Insurance Company, Brick Fist wondered what sort of moral or criminal transgressions were behind the fortunes that fueled these lifestyles. Yet, while contemptuous of the lies and hypocrisy that lay at the foundation of their riches, he was reluctant to condemn the impulse to grasp for as much as one could. For to do so, would be to ignore the cruel yet unavoidable reality of life itself. Consequently, comparing these scenes of wealth and influence with his own struggles, only served to whet his desire to get his share. For the moment at least, he felt reinvigorated.

As the yeoman-like beasts kept pulling their burden along the rails leading north, the commercial atmosphere began to give way to a more residential setting. Stepping off the trolley at Edward Street, Doyle bid a jaunty adieu to a somewhat startled driver.

Saint Louis' Catholic Church, mother parish of the Diocese, dominated the surrounding landscape. Doyle knew the area well, having spent the latter years of his youth as a resident of the Orphan's Asylum, located a couple of streets over. Although not the nurturing wellspring of a family household, it was a clean and sturdy environment. Moreover, it was an atmosphere in which young Danny not only survived, but prospered, owing in no small part to his street smarts and talent with his fists.

As he made his way down the hill, the setting was markedly different from what he had seen earlier in the day. Having left behind the cottages and tenements that housed the toiling masses, he was now amidst the homes of the executives and professionals who steered the engines of commerce or otherwise rode the economic juggernaut that was Buffalo. He paused at the corner of Franklin Street, in order to savor the scene. Looking up the road, he marveled at the sight of stately homes and manicured gardens, all under a canopy of majestic elms. The run-down farmhouses and empty fields from the time of his of his youth were now all gone. In their place was a landscape of domestic elegance that would rival the domains of the *nouveau riche* anywhere else in the country. Still, the most exclusive addresses were on the next street over; on Delaware, home to the city's moneyed aristocracy and site of the famous "Millionaire's Row."

Just past the halfway point of the block, Doyle arrived at his destination, the police force's newest construct, the Edward Street Livery. It was an impressive three-story brick structure, featuring an arched entranceway and matching front windows. Above the gate was a stone header engraved with the words "Mounted Police" and featuring bas-relief portraits of a horse and bison on either side. As he passed through the heavy oak doors thrown open in response to the rising temperature, he encountered an equally impressive interior that included, parquet flooring with matching tile along the walls, ornate millwork, brass fixtures and wrought-iron box stalls. One would be hard pressed not to conclude that the city fathers made every effort to ensure that the facility was in harmony with its luxurious surroundings, which by no coincidence was oftentimes home to themselves or their allies and benefactors.

Creeping past the empty front office, he silently watched as a mechanic worked on the springs of a gleaming carriage. After once more looking about, Danny yelled out, "What? They got ya workin' this place all by yourself?"

"The other fellas were called out to the main barn; and who's askin'?" the man in overalls replied before hesitating and turning around.

"Ah, don't worry, I'm a detective, see," Danny smiled as he pulled out his gold shield. "I was just passin' by."

"Sorry, I didn't mean to question ya." The bespectacled mechanic said, as he squinted in an effort to make out the stranger silhouetted against the sunlight rushing through the door.

"That's all right. A soul can't be too careful, even around these rich fella's parts. And speakin' of luxury, that carriage is a real beauty. Wait, don't tell me. The Commission's gonna start assignin' 'em to us bogtrotters," he laughed, loudly.

"Oh, no, this one belongs to Mister Prescott, the owner ..." Once more, he appeared to hesitate.

"For the life 'a me," Danny bellowed as he slapped his thigh, "he's sellin' the factory and joinin' the force."

"Well... ah... ah," the man stammered before regaining his voice, "My Uncle Pat... er... Captain Collins instructed me to fix the problem."

"No doubt, he has good reason. Anyway, so you're the one married to the Captain's niece, are ya? And it just so happens that I work for 'im, Sergeant Doyle, Danny Doyle."

"That's right, I'm married ta his niece. Kevin Toohey, here, and for sure I heard of ya, Doyle, Brick Fist Doyle." A puzzled look crossed his face before continuing on, "Listen Sergeant, I'd like to talk but I gotta get this done by five, so if ya'd excuse me."

Just as Toohey bent down to resume his work, Brick Fist grabbed him by the collar and flung him head first into a heap of manure piled high in a corner of an adjacent stall. Slamming the gate behind him and straddling the now stunned mechanic as he struggled to regain his bearings, Doyle snarled, "I'm here to pay ya a little visit. Ya been beatin' your wife, ain't ya!"

Fighting to catch his breath while trying to scrape the excrement and straw from his face, the little man whimpered, "Please! Ya got it wrong, sir!

"Shut your gob and take your punishment like a man," Danny growled as he leaned closer.

Throwing his hands up in an effort to forestall the inevitable rain of blows, he pleaded, "I beg of ya; they're lyin'; that prick Collins and me whorin' wife!"

Catching himself as he was about to wind-up and deliver a haymaker, Danny barked out, "Go on, and you better not be lyin', if you know what's good for ya!"

"The whole Collins family is no damn good! For the last six months she's been carrying-on right in front 'a me nose with that copper, Perry, Collins' fair-haired boy. Gone for days, not even carin' about our wee boys. The whole neighborhood knows. I can't take it no more. When I threatened to move me and the boys to my ma's, she warned me that I better not even try!"

Although still poised to strike, the sight of Toohey's beaten and sorrowful eyes convinced Brick Fist that he'd been used. "And ya ain't been beatin' her, now?"

"No! On the Sacred Heart of the Virgin Mother, I swear!"

Loosening his clenched fists, he bristled, "Collins and that whole clan are thievin', lyin', cocksuckers, ain't they!"

Toohey could only manage a rasping sob.

"Pull up your socks and get a hold a yourself, lad! I'll help ya. Tell your whorin' wife that I hammered ya good. Would ya want me to break your nose, Kevin?"

"No! No, that's all right. I'll rip me shirt. Ya already bent me specs."

"Sorry 'bout that. I suggest you get your kids out of there and over to your ma's. If anybody gives you trouble, especially that weasel Perry, come find me. Ya hear?"

"Monsignor Gillespie already told me I'd be ex-communicated if I left."

"Ah, yeah! Collins is always goin' on about his pal the monsignor. Probably each one playin' the barrel-boy. Maybe I ought to pay a visit to that little altar boy rat."

"No, please, Sergeant," the little man gasped, wide-eyed.

"Okay," he chuckled, "but if you'd like to, go tell your ol' lady that I can find her a spot at Big Tits! Kate's a good friend ya know."

That last remark finally brought a smile to Toohey's tired face. "I'll think it over, Danny."

"Good! Now go clean yourself up. Ya look like shit."

With that, Doyle headed out the door as quickly as he arrived; but as he marched back towards Main Street, he could feel his temper surge. He'd been used by someone that he hated. Of course, he had done "special assignments" for the Captain many times before, but it was always something he could live with and it was always part of a compact that, in the long run, was beneficial to both. In this case, there was something particularly shameful about further abusing a man who not only had been cuckolded, but who was trying to protect his children. All this only served to add to Doyle's toxic view of the world. As he spun this sordid tale around in his head, he was already planning how to deal with the good Captain, no matter how long it would take. After all, no matter how high and mighty, nobody screwed with Danny Doyle.

III

As she peered through the beveled glass that framed the entranceway to the mansion, Rebecca wondered what was keeping Charles. Perhaps the years were catching up on the old man and maybe it was time to consider a new position on the staff. Adding to her growing impatience was the fact that with the windows having been locked tight, the vestibule was little more than a marble barn; the air thick and stifling.

She began to question if her full polonaise had been the right choice, given the unseasonably warm weather; however, seeing her new diamond pendant set against the purple velvet fabric, convinced her that the dress was an inspired selection.

She returned to the window just as the shiny black brougham was turning onto the brick carriageway. By now, the butler, who had been busy instructing a new maid about the household protocols, heard the clattering of hoof beats and arrived in time to escort his mistress to the waiting driver.

Her frosty reminder of the hour prompted the driver to plead that the job had taken longer than expected. Ignoring his explanation, she merely cast a look that suggested time was wasting.

After watching old Mister Clark lower the steps and open the door, she deftly scooped up the hem of her billowy dress and climbed up. Yet, no sooner had she stuck her head into the coach than she abruptly spun around. Crinkling her nose, she demanded, "Who worked on this?"

"Mister Prescott said he'd been told the man was the finest mechanic on the force."

"I mean, what was his background? Was he Irish?"

"Indeed he was ma'am. From the cut of his speech, I believe he had roots in Limerick."

"Do you think he sat in it?"

Despite chafing at the direction of her talk, Charles knew he had little choice but to curb his tongue. "Perhaps he had to test it, ma'am."

"Well, he should have jumped up and down on the roof or on your little perch. In any case, it stinks! Air it out and wipe off the seats. And please, do it quickly; we're running late."

While Charles went about his task, she took rest on one of the polished marble benches that sat beneath the colonnaded portico. This latest incident reminded her of the tensions that existed between the Irish and the rest of proper society. It was a matter that she seemed unable to escape and it was becoming a source of both challenge and frustration to her. Many of the two hundred workers employed at her husband's factory were of the Hibernian race, as were most of their household servants. Although whatever contact she had with the help was cordial, she was always aware of the social chasm that existed between them, and as a consequence, preferred to maintain a definite distance. Her feelings were further colored by their circle of friends, whose dinnertime discussions often focused on the tidal wave of immigration that was threatening the very character of the country.

Although some of their number had achieved a measure of success, it seemed to her that the vast majority of the Irish wallowed in poverty and ignorance. Their oftentimes pathetic circumstances pulled at her heartstrings; however, she had to admit that most of this was their own doing. They followed religious beliefs steeped in pagan idolatry, and they embraced personal conduct fueled by the baser instincts and a lust for whiskey. Their neighborhoods were breeding grounds for disease and crime. Most of this could be traced to a sorry absence of basic Christian virtues. Still, there was reason to hope. At the very least, living among the God-fearing and industrious protestant citizens of this country could have a positive effect; nonetheless, more had to be done on a personal level by the good people of her community.

As was the case with a number of her relatives who delivered the message of the King James Bible to the heathen masses of China, it was the Christian duty of herself and others like her to bring enlightenment to these people, who had long been living in darkness. She was certain that much like little children, the Irish could be schooled to save themselves through hard work, abstinence and of course, the observance of true Christianity.

On occasion, she discussed this issue with Mister Prescott, but Alfred had proved resistant, having long held a considerably less sympathetic view. From his perspective, the Irish, by virtue of their dissolute and ignorant natures, were ordained to perform the type of bestial work spawned by the arrival of mass industrialization. For those clever few who had gained a level of success, their efforts were more the product of guile, better suited to criminal enterprises or the backroom realm of politics, than to the established world of business. Yet, unlike others of his station who readily displayed the "NINA- No Irish Need Apply" signs at their factory gates, he believed that through a stern hand, these people could function at an acceptable level, or more importantly, in a manner that contributed to maximum profitability. In fact, he suggested that a few could be saved and drilled in the tenets of respectable society; however, any attempts to expand upon this to the Irish masses would be virtually impossible and, at best, would be a long and difficult process better suited to humanitarian organizations. It was certainly not within the purview of business or government. While insisting the issue was not worthy of his attention, he did not forbid his wife from pursuing the matter at their church or some other appropriate charitable society.

Yet, as Rebecca once again stepped aboard the now purged carriage, she neglected to reflect upon a resentment that existed just beneath the surface. As the beautiful young daughter of one of the oldest families in the city, and as the wife of one of the wealthiest and most accomplished men in the area, she appeared to have it all; nonetheless, a failure to bring forth any children had become a source of great personal pain—along with having set off the wagging tongues among her social circle. Choosing to ignore a family history of few offspring or the fact that her husband was considerably older and often away until the wee hours, she instead focused her bitterness on the shear injustice of it all. She was especially jealous of the immigrant multitudes, who seemed to bear children at the drop of a hat, while she was forced to suffer the loneliness of an empty crib for what felt like ages.

Once she was settled, Charles lost little time snapping his charges into a quick paced trot down Delaware Street. With the windows pushed open, the warm breeze seemed to relax her mood. As such, she took the opportunity to admire the beauty of the neighborhood that she long called home. Passing the grand mansions that symbolized the opulence of the street, she recalled the fond times spent with the families who lived there. They were Buffalo's established elite; not only owning the vehicles of commerce and industry, but oftentimes wielding the power that controlled the levers of local government. And, they were her people.

By now, the arrival of dusk inspired the illumination of a host of lamps within the various estates, which, along with the flickering glow of the gas lights lining the curb, imparted a magical air to the surrounding streetscape. Noticing that Van Cleff's Jewelers was still open, she felt the urge to stop and make a quick purchase of some cufflinks. It would no doubt add luster to her plans for surprising and cajoling her husband into a fun night on the town; but in light of her late start, time was of the essence.

Although respectful of his position as a captain of industry and appreciative of his efforts to maintain a way of life befitting their class, she was growing increasingly frustrated over the cycle of routine that had encroached upon their lives. She realized that given his responsibilities as the owner of Prescott's Wallpaper Company, Alfred would have to toil at his desk well into the evening. Oftentimes, he would follow up with a business meeting or a trip to his club to relax over drinks. By the time he returned to his home, he was usually exhausted and ready for sleep. Too often during the three year course of their marriage, she would lay in bed primped up and poised for romantic adventure, only to be greeted by a cascade of snores resonating from the adjoining room. Of course, she understood such disappointments were often the price of a refined existence that celebrated sublime joys, as opposed to the profanities of the unwashed masses; but her yearnings to experience the full tapestry of domestic life, especially in terms of children, were beginning to overwhelm her.

Tonight, she was determined to change all that and rekindle the passions of their courtship. As part of her scheme, she had secured tickets to a light-hearted musical revue at the Majestic Theater. Hopefully, an evening of carefree escape would be a welcome change of pace and perhaps even set into motion a desire on his part to break the routine and embark upon a new course.

As the carriage entered Niagara Square, she took a moment to observe the big corner house that once belonged to President Fillmore. Once again, warm memories flooded her thoughts. Her father had been a close friend and confidante of the former Know-Nothing presidential candidate, and as such, he was a frequent guest at his residence. One of her earliest memories involved her introduction to the famous politician. Of course, being no more than three or four, she had no idea who he was, and upon seeing all the others paying homage to the white-haired old gentleman, she asked if he was god. Somehow her voice carried over the crowd, which inspired a deluge of laughter.

Gathering her up and onto his knee, the former President insisted he was just an old man and began to tease her about how such a "little chipmunk" could roar like a lion. Forever charmed, he always called her "Chippy" from that point forward. Over the next few years, as her love for music and proficiency on the piano grew, she would play for the old man whenever her father would visit.

As her carriage turned up Church Street, passing the new City Hall and proceeding along Pearl Street past Saint Paul's Cathedral, the tone of the surroundings changed abruptly. Gone were the lavish mansions and fashionable shops. In their place stood ancient office buildings, dour warehouses and brooding factories. Although proud of her city's robust standing and fully aware of what these buildings represented in an economic sense, she was always disturbed by their ugly presence.

Approaching the Liberty Pole at Main Street, she indulged her curiosity with a quick peak down Commercial Street, in the direction of the Infected District. By now, many of the harbor workers, having finished their shifts, had already descended onto its countless saloons and bordellos. Most of the buildings were ablaze with light, and spewing out a din of raucous music and loud voices. Straining her eyes to get a better glimpse, she could make out rolling crowds of revelers crisscrossing the streets in search of a good time. She could only imagine the depraved nature of their quests, before shaking her head in disgust and leaning out the window to demand that Charles quicken the pace. It didn't take long for the pervasive outside odor to begin penetrating the sanctuary of her cabin. Despite the prospect of being reintroduced to the lingering effects of the mechanic's earlier visit to the coach, she lost no time in slamming shut the windows.

Two blocks short of the Central Wharf, they turned onto Perry Street where Alfred's company was located. With the exception of the new steamer house sitting next to the plant, and O'Brien's Tavern, perched a block to the east, the street was occupied by a host of bustling factories; however, while one could clearly hear the rumble and strain of industrial machinery, the area was devoid of any human presence outside the plants' gates. A sense of isolation, made worse by the encroaching darkness, sent a cold shudder down Rebecca's spine. It was no wonder she rarely made the trip here, especially at this hour. Only after Charles rang the bell and the sentry came rushing out from the security shack, did her discomfort ease.

Recognizing his boss's brougham, the guard was quick to roll back the gate. "Good evening, Missus Prescott. How may I help you?"

Cracking open the window, she announced, "I'm here to see my husband."

"I just got here ma'am, but I'm sorry to say that I believe Mister Prescott has already left. Still, I can check with his office to make sure..."

"Yes, by all means check to make sure," she grumbled, frustrated as much by the man's vacillation as by the possible scuttling of her plans.

"I'll get a lad on it right quick, ma'am. I don't wanna hold ya up any more than needed." Hobbling towards the main building as fast as he could, the crippled guard yelled frantically at a couple of workers on the loading dock, who were securing some barrels onto a wagon.

Either ignoring his shouts or unable to hear above the noise of the presses, the pair appeared ready to set out when a third party arrived at the scene. While at first seeming to heed the guard's call, the new arrival quickly joined the others and headed off. Frustrated and embarrassed, the man limped back. "Sorry, ma'am. I'll run up to the office myself. You and your driver are of course welcome to join me, but with all the dust and such."

"No, that's all right. And your name is?"

"Kruger, ma'am; Otto Kruger."

Recalling the story of a former foreman who suffered an accident at the plant that left him crippled, she was swept by a rush of sympathy. "Please, Mister Kruger, take your time. We'll wait here. I'm quite comfortable."

As she watched the man literally hop towards the main door, she felt a sense of pride in the fact that her husband didn't throw Kruger to the wolves, but found another position for him. Unfortunately, his sad circumstances demanded a reduced wage. Yet, despite her request that the guard not hurry, as the minutes passed, she felt her earlier uneasiness return. With nothing more than an old man as her protection, she felt a renewed sense of vulnerability. Just then, she thought she saw a shadowy figure slip behind the carriage. Unnerved and unwilling to open the window, she yelled towards the roof, "Charles, did you see someone out there?"

"Probably just a dog or cat, ma'am. A bunch of 'em are around here to take care of the rats."

Hardly comforted by the reference to vermin or by Charles' doddering nature, she checked the doors' locks while keeping her eyes peeled. Finally, relief came in the form of the guard and another man. Unfortunately, given the shape of his profile, he was not her husband. Upon their arrival alongside the coach, Rebecca felt comfortable enough to slide open the window. She was immediately greeted by a young man who appeared the type eager to display his cleverness and proficiency; however, his fledgling status was betrayed by a cheap suit that given his exposed wrists and ankles, was at least a size too small. Clean and well groomed, he had a thick crop of blond hair, having the appearance of being freshly trimmed. He was tall and slim, and exhibited a fluidity of movement that went along nicely with a graceful manner of speech. His face exuded a relentless charm and was accompanied by a dazzling yet mischievous smile. Completing the portrait was a fine tuft of moustache; no doubt, its growth was an attempt to add a degree of gravitas. After affecting a slight bow, he spoke first, "Excuse me, Missus Prescott, I'm Mister Prescott's secretary, Lee Riley."

"Oh, yes, my husband expressed his satisfaction as to how you're coming along."

"Thank, you, ma'am. I'm quite privileged to be of service to him."

"Indeed you are; but don't let my words go to your head. Mister Prescott is a demanding patron who won't tolerate anything less than excellence."

"Of course; and I can assure you that I will devote all my efforts to that end, ma'am."

"Very good; now, may I assume you're here to take me to my husband."

"I'm terribly sorry ma'am but Mister Prescott left the premises not ten minutes ago. He said he was going to the City Club for a steam and a massage."

"Well, Mister Prescott certainly needs those opportunities to relax and get rid of the stress of working so hard. We were driving past Saint Paul's and thought we might drop by and surprise him; but perhaps some other time."

"Oh… ah… well … I'm sure he will appreciate your taking the time; and as for the pressures of his work, as his secretary, I'll try as best I can to help."

After thanking him, but before he had a chance to bid farewell, she shut the window. Although somewhat piqued by this lowly aide's air of presumption, and despite her disappointment at the collapse of her plans, she wasn't about to reveal her feelings in front of the help.

While lamenting her bad timing, she still couldn't understand successful men's fixation with their male bastions and corresponding rituals, especially when they so frequently intruded on their domestic lives; however, in light of his accomplishments and position, Alfred knew best how to manage the strains that came with his work, and as a good wife, she must accept her role and support him in every way possible. Still, it was a sad and frustrated figure who summoned her driver to return home.

As they left behind the gas-lit glow bathing the factory gate, she once more felt the menacing shadows of the street engulf her suddenly frail little carriage. Searching out the window for some signs of life, she could only find a solitary light flickering outside the steamer house, that otherwise looked locked down for the night.

Just then, she felt stomping footsteps race across the roof of the coach. The sounds of a scuffle and a blood-curdling cry quickly followed. Diving to the door nearest the tumult, she gripped the handle with all the strength she could muster. Yet before she knew it, a masked figure appeared at the opposite window, and with a swift, violent movement, smashed the latch and flung open the door. With lightening speed, he flew through the opening, grabbed her by the foot and pulled her to the floor. Despite a flurry of kicks and an ear-piercing screams that seemed to echo down the street, he was on her in an instant; and with a deft twist of his still-bloody knife, he ripped the diamond pendant from around her neck.

Panting like a galloping hound and stinking of gin, he leaned down. By now, every second seemed to burn itself into her consciousness. As he pressed ever closer, the sight of his blood-soaked eyes, filthy hands and stringy, red hair sticking out from his cap, nearly sent her into shock. Bracing for the worst, she could only manage a pitiful whimper.

Laughing in the face of her sobs, he sneered, "If I had more time, I'd give ya a big treat, ya rich whore!" With that, he delivered a sharp crack to her head, before bounding out the door.

Although in a daze, she managed to somehow marshal her wits and steady her legs. Stumbling onto the street, she caught sight of a groaning Charles, holding his face while lying in a pool of blood. Before finally collapsing onto the pavement, she could make out the figures of men rushing from the plant.

"It's Missus Prescott!"

"There he goes, lads. He's runnin' down Water Street!"

"Sweet Jesus! What's he done to ya, old man!"

Aware of a man's hands untying her bonnet and placing his jacket under her head, she finally felt safe.

Kneeling by her side, he bent down and whispered, "Are you all right, Missus Prescott? It's me, Riley. I'm here."

"Can't you see! Now get my husband!"

IV

"He could have killed her, Doyle! Do, you hear me!"

"Yes, sir; I know."

"Grabbed her leg! Put his filthy, stinking hand on her throat! Threatened her with a bloody knife, stole the diamond necklace that was my present and even dared to strike her! Lord knows what would have happened if my men hadn't come running out."

Danny was content to nod and let Prescott continue on. He knew something big was up when a messenger boy came rapping on his door just before dawn. The note merely read, "My office, now! Prescott."

"It isn't enough that I pay a king's ransom in taxes and then there's Collins…"

Prescott didn't need to worry that he let slip that Captain Collins was on his payroll. Danny didn't get where he was without knowing the terrain. He had long since discovered that the pious little piece of dirt was on the take, not just to various business types but to other, less savory players as well. In regards to Prescott, Collins' role was simple: monitor, harass and crush any union activity; and from what Danny could see, the man performed his job not just with earnest efficiency, but with great enthusiasm.

"In any case, I don't want to trust the police and all their rules. I want justice! Swift justice!"

Alfred Prescott was a man whose demands were rarely, if ever, denied. He was the son of a prosperous and politically connected, local physician. After earning his degree at Harvard, he set about making a small fortune at one of the premier trading houses on Wall Street. He paid a surrogate to take his place during the War and shortly thereafter, bought a failing wallpaper company in his hometown. Within a couple of years, he transformed it into one of the most successful in the country.

With salt and pepper hair flowing over his stiff white collar and dressed in an impeccably tailored English suit, the fifty year-old gentleman looked every inch the industrial lion that he was. A narrow stern face, along with menacing grey eyes set beneath bushy eyebrows, bore witness to a man not to be trifled with.

"And that's where you come in, Detective." For Alfred Prescott, Danny Doyle had come to be one of his instruments for getting his way. After having gotten wind of Brick Fist's ruthless reputation, the business mogul used his services on many occasions. Usually, it involved collecting on debts, since Prescott owned scores of properties both commercial and residential; or, if he felt someone had cheated him in business or cards, his personal passion, he'd send Doyle to straighten things out; and for situations where the need arose, he would task the detective to spy on rivals of his ancillary enterprises, such as lumber processing, coal distribution and ship's stores.

For his part, regardless of the circumstances, Brick Fist always got the job done. Unlike the case with Collins, Danny believed his efforts on behalf of the tycoon would never qualify as graft. Instead, he viewed his work as a second job, intended to augment his meager police wages. Besides, Prescott was a legitimate businessman. It wasn't as if he was in the employ of Fingers Carnahan or some other gangster overlord. Still, as he stood amidst the opulence of Prescott's second-story office, he was forced to hide his disdain for the man. Oh, he envied, and in many ways respected Prescott's wealth and power; however, he resented not only the man's ostentatious bearing, but his arrogant and dismissive manner as well. Most of all, he despised his attitude towards the Irish, for whom Prescott made no attempt to conceal his contempt. Nonetheless, he was paid handsomely, and in light of this, Danny was willing to bite his tongue and go along. Yet as he stood before the boss's desk, which sat in front of a large window overlooking the factory gate, he knew he was seen as little more than hired trash.

"And I want you to take care of this by any means possible, Doyle."

"This isn't going to be easy, sir. I've got my ideas, but there's a lot of thugs out there. I'm going to have to talk to your wife to get started."

"My wife? You can't be serious, Doyle. I'm not going to have my wife, a refined and sensitive lady, speak to the likes of you. Besides, she's under the strict medical supervision of my doctor for the immediate future. Lord only knows how this damaged her spirits."

"And what about the driver?"

"He proved to be quite the protector, didn't he! And that's another thing! Now what's he good for; a one-eyed, old-man driver! Not only will my wife make me come up with a new position for him, but I'll have to find another so-called trustworthy servant, who'll have to be trained. Good God that should prove to be quite the task, given that feeble lot."

"Well, he should be a good place for me to start. What's his name, sir?"

"Charles Clark, but don't expect too much there. Last night, he told my secretary, Riley..."

Danny could barely conceal the look on his face at the mention of Keena's boyfriend.

"So, you know my man, Riley, Doyle?"

"He's from the neighborhood, sir. Seems like a fine fellow."

"That's my impression, too. Hopefully, he has the makings to climb out of his unfortunate background. Anyway, Charles told him that he couldn't describe his attacker, since he jumped him from behind. On the other hand, my wife, though still ill-disposed, was able to provide me with some snippets of information." Prescott showed no inclination to slow down as Danny pulled out a dog-eared little note pad and a stubby pencil. "Despite his wearing a mask, she could tell he was... surprisingly... Irish," Prescott slowly intoned, with every syllable drippingly sardonic, "red haired, and this should narrow it down, significantly, reeking of gin."

"Don't you worry, sir. What you told me will be helpful. As I said before, I have me... er... my ideas. Anything to narrow it down is good. Plus, you can be sure I'll be beating the bushes."

After smashing down a fist that nearly sent flying a model of his yacht that was sitting on his desk, Prescott roared, "You bet you will!" Gone was his usual reserve. In its place was a blood-red face, with veins straining at the edges of his scalp. "You'll break every thick Irish skull in your way and scour under every scummy rock to find this fine member of your brethren!"

"Is there anything more you can tell me, sir?"

"Like I said, she's somewhat ill-disposed at the moment, but in the event further details surface, I'll let you know, detective. But in the meantime, you better make do with what you have!"

Ignoring the obvious sarcasm, Doyle fired back, "You can be sure I'll make do! There's a number of fine citizens who I plan to be meeting with!"

Preoccupied and barely listening, the still-seething tycoon shook his head in disgust, "Like my father always said, they're going to ruin this great country! Good, God, when are we going to be able to bring civilization to this rabble!"

"Is that all, sir," Danny chimed in, not wanting to endure another moment of Prescott's bigoted philosophizing.

"Yes, that's all; so, I'd suggest you get on with things," Prescott calmly stated, once more looking composed. "I have much work to catch up on. The entire morning has been taken up by this horror."

"In that case, I won't be taking up any more of your time. Good day, sir." As he turned on his heels, he paused to observe a box of Cubans sitting on a table next to the door

Noticing Danny's interest, Prescott interrupted, "Oh, go on, Doyle. Take one. I usually give them out to business associates, anyway; and one more thing, detective, don't ever again come here stinking of whores and whiskey!"

Gritting his teeth, Brick Fist grabbed one of the panatelas and made his way out. After shutting the heavy oak door emblazoned with the gold-leaf words, "President Alfred Prescott," Danny caught sight of the familiar figure of Liam Riley sitting behind the secretary's desk outside the office. Riley was in the midst of a conversation with an injured worker. The boy, no more than twelve, was still bandaged up to his elbow, the result of a scalding caused by the caustic spray from one of the presses. "Now, that's a good lad! The company has invested much in your training and expects you to man your post like a loyal employee. I know they wouldn't want to replace you; plus, bein' familiar with your ma's burdens, I know you want to earn some money again." Slapping the youngster on his shoulder, he led him to the stairs, "I know you have it in you to work hard and succeed. It worked for me and see where I am, Bobby."

Returning to his desk, the secretary affected a more serious, business-like demeanor, "So, did your meeting go well, detective?"

Ignoring the question, Doyle fixed his focus on the nameplate propped on the desk. "Mister Lee Riley! So, what did you do, change your name, Liam? Don't tell me ya became an admirer of that slave-owning traitor general who went by the same name? Or, maybe you took the soup and became a Protestant?"

"It's just a diminutive, Danny."

"Ah, diminutive, now that's a fancy word. I remember hearing it at Big Tits, when one of the girls yelled at a fella that he had a diminutive cock. But then, that's not you!" the detective bellowed out with a hardy laugh.

"Danny, lower your voice. Mister Prescott might hear you," Riley nervously whispered.

"Fuck him and fuck his cigar!" With that, Danny made a move to crush the cigar and throw it in the trash bin.

"Wait, do you know how much those cost?"

"About the price of that boy's arm, I'd say."

"I know. It's a hard world, Danny but at least he has a chance to make a buck and provide for his family."

"And it helps pay for little gifts for, how did he put it, ah, business associates."

"Here, before you break that panatela, let me trade you for a few of these candies." Making for an elaborate gift box atop his desk, Riley boasted, "Imported from France; cherry hard candy with a rich creamy filling. One of my few indulgences, and way beyond my budget. Yet, having them here reminds me that one day I'm going to afford these and a lot more. Besides, they make an impression with the bigwigs who pass through here."

As he slowly unwrapped the gold foil, exposing a shiny red morsel embossed with a *fleur-de-lis*, Danny cracked, "Don't bank on the likes of Prescott, Riley. You're not quite his type, if you know what I mean."

"I know enough about business to know that if you make things happen, you're rewarded"

"Good for you, boyo but I'm sure all the ward heelers in the family didn't hurt things for you."

"Those sorts of things never help with Mister Prescott. He only promotes on merit. And as for your reference to the Irish, the fact that we're here speaks for itself."

"As long as we're the hired help; but as much as I'd like to sit and chat, I got my work cut out for me."

"It's about the robbery of Missus Prescott, isn't it?"

"Good-bye, Lee."

Anxious to escape the reminders of his subservient role with Prescott, Brick Fist bound down the stairs that led to the factory courtyard. By now, a taste of winter had replaced yesterday's warmth. Turning up his coat collar, he looked towards the west, where dark clouds were rolling in off the lake. A backdrop of factories spewing columns of smoke into the sky only added to the desolate atmosphere.

Given the cold crispness of the morning air, the soot that was pervasive in this part of the city seemed to hang suspended before his eyes. All this served to feed his toxic mood; as such, Doyle was ill prepared for what was soon to greet him. He had barely passed through the plant gates, when he literally ran into a young policeman whose eager look betrayed the purpose to his presence. "Don't tell me. You're the yearling Collins was threatenin' to send over for me to instruct."

"Yes, Patrol Officer Hugh Costello. Captain Collins told me I was to accompany you on your rounds and learn from your example."

"He did, now? I find that surprising given his attitude about me; but I'm sure you're not some son of a political hack sent to spy on me. Of course not, are ya, lad."

"Actually, he's doing it at the request of my cousin, Lieutenant Broderick."

"Sweet Jesus, why didn't ya say that right off the mark?

"Well, I do now, sir."

"First of all, Costello, let's drop this 'sir" shit; but tell me, are you the son of Billy's cousin, Johnny Costello, the lawyer?"

"That's right, sir... er... Detective Doyle."

"For the sake of convenience, when alone, you can call me, Danny; otherwise it's Sergeant." Sporting a look of skepticism, if not, a lingering look of irritability, Brick Fist stepped back and took measure of his ramrod straight charge standing before him.

Clear-eyed and fair-skinned, young Costello had the face of a choirboy; however, he possessed a wiry frame that suggested a nimble strength and athleticism. An easy tendency to blush combined with an obstinate cowlick that refused to submit to the discipline of a comb, only added to his boyish look. Completing the portrait was a quick smile that captured the genial charm so often ascribed to his people.

Raised by parents who were pillars in the local Church, he reflected their beliefs in compassion and good works. Yet such attitudes did not interfere with his role as a copper. He could be no-nonsense and forceful in the application of his duties, showing the grit needed to get the job done; and as he stood there dressed in his perfectly assembled uniform, it was apparent that Officer Costello was anxious to look the part.

"Ya look like a seminarian. Do you know how to handle yourself?"

"I boxed and played rugby in school."

"Ah, so you fought by the Queensbury rules and you played that game in school, did ya? So tell me, sonny, do your school chums ever try to gouge your eyes out like some of those fine citizens on Canal Street?"

"Don't sweat your arse, Danny. I can handle myself," Hugh fired back with an edge.

Finished with his appraisal of the goods set before him, Danny paused for a moment before conceding, "Well, I suppose I can take you on. Besides, Billy Broderick wouldn't send me some sissy boy or more importantly, let loose a snake in my chicken coop."

"I'm here to learn and help, Danny."

"No, no, boyo. You're here to keep your gob shut, watch and do whatever I say! I'm no school marm and I ain't been needin' any help. My help is in my noggin, my two fists and my gun; and I don't like usin' the gun." Letting out a laugh, he added, "I can't say the same about my fists, if ya haven't heard!"

Ignoring the uncertain look that crossed Costello's face, Danny made a sweeping gesture to follow along. As they dodged all manner of conveyances through the crisscross of streets, Danny kept up the conversation, "I'm curious, Hugh, if I can call ya that, what makes a rich boy want to be a copper?"

"Well, I don't think I'm rich, Danny, but as I was finishing up at Canisius College, I got tired of all the books and studying."

"College! Don't tell me you're a college boy wastin' your time on this."

"I left before I graduated because I wanted to do something interesting and fulfilling."

"For Christ's sake! I suppose some might think that admirable, but for this former guttersnipe, I'm in it for what I can get out of it: mainly money. But just remember my young friend, this interesting work can get you killed; and if ya fuck up, me too. So, mark my words."

"Whatever you say, boss."

"That's a good lad! Now, I'm gonna show ya how we nab the thievin' rat who pinched Prescott's ol' lady outta of her jewelry."

After hustling down Water Street, they paused at the top of Evans, where Danny pointed out the object of their trek, a run-down liquor store with upstairs apartments. From the safe vantage point of an alley that ran alongside the shuttered-up Peking Saloon, the detective took time to observe any goings-on. He then proceeded to go over the details of the case with his new-found partner, before darting across the street.

After tiptoeing up the litter-strewn staircase, Doyle leaned his ear against the door. Satisfied that all was well, he whipped out his gun and kicked in the door. Charging into the room, he yelled, "Get your sorry English arse outta your pissed-soaked bed, Malcolm!"

Grabbing his whimpering target by his grimy nightshirt, Doyle slammed him against the wall with a force that made his head bounce. "Officer Costello, let me present the mysterious swami from the East, Babu Guru."

For Malcolm Blair, Buffalo's Infected District was the last sad outpost on a show business journey that took him from the docks of Liverpool to countless ports around the world. The self-proclaimed "holy man and seer" performed nightly at the Olympic Theater on Canal Street, just before the dancers would mount the stage. Despite an earnestness of effort, it was his ineptitude at magic that inspired choruses of laughter; thus keeping him on the fringes of employment. Yet this pervasive lack of talent, along with an inability to pry his hand from the bottle, left him teetering on the edge of the gutter.

"Ah, there it is," Brick Fist chuckled as he snared a greasy turban from the shelf of a barren cupboard. Plopping it atop the downcast head of his captive, he cajoled, "Now, Babu, I'd suggest ya conjure up what's goin' on with your pal Emmon Foley, if ya know what's good for ya! I'm sure ya heard what I did to your friend, Toots, the shell-game man, when he failed to mind my rules."

As young Costello lowered his eyes, unwilling to join in on the spectacle, the terrified rummy stammered, "Ah... ah... I saw him last night, Constable. If that's what you mean?"

"Stop wastin' time, Babu. I'm not a patient man!"

Catching his breath, he resumed, in an unmistakably refined English baritone, "He was having a grand time of it; spending money like a Vanderbilt; buying the house a drink on more than one occasion. He proceeded to secure the services of a couple of young damsels, if memory serves me right. He even had a goat tied up in the back room of the Olympic; said he bought it earlier in the day at the Elk Street Market, before announcing he was going to have a feast at his place tomorrow, that is, today." Letting out a sardonic chuckle, he added, "Called the beast, 'Shit a Brick,' if I'm not mistaken."

As Danny shot back a threatening look, the magician cried out, "Please, sir! I implore you. I just thought that you may find humor in the irony."

"Now, do I look like I'm interested in irony? Just tell me if he's still at his place down in the Beaches."

"As far as I know, that is the case, Sergeant. And of course you won't tell anyone that I told you."

"Don't worry. Ya done good, Malcolm," the detective replied in a somewhat weary tone. Despite knowing he had to squeeze the sad little showman to get results, he didn't feel good about it; consequently, he slipped a greenback onto the table before heading out the door. Yet no sooner had they left Babu Guru's squalid hovel than Brick Fist triumphantly announced, "We're off to the Beaches to catch a fish—a thieving bottom-feeder, our Mister Foley—getting ready for his party from his ill-gotten gains.

With the young patrolman hurrying to keep up, Danny hopped aboard a trolley that would take them over the Ohio Street Draw Bridge, and towards the area known as the Beaches. No sooner had they settled onto a bench near the back furnace than Danny turned to his new protégée, "So, seeing you had your first taste, you don't like my methods."

"You told me to keep my mouth shut."

"I bet those priests at college got you thinking about morality and all that. And for the record, I also told you to watch me. So what did ya see? Go on, Hugh. I doubt you'll hurt my feeling."

"You didn't have to humiliate that pathetic creature. You could've pressed him hard without the shame, and still gotten your information."

"His friends kill people. That should tell ya enough."

"Sometimes that attitude comes at a price."

"That sort of thinking is a luxury I can't afford. I just do what works, Officer Costello."

Arriving at their stop, they set out on foot. The Beaches was a community of squatters who lived in shacks along a sea wall on a barren strip of land between Lake Erie and the Buffalo River. The dreary scrubland stood barely above water level and was unsuitable for any practical use. Its tiny homes were constructed from all manner of reclaimed material, with little more than rags serving to fill the gaps between patchwork planks. One could only imagine what little protection these shelters could provide in the face of Buffalo's harsh winters. Still, many of them were well-kept and possessing a certain humble charm; a testament to the fortitude and hopefulness of their inhabitants.

Its residents were the poorest of the poor, making whatever qualified as a living as best they could; usually at the bottom rung of the wage ladder. Ironically, their prime earning days were in the winter, when the commercial fleet was iced in. Braving the withering elements, they would take their dogsleds onto the frozen lake, saw through the ice and bring in a catch that they'd sell to appreciative fishmongers and restaurants.

With no street names or house numbers, Danny and Costello wandered through a maze of cottages searching for their quarry. As luck would have it, fortune intervened in the form of Emmon Foley returning to his hovel after a visit to a community outhouse.

Ducking behind a collapsing shed that managed to serve as a barn, the pair stood back and watched as the carefree crook ambled back to his shanty, whistling the strains of the popular song, "I'll take you home again, Kathleen."

After edging closer and making sure the working girls or other guests were gone, the detective instructed his partner to circle around the back. Once his target was safely inside, Danny bolted across the overgrown patch that qualified as a neighbor's front lawn. Peering through the cracks in the shutter, he watched as Emmon danced a little jig while counting a wad of greenbacks stuffed into a ceramic fruit jar. With Costello's arrival around the corner, Doyle signaled a count of three before he drew his pistol and started smashing through the entranceway. No sooner had the makeshift door come flying off its hinges than Foley went leaping through a back-room window. Tumbling onto his feet with the agile grace of a circus performer, he turned and locked eyes with the startled sentry lying in wait.

In an instant the chase began. Hightailing it through a labyrinth of buildings, the wily thief performed as if executing a well rehearsed escape plan. By now, Brick Fist had joined the pursuit. Yet despite his size, he was able to keep pace and more importantly keep the pair in his sight.

Flinging anything that wasn't tied down into the path of his pursuers, Foley emerged from the yards and alleys of the Beaches and headed towards the Ohio Street Bridge. Once over, he hoped to find refuge within the adjoining network of granaries, wharves and rail yards; however, his scheme seemed thwarted when the bridge began to rise for an approaching lake steamer. Yet good fortune came to the rescue, in the form of a reluctant lift engine. Ignoring the lowered warning gate, Foley flew across the span with hardly a bump.

No such luck prevailed for the hard charging posse, as their arrival coincided with the reanimation of the bridge machinery. Despite cries from the operator, they churned up the incline, just before the widening chasm reached an impassable distance. As the ship's horn blared in the background, the pair made a mad leap and landed with a resounding thud. Scrambling to their feet, they scanned the terrain in an effort to pick up the trail. Just then, Danny spied a phantom figure duck down Saint Clair Street. As they resumed the chase, haste was at a premium, since the fugitive would soon be lost amid the industrial chaos.

The fleet-footed thief seemed to confirm Danny's instincts; however, as he turned into the labyrinth of train cars assembled in the yard, he failed to see an oncoming locomotive steaming from one of the grain mills. In an instant, a blood-curdling scream echoed off the walls of the nearby elevators. As the long line of cars crept towards a halt, the policemen could make out what looked like a pinwheel of arms and legs twisting alongside the engine. After rushing up to the train as it came to a stop, they met a distraught crew clambering down the ladder. Foley, lay bathed in a pool of blood, with his head smashed against the metal post of a track switch. The mangled remnant of his leg was caught within the gearing of the wheel, hanging by a thread from just above the knee. Moving quickly, Danny ripped off his belt in an effort to stanch the flow from the gushing wound. Ignoring the pleas of innocence by the engineer, he yelled out to Costello, "Get to the firebox, Hugh! And make it fast! The poor man's dyin'."

V

"Get outta here ya dirty pig! I told ya before about your language!"

The ever scrupulous barkeep was quick to excuse himself to his customers at the rail, before calmly grabbing a club from behind the bar. Needing no further prompting from the former war hero and champion boxer, the offending patron beat a hasty retreat to the door, all the while pleading forgiveness for his errant remark.

"This ain't no sportin' bar or stall saloon; they can go find that on Canal Street," he grumbled as he returned to his station next to the taps, where he always held court. There was never any mistaking who was the master of this realm. As the owner of Horgan's Hilt, Brendan, "Blinky" Shea was not only the strict arbiter of barroom etiquette, but he was also a commanding figure in the local Irish community, having eclipsed both his wartime and prizefighting fame.

Some ten years earlier, he had taken his considerable earnings from the ring and used it to start his own business. Despite the bar's working-class location, Blinky spared no expense in converting the one-time harness shop and drygoods store into the premier public house of the First Ward.

Stung by society's treatment of the Irish, Shea was determined to "spit in their eye," by providing a first-class setting for his patrons and brethren; and in that respect, he did not fail. Its centerpiece was a gleaming mahogany bar supported by massive Tuscan columns ornamented with an elaborately carved Celtic motif. Over forty feet long, it featured a polished marble counter, and a matching rail that was held in place by bronze lion-head fixtures. The fluted crown above the back-bar had at its center, a bas-relief of a regimental sword flanked by military emblems of Shea's wartime units. Prominently displayed in front of a mirror etched with the words, "Horgan's Hilt, B.T. Shea, proprietor," were framed portraits of the martyred President, Abraham Lincoln, the Holy Family and the Irish Nationalist, Daniel O'Connell. Occupying lesser spots along the mantel were tintypes of the boxing champion, Paddy Ryan, pitching great, Pud Galvin of the Buffalo baseball club and a group picture of the bar's regulars.

The tavern housed a spacious back room that often served as a community meeting space. Banners hanging above its archway identified a number of these organizations, including the First Ward Democratic Club, the Brotherhood of Railroad Workers and the Grain Scooper's Exchange. Since its inception, Horgan's Hilt had become a cultural hub for the Irish of Buffalo, attracting both the powerful and ordinary alike. More importantly, it was an oasis where hard working and largely immigrant masses could find respect, joy and respite from their daily toils.

Completing the grand tableau were parquet flooring, art-glass lighting and custom wallpaper. Much of the design plan had been conceived by Shea's late wife and their three daughters, the oldest of whom, Keena, worked out of a small office behind the bar. The rest of the tavern's staff was mostly comprised of his family and neighbors.

Located near the corner of Louisiana and Mackinaw Streets, the saloon was named after Shea's commander in New York's Eighty-Eighth Volunteers, Major William Horgan. Horgan was a hero at the Battle of Fredericksburg, and who despite suffering what would prove to be mortal wounds, urged his men forward by waving the hilt of his sword during the Irish Brigade's doomed assault on Marye's Heights. Shea's own nickname came about as a result of the famous attack, since his facial tic and crease across his bald temple were the only remaining signs of a head wound he suffered during the bloody charge. This battlefield reminder seemed to perfectly fit his overall image. A bulldog of a man, Blinky possessed a smashed nose, lantern jaw and a series of scars left from his bare-knuckle days. It all combined to suggest a tenacious strength and toughness. Still, he had a tender heart as evidenced by his ready smile and willingness to help others. Most of all, he was a devoted and loving husband, father and grandpa to a family that was the apple of his eye.

After one last interruption, directing his niece and barmaid, Kitty McCoy, on the placement of food trays for the free lunchtime meal, Blinky resumed his homily, "Now, as I was sayin', I heard from the reporter Joe Perkins, that they robbed Harmon's Chandler Shop and Kennedy's Foundry last night; took tools, supplies and whatever else wasn't nailed down."

Joining him on this day were the lawyer Tom Beahan, Father Pat Morris, an assistant at St Bridget's, Mike Nellaney, the ward boss and local political power, and Padrig Tierney, a night shift worker at Prescott Wallpaper. Sitting beside Tierney was his grandfather, Thomas, a patriarch of the Ward, who helped dig the canal in his youth.

"Yeah, I heard from the copper, Herm Krause, that they think it was one of the neighborhood gangs, like the 'Beach Bugs' or the 'Louisiana Street Rat Kickers,'" Tierney offered as he snipped off the tip of his five-cent cigar.

"Isn't that typical; our own people once more preying on ourselves; whether it's workers undermining workers, politicians backstabbing voters or crooks beating victim," Father Morris quipped.

"Or poor men doin' rich men's biddin'" Tierney added

"Ain't it always the case, gents," Blinky observed. "For the life of me, a goodly part of Georgia's Twenty-Fourth were sons of Erin. After that horrible charge up the heights at Fredericksburg, I remember lyin' there and hearin' 'em shout, 'Sorry lads, it was you or us'; half the time in the ol' tongue. Things don't change."

"Amen, Brendan, and knowing it's just us 'micks,' I wonder how quickly the big guns at City Hall will get on these robberies," the priest asked.

"Don't worry, I'll be seein' to that," Nellaney insisted. "But don't be so sure it's some of ours. Those gang thugs don't have the smarts, and I know whoever did it, pinched a number of places around town including Jewett's Stove Works and the Clark and Brown Distillery."

"Sweet Mother Mary, is the whiskey hurting," Tierney laughed before remembering Father Morris. "Ah, beggin' your pardon, Father."

"Don't worry, Padrig, it made my heart skip a beat, too."

"As Brendan can easily testify, I like the liquor as much as anybody," Beahan, the lawyer, interjected, "but we shouldn't be praising it like a sacrament. It's too often been a source of trouble for our people. The powerful still want to keep us under their boot. Like the English in the old country, they want to keep us poor, ignorant and liquored up; you know divide and conquer. That being said, I plan on talking to Captain Collins about these thefts. Neil Kennedy is a good friend of mine and he's had enough bad luck lately." Besides steadfastly defending the interests of an Irish community that was so often marginalized when it came to the law, Tom Beahan held a special status among his ethnic kin for having participated in the Fenian Raid on Canada that took place across the Niagara River from Buffalo, back in sixty-six.

The ensuing Battle of Ridgeway, involved over a thousand Irish Americans troops, mainly Civil War veterans, whose goal was to seize and hold Upper Canada in exchange for Irish independence. The doomed invasion was quickly quashed by British North American forces, but not before the loss of life on both sides. Eventually released through the diplomatic efforts of the United States government, Beahan and his madly heroic cohorts became the stuff of legend among their Irish brethren.

"Still," the priest insisted, "we always seem to be hardest on our own, like with yesterday's tragedy…"

Just then, the conversation trailed off, as Brick Fist and his young partner came walking through the doors. Grabbing a slab of ham and a thick slice of rye from the lunchtime tray, Danny slipped into a spot not far from the others. As Doyle began to peruse a copy of the *Commercial Advertiser* that he snatched from a stack of papers on the bar, the priest slid over to his side; but not before taking time to place an order. "If you would, Brendan; can you draw me another stout?"

Before the young priest had a chance to pull out change from his pocket, Blinky intervened, "And we'll be taking no money from you, Father. Thank you for seeing to the care of the three Kilcoyne boys up at the orphanage on Limestone Hill. The wee lads loosing both their parents in the same year; a cryin' shame. The ma and da were good folks, being neighbors an' all."

"And thank you for your generous gift, Brendan. Saint Joseph's Orphan Home is a fine place. My friend, Father Baker will take good care of them."

The discussion managed to catch the detective's attention, but before he had a chance to comment, Father Pat spoke up, "So, Daniel, are you reading about your exploits yesterday?"

"I did notice a story about some thievin' dog gettin' caught."

"So, once more you got your man, Danny; a man not a dog. And was his leg or maybe his life worth a pendant?"

"I didn't run into a train, Foley did."

"Just doing your job, eh?"

"That's right, Father."

"And leaving a path of destruction wherever you've been."

"Sometimes things get a little rough dealing with the dregs around these parts."

"Like an attack dog meeting out so-called justice."

"The fine citizens of this city want their streets clean."

"Don't give me that choirboy talk, Danny. I know you protect some of those upstanding businessmen in the Infected District and do the dirty work for some of those rich folk who don't want to get their hands dirty."

"Then take it up with my choirboy boss."

"No, that's not the bad part. It's your heavy-handed, cruel treatment of some of those desperate souls who find themselves on the wrong side of the law."

"I'm a success as a copper because I put my Irish arse on the line and get the job done. Those on the top know it and I make sure I'm rewarded for my efforts. I'm never gonna be stomped down and left poor and adrift like most of those who make their way to your church."

"Mark my words, Sergeant! It's not all black and white, and even criminals are God's children. You might be sitting pretty now, but you'll be finding yourself cutoff and empty; not to mention putting your eternal soul in peril."

"You're a good man, Father; and unlike some of your stinkin', black-hearted brothers of the cloth—"

"Danny!" a wide-eyed Costello gasped.

Brushing aside his partner, Danny kept on, "You're a credit to your calling. I like you, but don't go lecturing me on what I'm doing. Ya don't know what it's all about."

"You'd test the entire roll call of Saints, but I'll still keep you in my prayers, Danny."

"It's a free country but you're wastin' your time, Pat."

Having said his peace, the priest was content to make his way back to the now animated discussion, taking place among his companions, which at the moment seemed much less draining than his parrying with Doyle. No sooner had Father Morris turned to leave than Keena poked her head out from the office behind the bar. With the coast clear, she slid up to where Danny was standing. By now, young Costello had headed back to the buffet tray, intent on filling his plate from the assorted treats.

Ignoring the questioning look of her father, she spoke up, "I'm surprised at Father Pat, Danny. He had no right talking to you like that, at least outside the confessional."

"Ah, I suppose he has a job to do."

"But suggesting you're corrupt."

"I'm not at all ashamed to say I do favors for friends in position to offer me gifts. *Begorrah*, even the Church pushes for their gifts every Sunday, even from the poor."

"My, you're a hard one, Danny; but despite your wanting all that Brick Fist talk about you, I know you have a good heart somewhere in there. I know that little secret about how you do things for the widows and little children in the neighborhood."

"Please, I'm no goody-boy like your lovely Mister Riley."

"See! I pay you a compliment and you have to insult my friend, Mister Riley, whom I am quite proud of for his attempts to be a successful example to the young ones around here, and for his efforts to find work for them: like getting jobs at Prescott's for my cousin Kitty's two boys."

"Jobs for kids in that hellhole!"

"I know, but conditions will change, God willing and with hard work. In the meantime, they're not wee kids and those jobs will help a family in trouble. Kitty's crippled husband hasn't worked in a year since he fell from a scaffold while working on the German Insurance Building. My da tries to help, but they're proud people. With nine mouths to feed, the boy's pay will go a long way to help."

"And that's why I'm gonna make sure I'm never caught without money again. That's why I say, do whatever it takes to get results and cash in."

"Everybody wants to get ahead, Danny, but that's not the only thing in life."

"Getting ahead is everything. It's making sure you take care of yourself and all that's important to ya."

"And what about having the admiration and respect of the people around you."

"I have that when I keep order on the streets."

"But you can't take it so far that they're fearing and resenting you."

"Oh, for sure there's a lot of them that hate me," he noted as he looked down the rail, "yet I know what has to be done. That's what I'm paid for."

"We all want those sure answers, especially in a world that can be hard and confusing. But when we're too sure, we can shut ourselves off to the truth and to others."

"Ah, this is all dreamin' talk; and easy talk for you, what with your being the daughter of a rich man and knowing someday you'll have a husband to provide for you!"

"Don't go puttin' that on me, Danny Doyle! I help run this place, with the buying and bookkeeping and all. And don't you worry, I plan on making my mark in the labor movement."

"And I bet you're all sure about yourself when it comes to that!"

"I believe in what I do to help workers, but I know I can't and shouldn't expect to get all the results I want. Still, if there's justice in the world, and I believe there is, we'll move forward."

"Well, I'm not gonna twist myself up in all that thinking; but I got my goals too: simple ones. I want to get one of those nice Quaker farms out in the country. Nobody bothers you out there. I once farmed, you know, and I liked it."

"I hope your dreams are answered and..." Just then, she was interrupted by the arrival of Raphael Taglieri, one of her colleagues from the K of L. "Ah excuse me, Keena," glancing suspiciously at the detective, he whispered, "I was just passing by and I thought I'd check to see about the meeting."

After merely nodding, she said, "And I talked to the others."

Feigning a rush, the organizer quickly paid his adieus.

"I recognize him. He's that *eye-talian* troublemaker. You better be careful. I don't trust those anarchists."

"He's no anarchist; but you don't trust anybody, Sergeant Brick Fist. You ought to try it sometime," she smiled wryly.

"Always trying to convert me; like the waves pounding on the rocks. Sweet Jesus, you just might wear me down someday."

"I do hope so," she giggled.

"Say, what are you two all whisperin' about?" Kitty, the barmaid, asked as she showed up to replenish the lunchtime stores. "Ya look like you're plannin' to carve your initials in a tree."

"With her? I'd only end up hangin' myself on one of its branches."

"Don't flatter yourself! You'd be so lucky, Doyle."

"I don't know, Keena. I wouldn't mind those blue eyes staring at me in the mornin'," Kitty leered, "or those big boots sittin' under me bed." Although two years short of forty and having brought into the world nine babies, seven of whom survived, Kitty McCoy still had the sort of buxom yet lithe body that both men and women covet. Her jet black hair, emblazoned with a swath of gray down the middle, coupled with her wolf-like, eyes, gave her a beautiful yet dangerous look that seemed to perfectly fit her bawdy personality. All this served her well in the largely male domain of a saloon, where love-struck patrons would tip freely.

"The shame on you, cousin, both for your poor taste and the fact you're a married woman," Keena winked.

"And you're almost spoken for, girl."

"Thank you, Kit but she's just jealous you got real men payin' attention to ya," Doyle chuckled.

"Don't go spillin' your holy water, Keena. I'm just flirtin' with the famous Sergeant Big Fist. And by the way, is it true what they say about big hands, Danny?"

Nearly choking on his beer, the detective struggled for words.

"So what have you got to say for yourself, now, Mister Smarty-aleck," Keena laughed as she nudged her cousin.

Regaining himself, Danny fired back, "There's only one way to find out, but that would mean your uncle's shillelagh cracking my noggin."

"Well, I suppose I wouldn't wanna see such a pretty face bruised," Kitty sighed.

"Good God, the malarkey is getting a bit thick around here. Besides, I have to be getting back to the desk. I have a lot of work to do, plus my da has me organizing a group from the tavern to cheer General Grant when he comes to town next month; drums, a wagon, painted banners, the whole kit and caboodle."

"I thought your da was a Democrat?"

"He is, but he thinks the General walks on water; him being a war hero and all."

"Oh, yeah. Well, I have to get back to the street. It looks like I'm gonna have my work cut out for me trying to drag young Costello away from that barmaid he's talking to."

"That's my niece, Colleen," Kitty snapped. "So ya better be tellin' 'im to put any ideas right outta his head."

"He's got big hands like me, ya know."

"Oh, yeah! And I'll be headin' for my uncle's stick if ya don't hurry."

"No need to tell me more, ma'am. And here's for me and the kid and get one for your da's bunch over there."

Acknowledging the detective's gesture, the patrons offered their thanks with the customary Irish salute, "*slainte.*"

After bidding a smiling farewell to the ladies, Danny plunked down a greenback and headed towards the door. No sooner had he made his way out, than Keena turned to her cousin, "You're right though, he is a handsome lad."

"But there's a hurtin' quality about 'im."

"Yeah, I know."

VI

The pestilent eyes refused to stray from their targets as they watched the policemen pause on their way down Canal Street.

"Danny, before you go on about what you want me to do, those two fellas standing across the street have been following us since we left the precinct house."

"Thank goodness; I was beginnin' to think you might be going blind, Hugh. They ain't exactly been hidin'."

"So what do you think they're up to?"

They're the other Foley boys; just sayin' 'hello,' I suppose."

Leaning against a lamppost in front of the steaming shack that housed Ling's Chinese Laundry, the two kept their unflinching gaze riveted on the coppers. Despite the distance separating the parties, there was no mistaking the brothers' menacing intent, as each had a steely look of resolve etched across his face. Dressed in matching black frock coats, they had spent the night at Saint Mary's Infirmary, where their brother lay at death's door. Mike, the younger of the two had the usual Foley mop of red hair, but unlike the rest of the clan he was handsome and a natty dresser; enough so that he could easily be confused with any of the rising young business types making their mark on the town. However, he made no effort to conceal his brutal nature, as he pulled a Bowie knife from his belt and began to pick at his nails, all the while smiling straight at Danny.

Doc, the leader and muscle of the clan, was distinguished by his ubiquitous green flannel shirt and dirty flat cap. His pit bull frame aligned perfectly with his treacherous reputation. Bulging shoulders supported a massive head framed with mutton chops; nonetheless, the thick crop of whiskers failed to obscure a scarred-over, missing chunk of cheek, bitten off by his mistress cousin, enraged by his holding back on her cut of the spoils. Rumor had it that the unfortunate hell-fire was chopped up and dumped into Lake Erie.

Now aware that his targets had taken notice, the elder Foley pulled an object from his pocket and began tossing it into the air. No sooner had Danny returned a piercing glare than Doc flung the gyrating orb towards the detective. As it skidded to a stop at his feet, Brick Fist leaned down and observed, "Dead Rabbit."

"A rabbit's head? What in the world?" Costello wondered aloud.

"Didn't your nuns and priests teach ya nothin' about our people in this country; like how they had to fight when they got here?"

"Oh, yeah, now I remember. Wasn't the "Dead Rabbits" an Irish gang in New York?"

"And a fearsome lot they were; used to stick a dead rabbit on a pike and carry it before 'em as they'd go into battle. I remember hearin' ol' Buck Foley, the dead patriarch of that blighted clan, was a member of the gang, long ago. He got kicked out because they had no room for thieves bein' among 'em. He high tailed it up here, where the family continues their fine traditions. Anyway, this here is a message. Apparently, I should be shakin' in my boots that they want to do me harm." After the detective cast a disdainful look towards the brothers, the pair returned sneering salutes before ambling off in the opposite direction.

"They can't be threatening a city detective! Let's go drag 'em in and grill 'em.

"That won't do no good. No, I just gotta be on my toes. In the meantime, I'll figure out something to take care of my friends the Foleys."

After kicking the animal head into the gutter, Doyle resumed his instructions to his charge, "Now, as I was sayin' before we got interrupted, I want ya to go over to Harmon's and then to Kennedy's Foundry and talk to the bosses about the thefts. Ask about anybody they fired or about any bellyachers on the payroll; or anybody lurkin' around or acting suspicious. Poke around and use that block a wood on your neck; you're the college boy. And keep your head up! The Foleys know you're my mate."

Smiling at the reference to a "mate," Costello adopted a more familiar tone, "And where will you be, so I can meet up with you, Danny?"

"Never mind about me; you just do what I told you and I'll find ya; besides, I got a bunch of street hawker kids who deliver my messages if I need to get in touch with ya."

As the patrolman hurried to Main Street, where he could catch a trolley to the Ward, Brick Fist made towards the industrial area near the mouth of the harbor. As he sidestepped his way through the growing pedestrian traffic, he noticed more than a few turning heads, no doubt in response to his run-in with Emmon, one of the more notable habitués of the street. Heading past the grain elevators and steam engine works on Norton Street, he sneaked behind the New York Central Depot and followed the tracks to where Carnahan had a lumberyard next to the canal. Looking down from a vantage point of a trestle spanning one of the slips, he searched for any signs of a missing shipment of Canadian lumber that Prescott insisted was hijacked by Finger's men. Convinced that no one was around this section of the yard, Doyle decided to slip through the fence and examine a tarped-over load of wood in the hope of finding the exporter's stenciled markings. No sooner had he begun to pull back the canvas than he heard the strains of a popular sea chantey, "Blow the Man Down," being whistled behind his back.

"Well, I'll be damned. The famous Sergeant Doyle robbin' lumber."

"You couldn't be more wrong, Mister Marley. I've been chasin a pickpocket for blocks now, and I'm sure he ducked under this coverin'."

"Ah, ya missed 'em, Danny. I saw a fella pop over the wall into that brickyard. He musta seen a chance when ya were taking a break on the trestle."

There was no missing George "Harpoon" Marley's six-foot, four-inch, three hundred pound frame. As Carnahan's number one man, he had a reputation that was as fearsome and overwhelming as his physical presence. As a child, the gentle teachings of a Quaker upbringing failed to quell his unruly spirit. Later, his taste for violence was nurtured on the bloody decks of a New England whaler, and brought to full fruition during some of the most savage fighting of the Civil War. It was on one of those battlefields that Sergeant Marley saved the life of his commanding officer, Major Finbar Carnahan. The two had been as thick as thieves ever since.

Tattooed from top to bottom, his usual choice of clothing included a sailor's pea coat, corduroy trousers and English riding boots. Perched atop his shaved head was his ever-present Union kepi, embroidered with the ensign of his former unit, the Seventy-Ninth New York Volunteers. A wide leather holster completed his outfit, and it always held his trademark pistol, unique for its whalebone scrimshaw grip. Needless to say, there was no mistaking this man for a grocer or a clerk.

"Maybe the bugger stashed his pickin's here. You don't mind if I take a quick look, Georgie." Without waiting for an answer, the detective drew back the tarp, only to discover a stack of raw timber.

"I'm sure you'll catch the thievin' rat the next time, Danny; but ya know, this is good fortune, my friend. I was about to go lookin' for ya. The boss would like to see ya."

Knowing that they wouldn't try anything funny with a police sergeant, and more importantly, knowing he could handle himself in any situation, even when confronting the likes of Harpoon Marley, Doyle showed no hesitation. "I'd like to see Fingers, too."

"I don't have to remind ya of the name, Danny."

"Ah, forgive my slip. I mean Major Carnahan, of course."

"He's back at his place. Why don't we grab me wagon." Barely settled onto the buckboard, Marley launched into one of his colorful anecdotes, the themes of which usually revolved around whiskey, women and fighting. Despite the man's ferocious reputation, Danny always found the hulking enforcer to be an engaging and friendly companion; however, given a disposition that could turn on a penny, the policeman always remained vigilant.

Finger's warehouse headquarters, located down the street from the Central Wharf, was both his professional and personal lair. Rejecting the lure of a more than affordable mansion on Millionaires' Row, the crime lord preferred to be closer to the heart of his commercial interests. He secured the property at a bargain price from the previous owner who had the misfortune of sustaining considerable loses at Finger's tables. It was said that the transfer was coaxed along by the barrel of Marley's pistol pressed against the man's temple. He was told to sign the deed or end up food for the sturgeons.

As Danny was soon to discover, Finger's domicile was hardly Spartan. While the first two floors were typical of an industrial warehouse, complete with docks, crates and all manner of lifts and conveyances, the top story would rival the interiors of any of city's great homes. As Marley led him through the apartment, he found himself amidst a sea of luxury, including, plush carpets, ornate millwork, and furniture and artwork from around the world. Arriving at the grand parlor dominated by a massive

crystal chandelier, Doyle followed his escort to the far corner, where
Carnahan sat behind his desk, surrounded by cabinets filled with books.
Rising, the gangster flashed a bright smile before thrusting out his hand,
"Good to see you, Sergeant Doyle! It's been too long."

"Likewise, Major Carnahan."

"I think we can dispense with the formalities. We've known each
other too long, Danny."

"You're right, Finbar."

Dressed in a red, silk smoking jacket and dark wool trousers, he cut
the figure of an urbane Victorian gentleman. Over six feet tall, he had a
narrow, porcelain face crowned by thick gray hair slicked back with a hint of
pomade. He sported a thin black moustache of the continental style and
while too long a nose would preclude his being considered classically
handsome, he had a look that was lean and distinguished. But what set him
apart were crystalline blue eyes that seemed to bore through those with
whom he talked. "Please, join me in some tea, Danny. George, could you
ask Min if she'd bring out a pot and cups; and then, if I could be alone with
my friend."

"Sure thing, Major." After a quick sidebar conversation with his
boss, Marley proceeded down the hall.

"I hope I'm not interrupting your reading. So what's that, Sch...
Shooo..."

"Schopenhauer, a German philosopher."

"'Soup in an hour,' sounds good to me! Ah, there I go showing my
ignorance."

"I know better than that, Danny. Despite the rough and tumble
image, I know you're damn sharp. A lot smarter than your bosses."

"That's mighty generous of you, Finbar, but I..."

Just then he was interrupted by an older Chinese woman dressed in traditional native garb and carrying a tray with tea service. Her lavender scented bun evoked in Danny distant memories of similarly perfumed hair.

"Before we go on, may I introduce, Madame Woo, my cook and supervisor of the household."

After bowing with a delicate smile and exchanging greetings with the detective, she quickly exited.

"As I was going to say, I'm curious about what's on your mind, Finbar."

"We'll get to that but I wouldn't be a good host, if I didn't show you around. I hope you allow me to indulge a little of my pride."

After leading Danny about the room and pointing out the various pieces of art, he stopped at a strange looking apparatus sitting next to the grand piano. "I think you'll like this. It's a mechanical organette. I first saw one at the Philadelphia Exposition. Here, listen." As he cranked the handle of the polished cherry box, out came the melodic chords of an organ sonata. "Bach, you heard of him, a musical giant; it's done with perforated rolls of paper." Taking one out from the bottom of a bureau, he handed it to Doyle.

"Most amazing; and over there, is that one of those telephone machines? I see them stringing wire around town."

"Indeed. It's down right now, but when it's working, I can pick it up and talk to my manager downstairs, or even to Mitch over at the Olympic."

"No telling how that will change things."

"And here is one of my prize possessions." Picking up a picture sitting on a shelf, he passed it to Danny, "No doubt, you recognize General Sheridan; and that peach-fuzzed officer is yours truly. I eventually found my way onto his staff. He's a great warrior and great man."

"And a great Irishman, to boot."

"One more reason to be proud of our people. We should never forget our people, Danny. They suffered greatly in their journey here. My own dear mother survived one of the coffin ships. Widowed young, she worked like a dog in those dives up the street to provide a life for me. Yet we're beginning to make our mark, no thanks to those greedy blue bloods who exploit our kinfolk and then try to justify it as some saving mission. They think they can wrap their turds in pious homilies and it won't taste like shit."

"I can tell you they won't be forcing it down my throat. I'm making sure I get my cut of the pie."

"Good, you're like me; take care of yourself while not selling out your people like some of those rats out there do. You know, you should be working for one of your own, Danny; but then we've gone over this before."

"And as I said before, I follow my own way, Finbar."

Noticing Doyle's renewed interest in his regimental regalia mounted on the wall, Carnahan changed the subject. "An important part of my life; and yet, I never asked if you served?"

"Sure, I got conscripted. Obviously, I couldn't buy my way out."

"Unlike most of those fancy-pants sons of the captains of industry."

"Ain't that so. Anyway, I didn't see much fighting, but I did my job. Still, my absence ruined my little farm. Even when I came back, it couldn't recover." He paused for a moment, appearing lost in thought. Continuing on he added, "Burned my arse knowing I fought to free slaves who would work cheap and take the jobs that remained."

"The money barons must have been licking their chops, thinking of that."

"Luckily for me, I eventually found a job as a copper."

"And quite an effective one at that; which leads me to wonder why you, of all people, are wasting your time snooping around my lumber yard for a prick like Prescott."

"Georgie knows I was chasing a snatcher."

"Come on, Danny. I heard about the stealing going on at his operations, including that recent shipment of lumber. My business is going great and I don't have to be pinching crumbs from him. Still, the rich bastard can't scratch his fat arse without thinking that I somehow planted the piles. Maybe if he paid his workers a little better, he wouldn't have this problem."

"He's like all those rich Prots, but still, he pays me and there's theft going—"

"Listen, you know why my people work hard and are loyal. Mainly, I pay them decently." Not only did Fingers take care of his workers, both in the legitimate and underbelly parts of his enterprise, but he was admired, if not esteemed by most of the Irish community for his philanthropy, such as his endowment of the schools at Saint Bridget's and Saint Pat's, and for his support of the Irish Republican Brotherhood, back in the old country. "I share the wealth not unlike those groups like the Shakers or those Ebenezers, who were chased out west for not wanting to fight in the War. But mind ya, lad, the big slice of the cake goes to me. After all, I should be rewarded for my expertise, planning and investment risk," he grinned slyly, before turning serious. "Yet it's not just about sharing the wealth. In my business, you have to watch your back. A happy comrade is less likely to slip ya the shiv."

"Nature of the business, I suppose."

"Which brings us to the purpose of our little meeting. You had a run-in with one of my employees, Mister Emmon Foley."

"You're damn right. I bagged the thieving rat for pinching Missus Prescott's jewelry. And that's not to mention his wounding her poor ol' driver and scaring the wits out of her while conducting himself in an ungentlemanly fashion."

"You should have come to me before letting this get out of hand."

"Come to you? I figured you weren't involved and he was working on his own. Besides, time's important. I have a job to do whether or not, as you say, it gets out of hand."

"Of course he was acting rogue; and that will be addressed with him and his brothers, assuming he survives. But there's a bigger issue at hand here and you mentioned it before: the nature of my business. As you know, my enterprise has many elements, one being, let's say, the entertainment branch, where I supply people with little diversions from their miserable toils."

"And some might say, separate their wages from their pockets," Danny chuckled before adding, "Let's not go makin' a saint outta ya, Finbar."

"More likely being sent in the other direction," he laughed. "But I can't control customers foolish conduct, and I certainly don't encourage blowing their rent or grocery money."

"And once again, just the nature of the business, eh?"

"Yes, and I take that business very seriously. Not only do I rather enjoy its benefits, as you can see, but I'm also responsible for the welfare of many people who work for me. I won't abide anything that could threaten that. You see, one of the principal components of my business involves insurance. I and my team of associates provide protection from risk; a need fundamental to any commercial entity, whether big or small. It's a highly lucrative service that we perform quite well; however, when it appears the insurer is unable to protect one of its own 'assets', as in the case of my agent,

Mister Foley—and for him I use the word 'asset' very loosely—it strikes at my credibility in terms of delivering this important service. And of course, that could have a serious impact on my profits."

"It looks like ya have a bit of a problem there, Finbar."

"Well, as I see it, we both have a problem; but I have an easy solution to it. One way to prevent a recurrence of that unfortunate situation is for you to see me if one of my agents, acting in his own interest, causes a problem for you. I can assure you that the matter will be promptly taken care of."

"As with you, I like what I got going for myself. Part of the good deal I have, is that I get the job done. Swiftly! I can't be wasting time when, how'd ya say it, rogues like Foley fuck up."

"And my suggestion makes sure the likes of Foley keep in line."

"Like today, when his brother Doc tossed a dead rabbit in my path, which only made me laugh."

"I'm sorry, but see, that's exactly what I'm saying."

"All I can say, Finbar, is that everybody out there knows I got my rules, simple rules. And I know how loyal and dutiful your lads are. I know if you put out the word, none of 'em will be causing any rogue trouble."

Fingers didn't say a word, as the intensity showing in his eyes came to full force. After a moment, he slowly proclaimed, "I like and respect you, Danny, but never forget that I take business seriously and I will use all means at my disposal to solve any problems that threaten it."

"I know you respect that I can handle myself, and not always by the book. While I'm not the most popular fella on the force, I know the lads would not cotton to a brother officer havin' troubles. They'd get all worked up. I'm sure that would be bad business, too."

"Well, Danny, I'm also a firm believer that reason always prevails; especially when people take the time to reflect, but enough of this business talk. I want to show you the rest of the place; but more importantly, I just happen to have come upon some cases of Jamison's, straight from Dublin. I think they may need a little sampling."

"Ah, you're sendin' me heart a soarin,' Finbar."

VII

"I won't have people feeding off me, whether it be stealing or using those god-forsaken unions or brotherhoods or whatever they're called, to hold me up for excessive wages! Of course, insurance will cover my theft losses, but that's not the point. It's the principle! No one takes advantage of Alfred Prescott! Do I make myself clear!"

"I certainly understand, sir."

"But it's not just about my own circumstances. I have a duty to discourage sloth among the rabble. I must use my position and resources to imbue in them a spirit of discipline and hard work. Of course, for the most part, they're incapable of the drive and industry necessary to succeed in the business world, but they can contribute their labor. And perhaps our efforts will help reduce the crime that's so rampant, and which as you know," he thundered while slamming his fist on the desk, "was visited upon my own wife, so recently!"

"Indeed, Mister Prescott; and I can assure you that I will—"

"Yes, yes; we've gone over what I want, Collins. Now, get it done! And must I remind you, that I provide you with a more than generous stipend every month. Mister Riley, who's waiting outside with your associate, will escort you down to the factory floor. Now, if you will excuse me, I have to meet some friends for dinner and cards."

Knowing his place, the captain quickly withdrew to the company of the others waiting outside. Upon the group's arrival at the press line, a foreman blew the shop whistle signaling the workers to assemble along the banks of machinery. The laborers were the first to show up, while the skilled tradesmen, such as die formers and engravers, needed prodding from their bosses. Although production had come to a halt, the noise was still pervasive as massive lines of equipment continued to seethe and belch. As such, at Riley's urging, the scores of workers formed a tight semicircle around the contingent of police.

Once everyone was settled in, Riley wasted no time in introducing Collins. Anxious to command their attention, the Captain climbed atop a nearby box of gearing grease. Dressed in a crisply pressed uniform with gleaming buttons and gold shield, he was the very picture of authority. "For those of ya who don't know, I'm in charge of the police around these parts. I make it my job to run a tight ship, but right now, I'm not happy. My good friend, Mister Prescott, tells me that he's had some thefts of tools and such. That situation is going to stop, now! And you best remember, when they're stealing from Mister Prescott, they're stealing from you! After all, this company puts roofs over your heads and bread on your tables. For anyone found stealin,' you will be fired, but that's not the worst of it. You'll have to deal with me, and I hate a thief. You better believe you'll be beggin' to be off to jail after I get through with you! So, if you see or suspect some rat, come to me and I'll guarantee that you'll be protected and rewarded. Now, you've been warned. Do you have any questions? From the looks of you, you all understand; now that's good, but that's not the half of it.

We have an even bigger problem with all this talk of unions. That's gonna stop too! This ganging up and making demands is nothing short of stealing by extortion. It's un-American and I won't stand for it in my precinct. These so-called organizers—I call 'em trouble-makin' conspirators—they're anarchists, hoping to bring down this great country and cause chaos and ruin, not only for business but for you workers, too! Once more, remember, punishment will be severe and swift! And once again, I remind you to come to me with any information; but keep in mind that we'll be watching, not only here but on the streets and in your neighborhoods. We're gonna make sure we nip this in the bud!

Now, I hear some of the young clergy in the city are sayin' these so-called unions are O-K. Don't believe a word of it! They're either stupid, or black-hearted disgraces to their calling. In either case, they're risking their eternal souls. Scripture is quite clear on the matter. Luke, three-thirteen says, 'be content with your wages,' and chapter three, verse twenty-two of Saint Paul's letter to the Colossians says, 'work for your master as if you were workin' for the Lord.' And don't forget these are secret societies, like the freemasons, who seek to replace the one true Church!" Basking in triumph, the Captain bellowed out, "It's an affront to God and a fight we cannot lose, lads!"

Just as Collins was lifting himself down, a voice came floating from the back, "I didn't know Jesus was a capitalist;" to which a wave of laughter came rolling through the crowd. With his face exploding into a crimson red, Collins screamed out, "So, someone wants to be an entertainer!" Feverishly bobbing his head in an attempt to identify the perpetrator, he was finally forced to command his deputy, Spit n' Polish Perry, "unless ya spotted 'im, grab one near the pole."

As his fairhaired boy made his way through the pack, Collins nervously scanned the others. "And you with the smirk on your face. I know you! Come here, Young Tierney!"

"That's right, Paddy Tierney."

"Sweet Mother Mary, the grandson of Tommy Tierney chucklin' at a blasphemer! So, ya think it's funny, boyo!" With that, he pulled a club from his shiny leather belt and let loose a withering crack to the back of his leg, which instantly brought Tierney to his knees.

As the worker lay writhing on the floor, Sergeant Perry arrived with his catch. "The joke came from where you were standin'," Collins admonished as he nodded towards his subordinate's captive. In the blink of an eye, Perry hauled back and delivered a blow to the face that lifted the man off his feet. Although his eye was already beginning to close, the victim scrambled to his feet and made a move towards his attacker.

"Watch it, boyo! Ya don't know what you're bitin' off," Collins thundered as the man stopped dead in his tracks. "Tierney, get off your lazy arse and get back to work; and consider yourself lucky! As for you, mister, get goin' home. Now, if you want your job back, come to the station house with the name of the comic who caused ya all this trouble."

Bounding from the box, Collins yelled out, "I didn't want it to come to this, today, but that was just a taste of things to come if any of ya want to follow the crooked path of theft and unionism. So mark my words, fellas!"

With that, the policemen turned on their heels and marched out the door. While some of the workers, including most of the children, quickly returned to their posts, a large contingent gathered around their injured comrades. Soon grumblings escalated into angry shouts and invectives, as the men chafed at the brutal and threatening tactics. Finally, cries of "we're not gonna take this!" and "let's walk out," began to echo through the crowd.

Sensing the potential for disaster, Riley moved quickly to diffuse the situation. "Lads, lads, listen to me, please!" Knowing that with few exceptions, workers constantly lived on the edge of ruin, Riley was certain that the wives back home would not welcome any sudden walkout. As such, he figured time was on his side and he was determined to buy some of it. By tomorrow morning, the bravado of the worker's solidarity would be replaced by a cold-eyed realism and a desire for domestic tranquility. "Let's not let things get outta hand. I know Mister Prescott knows you're good workers and good fellas. I'll be speakin' to 'im tomorrow and nobody's gonna get sacked over this. And as a show of good faith, I'm gonna see to it that there's an extra two bits in your pay this week." His remarks appeared to calm the waters but the grumbling continued. "What about Collins," someone yelled.

"He's got a job to do and he had some important things to say, but for god's sake, he's worse than a monsignor, when it comes to the Church. Believe me, I'll unruffle his feathers about the joke, and actually, it was a pretty good one at that, boys," he laughed.

Tempered by his words and urged on by their foremen, the remaining workers began to slowly filter back to their stations. Feeling assured that he put to rest any chance of an uprising, Riley headed back to his office; nonetheless, he wondered if he'd bitten off too much in what he promised the troops. Still, although he had taken a risk, he believed he managed to gain Prescott's trust since assuming his duties, and despite his status, he had delivered on some key issues for his boss as of late. Besides, his judgment had been sound in this case; consequently, he felt a renewed sense of confidence as he watched the dismissed worker collect his belongings and head to the door. Just then, as he was about to pass the calendaring station, one of the roll tenders, a boy of no more than twelve, came rushing towards him. "Mister Riley, that's me da, leavin'," he cried as tears rolled down his cheeks. "What will we do? There's me ma and six little ones at home!"

Bending down and placing his hand upon the boy's shoulder, he consoled, "Don't be worryin', now. I'll take care of things. Besides, I saw that joker. It was that fella …"

"McGurty, he's always jokin'," the boy sniffled.

"Yeah, Kiernan McGurty, he's somethin'," he smiled as he patted the child on the head, before continuing on his way. Yet at that same moment, the wounded Tierney limped back to his machine with a dark look of vengeance etched upon his face.

VIII

Despite it being a pleasant autumn night, the cabin, which ran almost the entire length of the narrow, eighty-foot vessel, was hot and stuffy. One could only imagine the conditions when as many as one hundred passengers were stacked onto drop-down cots on a blistering summer night. Yet on this evening, it was the perfect venue for a clandestine meeting.

The canal packet boat was berthed in the brackish waters of the Ohio Street Basin as it awaited storage for the winter. Located at the western edge of the Ward, the basin was an ideal setting for a secret gathering, being dark, isolated and largely devoid of activity at this hour.

Present at the meeting were Raphael Taglieri and Keena Shea of the Knights of Labor, and a quartet of workers from Prescott Wallpaper, including a still-lame Padrig Tierney. A strategy session took up most of the night, and covered a wide range of topics, such as recruitment and demands for better wages and working conditions. As the little party prepared to leave, they went over some final details.

"So, Neil and Dick, you'll be putting together a list of people we can meet at home."

"Sure thing, Keena; and both you and Ralph are gonna be available?"

"That's right, Dick and Paddy and John, you'll be feeling out who else is sympathetic on the two shifts? And also, who might be a rat!"

"Yeah, and good point, Keena," Ralph added. "Ya gotta keep our wits about ya. As ya saw the other night, they're not playing around; but Shaddock's back, right?"

"Yeah, but McGurty, who made the joke was sacked just yesterday… for bein' late!"

"Somebody ratted 'im; but we can use it to our ends. Work it up!" Taglieri bristled.

"And Neil, thank the custodian for allowing us here."

"Don't worry, Keena, he worked at Prescott's house, hates the bas… er… fella."

"That's all right, he is a bastard; but we'll be fixing that," she smiled.

As the group scrambled out to the dock ladder, they relished the fresh nighttime air. Yet before scattering in different directions, Ralph called over to his partner, "Keena, let me walk you home, it's pretty late."

"It's only a few minutes up the street, Ralph. Besides, I won't be lollygagging around here. The place gives me the chills. Back when I was in school, a bunch of young children in the neighborhood died of fever. Some of the doctors blamed it on these stinkin,' diseased waters. So, I'm in a hurry to leave it in my dust. Now, get going. I'll be fine."

No sooner had they parted company than she was already having second thoughts. A thick patchwork of clouds not only cast a pall on the moonlit night, but it obscured her path through the unfamiliar terrain. As she picked her way across a cluttered corner of the boat yard, she nearly jumped from her skin when a well-fed rat leaped out from an ancient fur-trader's bateau that lay crumbling in a clump of weeds. Unfortunately for the scurrying creature, a harbor cat, hiding behind a rusted anchor, quickly snared it for dinner. Catching her breath, she made haste to leave the unsettling scene in her wake. Finally, after squeezing her way through a break in the fence, she once more found herself within the familiar streetscape of the First Ward; however, her relief was tempered by the deserted vista stretched out before her. Louisiana Street was absent any signs of life, as all the businesses and homes were shuttered up and dark. Even the scattered streetlights only added to the sense of desolation as they cast their glow on nothing but empty space. Still, she assured herself that this was her neighborhood and as a longtime resident, there was no need for alarm. Yet this attitude proved fleeting. Just as she crossed Republic Street, she heard a rattle of cans coming from the alley that ran parallel to Louisiana. Blaming it on the noisy wanderings of a stray dog, she continued on her way, albeit at a brisker pace. As she paused at O'Connell Avenue, her sense of caution was becoming fully engaged. Looking up and down the street, she was relieved to observe nothing of concern; however, a moment later, something stopped her in her tracks. With the pervasive silence serving to amplify any surrounding noise, the sounds of rushing footsteps and the muffled rumblings of male voices were unmistakable. More disturbing was the impression that whoever it was, he seemed to be following a path parallel to hers. Once more increasing her pace, she finally felt some measure of calm upon seeing her father's tavern. Yet despite what was now her noticeable panting, she could hear the strained groans of a fence being climbed, followed by a resounding thud. Needing no further prompting, she grabbed her hem and made a mad dash to her house behind the bar.

Rounding the corner of Mackinaw, she ran straight into a man's arms. Her spirited struggle to escape froze dead upon coming face to face with her captor, Liam Riley. Relieved yet fit to be tied, she screamed, "You scared the hell outta me!"

"Sorry, but what are you all worked up about? Ya came flying around the corner like a banshee."

"Were you following me down the alley? I heard noises!"

"I've been waiting here. You said you'd be late with your meeting. Those noises were probably some dog."

"That was no dog!"

"Want me to check?"

"No, let's just get to the house."

Creeping up to her back door, he whispered, "Ya know, I like this. You bein' all flush and your hair bein' wild. No one's back at my house. Da and Bobby are on the Cleveland run tonight." With that, he lowered his mouth to hers and made a move to lift her skirt.

Breaking away, she implored, softly, "I'm sure my da's still up waiting." Perhaps it was the circumstances of her trek home, or perhaps it was the report of his complicity in the events with Collins at the plant, but she was in no mood to play. Adding to her weary disposition was her growing frustration over their relationship, including a sense that he was not really committed, but merely content to enjoy the prestige of a beautiful, high-profile girlfriend and a steady "roll in the hay."

Things were different in the past. She was an incredible catch, and he used everything at his disposal to work his way into her heart. Given her stunning looks and neighborhood pedigree, she could have had her pick of the crop among the city's Irish bachelors. So, it came as a surprise to most, when she settled upon Riley, hardly one of the local luminaries. Although fairly handsome and on an upward career path, what set him apart was a relentless charm that more than a few viewed as disingenuous and self-serving. Despite being dubious at first, she finally agreed to see him after a long and persistent pursuit. They had now been courting for the better part of two years; however his insatiable ambition and occasional willingness to play loose with the rules had given her pause more than once. Lately, these issues had become a growing concern; yet she was committed to trying to keep things together.

"Tell ol' Blinky ya were at my sis's to help with the twins. Besides, it's been a week. Come on, we're both randy, my lovely flower of Erin," he cooed with a mischievous smile.

"I told you, I don't like that name, 'Blinky,' and I won't lie to him."

"Ah, it's not a lie when we need to fulfill our yearnings."

"But I'm beginning to feel uncomfortable being the way we are; and having no ring after all this time. I'm an independent woman, but I want a home and family."

"I'll say you're independent with all that suffrage talk and all that marching and what not."

"I have my beliefs that I stand by, like my work, my family and God; speaking of which, you don't join us at church anymore, and Kitty said she saw you coming out of Saint Paul's."

"I've been too busy, and as for Saint Paul's, I was just drivin' Mister Prescott and his daughter to their services, and they asked me to join them inside."

"She's the one who just graduated from college in Boston?"

"That's right, but what's this about, you not being comfortable with our loving an' all."

"It's going nowhere. I love intimacy but without a goal of marriage, I don't feel right. I'm not just about bangin' the headboard. I'm worth more."

"And I don't feel comfortable about all your union nonsense. I have my plans at Prescott and I don't want to jeopardize them." Frustrated by her sudden reluctance to proceed to the bed, he scowled, "A woman should follow her man; not the other way around!"

"Don't use that tone with me, Liam. I don't tag behind any man, but I understand your situation. If we were betrothed, I'd step back from any work that could involve Prescott."

"So you're sayin' you're going after my workplace?"

"Oh, no! I'm not saying anything either way. I hope you respect that."

"Well, no matter if it's Prescott or whoever. There's no secrets among the business community in this town when it comes to the unions, and it would reflect badly on me."

"I sometimes feel it's all just an excuse. You knew my work and beliefs long before we started courting. You have your plans; well, I have my principles."

"Good god! Principles, ack! Ya better smarten up if you want be married. I don't know any man who has a woman carrying on like this!"

"I'm no man's woman. I'm Brendan Shea's daughter. I'm educated, steadfast and not hard on the eyes, and I won't be dismissed or ruled."

Grabbing her by the arm, he snorted, "Come on, you'll feel different in the morning."

Quickly wrestling herself from his grip, she glared, "You know me! You shouldn't have done that, Mister Riley!"

Eyes flashing with anger, he turned on his heels and headed into the dark.

IX

The smell of kerosene hung thick in the air as the crush of marching clubs, bands and decorated wagons assembled near the Liberty Pole for the torchlight parade up Main Street. They were there to pay tribute to the legendary General and former President, Ulysses S. Grant, who was making a campaign stop in the city prior to the following week's national election. Leading the procession of ten thousand marchers were various chapters of the Republican "Boys in Blue" veterans clubs; however, this was no mere partisan affair, for on this night, the area's grateful citizenry had turned out in record numbers to honor the "Hero of Appomattox," regardless of their party allegiance. They came not only from the surrounding counties, but from Pennsylvania, Ohio and even neighboring Canada, such was the reputation of the great commander. By seven o'clock, the area between Court and Mohawk Street, where Grant was to review the spectacle from a stand in front of the Tifft House Hotel, was so densely packed that the street cars could no longer pass, and more than a few onlookers had fallen ill and needed evacuation.

Making his way through the deluge of people, Brick Fist was intent on preventing any incidents from escalating into something that could turn a crowd into a riotous mob. Accompanied by his young partner, Costello, he had already eased away a couple of drunken revelers whose boisterous and aggressive behavior spelled the potential for trouble. At the same time, he was keeping his eyes peeled for the type of petty theft that such events always attract. After snagging a pickpocket sliding his hand into a dowager's purse, he began hustling his captive to a command post at the rear of the hotel where his friend, Lieutenant Broderick was coordinating security efforts. Yet no sooner had he turned the corner of Main, than he ran into the two Foley Brothers stationed beneath a streetlight. After ordering Costello to deliver the prisoner to the booking tent, he strode over to the pair. "Come to see what all the ballyhoo's about, eh gents?"

After some wait, the dapper brother, Mike, observed, "Just watchin' the goin's-on."

"Yeah, should be a fine night. No trouble," Danny replied with a casual air.

"Maybe," the pit bull, Doc, fired back. "I see ya been hustlin' off some rowdies. Never know with a crowd like this; a fella could get hurt … or worse."

"Ah, you know me. I can take care of myself. I'm sure me and my mates on the force will keep the peace; but enough of me. How's Emmon? How's that poor soul doin'?"

As Doc stood silent, virtually shaking with rage, Mike finally answered, "He's in the infirmary; all messed up in the head."

"The head's a fragile thing," Doc added with a threatening sneer.

"Yeah, don't I know. A couple of times I had to shoot some fellas in the noggin who wanted to kill me." Opening his jacket, Danny announced, "Still got me old army revolver."

"Never know when ya may need it," Doc smiled, as he pulled out a knife to pick a seed from his teeth. Nodding to his brother, he picked up and headed towards the teeming mass of people.

Just then, Billy Broderick came marching up with a squad of patrolmen, along with a detachment of mounted constabulary poised to clear a path for the upcoming procession. But before Danny had a chance to greet him, Broderick barked to a couple of subordinates, "Goetz, Regan, keep those two in your sights at all times. Got it!" After watching the pair rush off to follow the Foleys, Billy asked his friend, "What was your little meetin' all about?"

"Just sendin' a reminder that they're out to get me."

"Well, keep your powder dry and don't underestimate 'em."

"Don't worry, I dealt with a lotta bad ones over the years."

"I don't know anybody worse than the Foleys, and remember, nobody's invincible."

"That's not what I hear about that young fella from Boston, John L. Sullivan"

"They don't shoot ya in the ring, Danny," he scolded as he shook his head in frustration.

"Anyway, I see ya arrived with the cavalry."

"Just in time, I see; although I ain't surprised. He's such a great man, Danny."

"Puts his pants on the same as the rest of us."

"Holy *Cathú*, are ya ever not the cynic, Danny," Billy sighed before catching himself. "Anyway, I'm glad to get up here, away from the command post. I got tired of dealin' with all them bigwigs. Besides, I figured I'd better get outta the way of Collins' stiff as he kisses all their arses."

"Thanks for the warnin', I'll keep it in mind when I round up your cousin."

"Yeah, he's back there writin' up that thief. And how's he workin' out, Danny?"

"Pretty good, even though I tell 'im he's a pain in the arse."

"Not like us, way back when," he smiled as he slapped his old partner on the back. "Oh, and before ya go, Clare wants ya over for dinner. Ya know, we got a pretty new neighbor."

"Okay, but dinner only. I got all the company I need down at Big Tits'."

After bidding farewell, Danny set off to retrieve his charge and get back to the evening's action. As he approached the rear driveway of the hotel, he was greeted by a line of luxury carriages stretching down the block. He immediately recognized Prescott's brougham as it arrived at the entrance portico, and watched as the tycoon's wife made her way out with the help of her driver. Dressed to the nines in a blue taffeta gown, she was a portrait of aristocratic beauty, and her emerald collar broach, newly purchased as a replacement for the recently purloined necklace, was the perfect accessory for highlighting the flawless quality of her porcelain skin. Yet there was no hint of a smile as she chafed over Alfred's refusal to join her on this grand occasion. Once again, he preferred dinner with his business cronies, and a late-night game of cards. The ensuing argument accomplished nothing, other than to further alienate her increasingly buffeted affections. In her husband's absence, she was accompanied by her older brother, Powell, who, as with all the members of her family, had been a steadfast abolitionist and supporter of the Union.

For what seemed like moments, Danny could barely keep his eyes off Prescott's wife; however, his fixation was eventually broken by the arrival of the next carriage. Sitting atop the driver's bench was Harpoon Marley, this time dressed in a formal coachman's livery, except for his ubiquitous army kepi.

Not waiting for the hotel doorman, Carnahan flung open the door and climbed out of the cabin. Dressed in the latest English formalwear and sporting a crimson-lined cape, he cut both a wealthy and dashing figure. As the crime lord stood on the carriageway fixing his top hat, Danny, being ever mindful of an opportunity, made straight for his side.

"Admirer of the General, I see," the detective observed.

"Indeed, and you too, I see."

"Dead-on; but I'm here on work, you know; making sure everyone's behavin'. Which reminds me, I ran into a couple of your employees in the crowd: the Foley boys.

Despite his effort to appear unruffled, a look of aggravation managed to creep across Finger's face. "Excuse me, Sergeant. I just remembered something that I forgot to tell George." Beckoning Marley's attention, he walked over and exchanged a few words. Upon returning, he was once more his engaging self. "As I was about to say, I gave all my men the night off. I'm sure a number of them want to see the great man. Speaking of which, I'm in a hurry to see him myself. So, if you would excuse me, Sergeant."

"One more thing, Major; knowing you like to be informed, I want you to know I won't be allowing any shenanigans by any of the rowdies out there, including your boys."

No longer showing even a trace of smile, Carnahan merely cast a quick nod before marching past the sentry at the door. Anxious to get on with the evening, he entered into a lobby, that was the embodiment of Victorian elegance, encompassing a landscape rich in ornamentation and housing an eclectic mix of expensive furnishings. Standing beneath a massive, crystal chandelier, he exchanged pleasantries with a number of acquaintances before making his way to the grand staircase. The stairs led to the main ballroom on the second floor, where a reception for Grant was in progress. Marching up the steps, he immediately noticed the shapely blond nearing the top of the landing; however, her graceful ascent came to an abrupt stop when the heel of her shoe caught the hem of her billowy gown. Only fast action, in the form of Carnahan's headlong rush to catch her fall, prevented catastrophe.

Although shaken at the thought of nearly tumbling over the banister, Rebecca was effusive in thanking the heroic stranger; and after regaining her composure was quick to introduce herself and her brother.

After affecting a graceful bow, the gangster replied, "Major Finbar Carnahan, local businessman and late of the seventy-ninth New York Volunteers. I am most honored to be of service to such a lovely lady. But you must still be quite unsettled. Allow me to join your brother in helping you to that settee in the hallway."

Please do, kind sir. I'm still a bit ruffled. I must be more careful. I'd rather be playing that lovely piano down below than to be landing on it." Despite recognizing his infamous name, Rebecca refused to react with shock or disgust. Instead she maintained a welcoming air. After all, he may have saved her life; and besides, he displayed a refined manner, quite at odds with his reputation.

For his part, despite realizing she was the wife of a man he reviled, Carnahan was taken not only by her beauty but by her winsome spirit as well. "While charmed by your intrepid spirit, I cannot bring myself to imagine that second possibility, but I would relish the first, being certain that you would create the most beautiful music, playing on that grand instrument."

"I love music and indeed, I do love playing the piano, although, I suspect not at the level to which you flatter me. But I only play in the privacy of my home. My husband doesn't permit me to perform in public."

"I'm sure your husband's pleasure is a loss for the rest of us," Fingers replied with a none too subtle edge. After helping her to the chair, he added, "I, too, love music. I struggle at home with the violin; but then I'm content to revel in the talents of true artists. In that regard, I've managed to secure a box at the Academy of Music for the last few seasons."

Being from out of town, her brother had no idea as to Finger's criminal background; consequently, when he spotted a couple of old school chums, he excused himself and headed in their direction.

After Carnahan joined her on the sofa, they kept up their discussion, delving not only into music, but into such subjects as literature and the beauty of nature. Surprisingly, she still felt little concern about engaging with the reported gangster. Perhaps it was because he was unlike any Irishman, or for that matter, anyone of that background, she could imagine. After all, he was educated, charming, handsome and wealthy. In fact, the more they talked, rather than being repelled by the nature of his work, she found herself intrigued by his outlaw image and willingness to break the rules.

In the eyes of Finbar, here was a woman who was not only beautiful and charming, but intelligent and culturally aware, qualities he found in short supply in either of the worlds he straddled.

Just as they were about to discuss their mutual admiration for the night's honoree, a man came rushing over from the head of the receiving line at the entrance to the ballroom. "Major Carnahan? Major Finbar Carnahan?"

"Yes, that's me."

"Sir, I'm an aide to General Grant. He recognized you sitting out here and he would very much be honored if you and your wife would join him and his party on the reviewing stand. But first, he would like the opportunity for a private chat prior to the ceremonies."

After acknowledging the eager look on Rebecca's face, Fingers was quick to reply, "Indeed, sir! My friend, Missus Prescott, and I would be most honored to accept the general's gracious invitation."

"Very good, sir. Missus Prescott, Major, if you would please follow me."

As Carnahan offered his arm, Rebecca not only found herself marveling at the level of his access, but was quickly abandoning herself to the excitement of the moment. After being whisked through a series of back hallways, they arrived at a spacious suite adjacent to the balcony leading to the reviewing stand. Already, a host of elected officials and local dignitaries were waiting in their seats on this brisk and beautiful October night. Inside, a bevy of aides and party functionaries were rushing about, preoccupied with last minute details.

As Finbar and Rebecca looked out the window, they feasted on a scene that would excite the senses of even the most jaded of observers. Bathed in the glow from multiple stands of limelights, a churning sea of humanity crowded into the two blocks surrounding the hotel. Thousands more lined Main Street, as endless cohorts of flaming torches crept along the parade route. Framing the panorama were the towering silhouettes of uptown buildings, their windows ablaze with all manner of light.

Not to be outdone, virtually every shopkeeper had adorned their storefronts with billowing streams of patriotic bunting and banners. It was if the entire city was determined not only to honor the great general, but to create a spectacle for the eyes as well.

With the crowd growing anxious for the arrival of its hero, chants of "U, S, Grant," "Unconditional Surrender," and "Long Live the Union," began to rise above the pervasive din of the assembled masses.

Finally, as the clock neared nine, the sounds of hurried footsteps and the clamor of lively voices came rumbling up from down the hallway. A moment later, the surprisingly short Grant came striding through the French doors, surrounded by a phalanx of official ushers representing the local business elite. No sooner had he begun to scan the room in search of a receptacle for his ever-present cigar, than he spotted Fingers standing near the window. "My old comrade-in-arms, Major Finbar Carnahan! I haven't seen you since the war. How are you doing, my boy?"

"I'm doing quite well, sir. It is a great honor to see you again, General. And may I introduce my friend, Missus Rebecca Prescott"

"It is my turn to be honored by meeting such a beautiful lady," he replied with a courtly bow.

"You are too kind, General," she blushed. Regaining herself, she beamed, "I cannot put into words my feelings at meeting the man who did so much to end the abomination of slavery and save the Union."

"It was the inspired leadership of our martyred President Lincoln and the heroic actions of thousands of men like Major Carnahan that brought about our national triumph. I was merely a coordinator of the effort."

"Your humility does honor to your greatness, General."

"Thank you for your generous words, Missus Prescott. It's such thoughtfulness that warms the heart of an old soldier as the end of his campaign draws closer."

"And may that not come for many, many years, General," Finbar replied as he beamed with happiness.

"I'll drink to that," the general smiled as he grabbed his old aide by the shoulder.

By now, members of his escort could barely hide their revulsion at the sight of someone like Carnahan rousing the General's affection. Even more disturbing was the fact that one of their own, Rebecca Prescott, the wife of a local captain of industry, was in the company of not merely a gangster, but a dreg of the Irish underclass. Their less than subtle reaction was not lost upon Rebecca; but she didn't care. Despite his notorious reputation, she felt that Carnahan was a gentleman and more importantly, was a man who showed a genuine interest in her person. Had her husband shown an even marginally similar inclination, the condition of their marriage would not be fast eroding.

Brushing aside their glares, Finbar felt nothing but contempt for these so-called pillars of society. None were veterans of the Great War and all owed their stations in life, not to industry and hard work, but to the good luck of a wealthy lineage. More importantly, they maintained their fortunes in a manner that flew in the face of their pious posturing, principally through the exploitation of the working masses, many of whom were Finger's co-religionists and ethnic kin.

"And speaking of drink, I was always amazed at how Finbar could always manage to secure Cuban cigars and Irish whiskey; even under the most wretched conditions."

"You once said, 'if men in war slavishly obey the rules, they'll fail.' I merely followed your advice and was creative," he said with a wink before adding, "And it doesn't hurt to have a lot of Irish friends."

"Hoisted on my own petard," Grant laughed as he turned to Rebecca. "But don't get me wrong, Missus Prescott, Major Carnahan was an outstanding cavalryman and staff officer, a view shared by all, including my dear friend and national hero, General McPherson… Jim's death pains my heart, even to this day."

"It was just like him though, he wasn't about to be captured."

"Well said, Finbar; and thank God he didn't buy into Hood's evacuation feint. He correctly predicted to Bill Sherman that they'd try to attack us at the rear."

"A singular honor to have served under such a great soldier; and great man."

"'We few, we happy few, we band of brothers;' I can assure you, my young friend, that whenever I walk onto the stage on such an occasion as this, I always have their memories with me. For it was only through their noble sacrifice that we find ourselves here." With that, General Grant bid his farewells, but not before grabbing the hand of his comrade-in-arms and pulling him into a strong embrace.

Following the escort party onto the reviewing stand, the pair watched as the old warrior ventured out into the tumultuous roar of the crowd. Unable to be heard, or perhaps more importantly, unable to speak, the Victor of Appomattox turned across the stage while tipping his hat in appreciation. Needing no further words, Finbar and Rebecca merely exchanged heartfelt looks.

X

By the time he landed on the pavement, the clap of gunfire was still resonating in his ears. Watching as his derby rolled into the gutter, Danny quickly flipped to his side, while pointing his revolver towards the source of the shots. He feverishly scanned the landscape but all he saw were scattered revelers hunched in terror against the walls of nearby buildings. After leaping to his feet, he raced up the street, all the while barking at the cowering bystanders to stay down. Creeping along the edge of a shuttered storefront as he approached Mohawk Street, he slowly peered around the corner, only to meet the benign sight of straggling spectators strolling home. Frustrated at his assailant's escape, he walked back and picked up his hat, which was now sporting matching holes on both ends of the crown.

Just then, Billy Broderick came rushing up, accompanied by Hugh Costello, who, moments earlier, had delivered one last troublemaker to the police tent. "What's goin' on with the shots! Are ya all right, Danny!" the lieutenant yelled.

"Just me hat's hurtin'," he smiled sardonically as he showed them the derby.

"Had to be the Foleys. They managed to give the slip to my boys."

"I saw nothin', but let's see what we can get from these folks while we got 'em here."

After announcing that all was safe, the officers began to question some nearby witnesses, however, still feeling unnerved, they could offer little more than that a lone gunman ran up Washington towards Mohawk. Seeing a little boy sobbing at his mother's side, Brick Fist leaned down and assured him that all was well. Yet the thought of children in the line of fire only served to further enflame his hatred for the Foleys.

"Danny, let me put a man at your back until we take care of this," Billy suggested.

"As we saw tonight, that didn't work. No, I can take care of myself, just fine. And don't worry, the Foley boys are gonna botch things up, and when they do, I'll nab their arses."

"Just the same, we're gonna put an end to this, whatever it takes," Billy replied with a look of concern etched across his face.

Anxious to get some rest, Danny was quick to leave after saying his goodbyes. As luck would have it, the Washington-Ohio Street trolley, on its final run to the Ward, was pulling up to the corner. The last remnants of parade watchers packed its seats, and in light of the crowded conditions, Brick Fist was more than happy to take up his usual perch alongside the teamster. Still primed for a crack at the Foleys, he began to survey the faces in the cabin, but much to his delight his eyes settled upon Keena sitting on a front bench. Jumping at the chance for some well-earned cheer, he abandoned his station and elbowed his way to her side. Given his formidable look, he encountered no resistance.

Keena, as with most others on board, was returning home after watching some of the parade and catching a glimpse of the great general; however, on this night, her main mission had been to attend a strategy session regarding union efforts at Prescott Wallpaper. The meeting took place earlier that evening in the basement of Saint Michael's Church, where a sympathetic Jesuit had offered the workers space for their secret gathering. Despite being weary after a long day, she was happy to see her friend Danny.

As Doyle slid alongside, he took note of her tired appearance. Yet for whatever reason, it only added to the endearing character of her beauty.

It also rekindled memories of unadorned and stalwart loveliness, which was so unlike the gaudy look of the professional girls he had long frequented.

"So you've come to see the General; but why ain't you with your Da and his party?"

"Party, no doubt! I'm sure he's still carousing with the boys at some Uptown watering hole. I had some other business tonight, but I stopped to watch the festivities."

"More of your union troublemaking, I reckon," he chuckled.

"Let's not talk of it, Sergeant."

"Ah, I sense you don't trust me."

"Danny, I know you're not one of those union-busting thugs like your Superintendent and his cronies like that Collins. I even heard you didn't shoot during the confrontation with the railroad strikers back in seventy-seven; but some of the folks you work for, let's just say I have no use for them."

"I'm glad I didn't shoot. They were just working folk, and a lotta young ones at that. As it was, I knew the father of the Lyons lad who was killed. I don't want to see that kind of pain visited on anyone. Still, I understand your feelings about some of the folks I do business with; but just the same, I'd never betray a friend and I don't have any problems with workers trying to better themselves. I got to be honest with ya though, I don't see what you want, happening."

"Danny, you're a hard working fella, but wouldn't you like fair treatment with overtime; forty- hour workweeks; vacations; no arbitrary firings; safe working conditions?"

"Slow down, Keena. My job, by the way it works, is a wee bit dangerous," he teased. "As for all the other stuff, I'd like to have a spring of gold and a flying horse, to boot; but life and its labors are a bitter road at best."

"Well, workers all over the country, and even all over the world, are beginning to band together and fight to change all that."

"I don't have to join arms with nobody. I, alone, make sure Danny Doyle is taken care of. Besides, I don't see you beating all the money and power that's set against you."

"Great goals are worth the fight. After all, the man being honored tonight beat the odds when things looked bleak."

"So, you're trying to catch me at a weak moment," he smiled. I have to admit it touched me tonight, knowing how he brought an end to the War; and then seeing how old he's gotten, as he stood up there saluting the men he fought beside."

"See, once again I can see a heart beating under that rough and tough armor. And even though I'm a Democrat, I share your feelings about the man. Besides being a hero, I believe he cares about the little fella; the same way he cared about his troops. Why just this summer, he said while speaking to unionists in London, that 'labor is the author of all greatness. Without labor, there would be no government, or no leading class, or nothing to preserve'."

"I know your heart is into it, and you work hard for all the fellas, but good luck getting them to join. Men bend to the powerful people who hold all the cards. It's like those Johnny Rebs we fought, poor as church mice, barefoot and wearing rags, but willing to fight like the fearsome *Fianna* to prop up plantation-living, slave-owning, rich men."

"Fear and ignorance; that's what these owners rely on. That's how they can fire workers and slash already slave wages at will; or convince poor farmers like the Rebs, that it's better to keep another man in bondage than to follow their own interests. But unions can help change that; whether through unity and strength in numbers to fight abuses, or by educating workers about their own interests."

"It's all quite worthy, but I don't think the likes of your Mister Riley's boss will be moved to go along."

An awkward silence ensued before Keena finally spoke up, "I'd rather not bring the subject of Mister Riley into the conversation. We are no longer seeing each other."

"I'm sorry, Keena, I didn't know."

"That's okay," she answered, while trying to stifle the catch in her throat. "It was meant to be."

As Keena was busy searching for a handkerchief in the overflowing carpetbag anchored at her side, Danny struggled for something to say. Resisting the urge to denounce her old boy friend, he settled upon the limp response of reminding her that her stop was coming up. After helping her up, he offered his arm, "It's pretty late, Keena. Let me walk you home."

"It's out of your way, Danny," she said before adding with a mischievous grin, "Besides, I'm no sissy-girl and I need a little quiet to go over all those evil plots from tonight's meeting."

"Good lord, woman. I actually feel pity for those poor owners."

After exchanging goodnights, he watched as she followed others out the front exit. Every movement of her flawless body seemed to exude grace as she floated down the steps. As he watched her long, slender fingers slowly release the rail, he could almost feel them unbuttoning his shirt. But as the driver waited for a few more riders to leave from the rear, Danny also found himself relishing her spirit; a spirit that was not only captivating, but steeped in goodness as well. Still, it was no wonder he cut short his musings, knowing that such a prize would always be beyond his grasp.

No sooner had the horses begun to pull the car down the tracks, than Keena stopped to inventory the contents of her bag. Although confident that she packed all the documents from the meeting, she wanted to make sure, knowing that tomorrow she would start contacting people and implementing plans. Satisfied all was in order, she resumed her trek; but by now, the other passengers had dispersed in all directions. As she walked down Mackinaw Street, she became preoccupied with going over details of the meeting; however, she couldn't help but hear the sound of phantom noises that seemed to be following her. Not wanting a repeat of her frenzied reaction of last week, she dismissed it as a wayward dog and continued on her way. As she approached Curtin's Blacksmith Shop, she was nearly startled out of her skin by a figure emerging from the shadows of the building. Yet her fears were put to rest when he thrust out a city police badge. "Miss, who are ya, and what are ya doin' out at this hour."

"I'm Keena Shea, Brendan Shea's daughter and I'm coming back from the parade."

"Can I see that bag ma'am. There's been some pickpocketin' and purse snatchin', tonight."

"Handing it to him, she snapped, "I am who I said I was. There's some grocer's receipts with my name and the name of my father's tavern on 'em."

After snatching open the satchel, he began to rifle through its contents. Upon discovering some papers, he slowly pulled them out and read their notes.

"Here, let me show you where the receipts—"

"Shut up!"

"Don't you—"

"Now ain't this interestin'. Looks like a conspiracy to incite a riot and disrupt the public order."

"You have no right—"

Pulling her into the alley beside the deserted shop, he slapped his hand across her mouth and shoved her against the wall. Not one to go quietly, she put up a violent struggle before he managed to subdue her.

Pressing hard against her body, he whispered, "No right? Why Miss Keena Shea is a lawbreaker! There's evidence in there about plottin' crimes, not to mention conspirin' on packet boats with greasy dagos. Hell, maybe she was fuckin' blackies in the basement of Saint Mike's tonight."

With that, she squirmed to raise her foot, before digging it deep into his shin. After almost biting through his lip in order to hold back a scream, he snarled, "But if ya were that uppity Miss Shea, ya wouldn't be fightin' like a whore." As he slid his hand onto her breast, he leered, "I see ya like the rough stuff, but afterwards, I'm still gonna haul your ass in as a strumpet plying her trade." His smirking chuckle ended abruptly when a hulking shadow came flying into the alley and delivered a crushing blow to his face.

"You piece of shit," Danny bellowed before yanking him up by the collar. "Spit 'n Polish," he gasped before launching another haymaker, this time, to the opposite side of his now-swollen face. As Officer Perry lay sprawled on the ground, Brick Fist rushed over to Keena's side. "Are ya all right, dear girl?"

As he wrapped his arm around her shoulder, she sobbed, "I'll be fine," before catching herself and firmly adding, "he's been followin' me because of my union activities."

After seating her on a little bench in front of the smithy's and offering words of comfort, he returned to her assailant.

By now able to prop himself up on his elbows, but showing no remorse, Perry spit out, "There'll be hell to pay for you, Doyle! I ain't sayin' nothin'! Talk to Collins; they're plannin' insurrection."

"I'm shakin' in me boots, boyo! I'll deal with Collins, but you gotta deal with me first! So, ya like grabbin' honest women. Did ya get a stiffy when ya did it?" Not waiting for an answer, Danny let loose a kick to the groin that produced a wail that reverberated between the walls.

Jolted by the cry, Keena came running back, only to see Perry rolled up in pain and Doyle looming above, ready for more. "Danny, stop it; please!"

Although biting at the bit to press on, he complied with her wishes, "Ya best be thankin' Miss Shea for keepin' ya from gettin' it worse. Now quit your bellyachin'. Missus Toohey can rub some balm on it. Ya won't be tryin' that again, will ya?"

His question elicited a barely audible whimper from the prone officer. Leaning closer, Danny whispered, "I didn't hear ya, but if it happens again, I'll break your back, so ya won't be havin' to deal with that little noodle in your pants, no more."

Straightening up, he announced "You'll have to excuse us, now. I'll be taking Miss Shea back to her house, and by the way, Sergeant Spit 'n Polish, your boots are scuffed. They'll be needin' a shine." With that, he turned and was met by Keena trying to hide a guilty smile.

XI

The sweet, smoky smell of burning leaves hung over the city as traffic rushed up and down a gas-lit Main Street. Another interlude of Indian Summer was making its presence felt; and as a result, the theater and dinner crowd needed little more than light coats and capes on this beautiful autumn night.

It was a few minutes before seven and a line was already forming when Prescott's buggy arrived under the marquee of the most exclusive restaurant in the city, Delmonico's. Whisked into the lobby by a familiar doorman, he all but ran into Fingers Carnahan. The crime lord was in the company of a small party, including former mayor Scheu and his wife, Wilhelmina. Scheu, a grocery magnate and Democratic Party power, was a longtime beneficiary of Carnahan's campaign largess. On this night, he and his wife were to be the guests in Finger's private box at the nearby Academy of Music, for a performance by the rising young soprano, Ada Adini.

"Ah, Alfred, you and your Republican friends must be delighted over Grant's reception on Thursday night," Scheu remarked with a slight accent that bore witness to his Bavarian roots.

"Indeed, Mister Mayor; a wonderful event; unfortunately, I had other commitments."

"You know Colonel Weber and his wife, and the Carltons of course; don't you?"

"Yes, yes; how are you all?"

"And of course, our host tonight, Major Finbar Carnahan."

"I've never had the... opportunity."

After greeting Finbar and exchanging pleasantries with the little circle of friends, Prescott interrupted, "Excuse me, all, but if I may have a brief private moment with Mister Carnahan."

After leading Fingers to a side hallway off the vestibule, Prescott's expression turned from genial to openly hostile. "Three things, Carnahan, or Fingers or whatever your gangster friends call you: don't ever go near my wife again; don't ever put your filthy, Irish presence near me again, and most importantly, you don't scare me. I've got my own people who are quite adept."

Resisting the urge to grab the smug little aristocrat by the throat and pummel him into the ground, Finbar instead struck a calm demeanor. "Before I say anything, since you are unable to refrain from keeping the subject of your wife out of the discussion, I will do it for you. As for my reputation, I could care less what a man like you thinks about me. People in my line of work accept the aspersions that come with the job. Unlike you and your sniveling ilk, I don't hide behind the law to prey on the innocent poor and then crow about my piety." Pressing closer, Finbar could detect a growing look of panic in his adversary's eyes. It was a look suggesting that the man realized he had bitten off too much. Having no access to an exit, Prescott could only stand and listen "Say what you will about me, but watch what you say about my people. We were preserving the works of civilization when your Anglo-Saxon forbearers were picking bugs off each others' asses. We built much of this country by the sweat of our backs and helped win the war by shedding our blood. A war for which I understand you somehow failed to hear the call. I've seen men explode and had human brains sprayed across my jacket. So please don't make me laugh with your threats about … how'd you put it? Oh, yes, having your own adept people. Interesting. Incidentally, I suspect those adept people of yours know of me, or are in fact on my payroll. No, I don't make threats, Mister Prescott. If someone wants to do me harm, the situation is merely taken care of. That being said, you must allow me to get back to my guests. Good manners require that I not keep them waiting any longer." Just as he was about to turn and leave, he thrust his finger in Prescott's chest and said, "Nice to meet you though," before withdrawing it and laughing, "fingers, useful little instruments aren't they?"

Ashen-faced and feeling a tremble in his arm, Prescott watched as the crime lord returned to the welcoming company of his friends. Although shaken by the reminder of Finger's power, he remained unrepentant. In fact, the incident only added to an anger that had been building since his earlier row with Rebecca: first, the impudence of a woman, and now, a lecture and veiled threat from a social and moral inferior. It was something that a man of Prescott's standing refused to accept. Barreling forward, he came upon a freckled-faced maitre d' who was preparing to seat an elderly couple.

"Take me to the private room where my friends are."

"Of course, Mister Prescott, but first let me take care of these nice people."

Grabbing him by the arm, the tycoon whispered, "That's all right, I'll deliver myself; and by the way, I'd suggest you prepare to find a new position after I talk to the owner tonight."

As the unfortunate attendant stepped back in shock, Prescott hurried down the hallway toward the site of the clandestine game. Still stinging from the evening's controversies, he was anxious to find some respite in whiskey, cigars and his beloved card games. After rapping out a series of secret knocks, he swung open the door, revealing a cast of familiar faces: the jeweler, Robert Van Cleff, Doctor Oscar Halpin, a prominent local physician; William Bingham, a brass works owner and commissioner of the city's newly formed professional fire company, and Richard Marvin, an industrialist who owned a malt house and metal working factory. Wasting no time, Prescott poured himself a drink and found a place at the table.

"Where's Jewett?"

"The wife's keeping him at home after all that time he spent preparing to host the Grants," Marvin smirked.

"Figures," Prescott huffed.

"So, Alfred, anything new with that incident involving your wife," the jeweler asked.

After stumbling at the reference to an incident involving his wife, Prescott quickly recovered. "Oh... ah... yes, the police arrested an Irish hoodlum. He was severely injured during the chase. He's in Saint Mary's Infirmary, all sick in the head; but unfortunately, they couldn't find the necklace. Thankfully, it was insured."

"Well done. I'm sure our friend Mills will be happy with how his constabulary is working," Doctor Halpin observed. "But speaking of the infirmary, I heard that one of the patients may have contracted typhoid fever. She came from the First Ward and I can't help but think that the canal basin is to blame. They should fill in that pestilent sewer."

"Business is not your bailiwick, doctor. One must not trifle with anything affecting lake commerce. Just put a sign up telling the canal scum and the neighborhood Irish hordes to stop pissing and shitting in the water," Prescott groused as he went over his cards.

After the usual back and forth during the course of the hand, a voice chimed in, "Ouch! That's a tough one to lose, Robert."

"What did Dickens write," the jeweler calmly replied, "'the pain of parting is nothing to the joy of meeting again.' If not at the table, those dollars will make their way to my store at some point. Alfred is one of my best and dearest customers." Besides fancying himself a literary expert, especially in terms of his favorite, Charles Dickens, Van Cleff was a consummate man-about-town, and a regular presence at all the premier events on the city's social calendar. Money, coupled with an ever-present but fawning charm, had proven to be his passport to these exclusive circles. Despite a humble background that included stints as a telegraph operator and an apprenticeship with a watchmaker, he parlayed an innate sense of business, along with some dubious financial schemes, into a successful retail enterprise that included tobacco and liquor stores, millenary shops, and a thriving jewelry store that catered to the high-society set.

Glaring at the oftentimes overly familiar upstart, Prescott declared, "We don't discuss personal business dealings at these proceedings. Besides, you talk too much, Van Cleff; as you know, I'm only here two hours, win or lose."

Ever the diplomat, Doctor Halpin was quick to change the subject, "By the way, Bill, congratulations on your appointment as the Chief Fire Commissioner."

"Why thank you, Doctor. It's quite an honor and responsibility."

"And how is it progressing so far?"

"Quite well, we're in the process of opening some new facilities. In fact, we just opened a new steamer house next to Alfred's place on Perry Street; good location, protecting all those iron works and Jewett's stove factory."

"Just more taxes and a spoils haven for the families and friends of the ward bosses," Prescott grumbled.

"Sure, most are Irish or immigrants, but they're good lads; happy for a job; strong and from what I can see, courageous," Bingham suggested.

"We'll see;" the wallpaper tycoon snorted. "but you better have strict rules and discipline with that lot. I have experience and can vouch that you better not be too generous. It will only inspire them to revert back to their lazy natures."

After the industrialist Marvin insisted that they get back to the business at hand, they played two more big-kitty hands, with Van Cleff winning both. On the second, Prescott detected what he thought was cheating on the winner's part. From his perspective, there was no greater sin in the litany of offenses. And no one, absolutely no one, took advantage of Alfred T. Prescott; nonetheless, he had no proof, and lacking such evidence, any unfounded accusations would be greeted with disdain and ostracism from among his set. Still, as he sat and boiled, he plotted retribution. Yet for his part, Van Cleff appeared unruffled as he swept up his winning pot and merrily slapped a dollar chip into the hand of his young waiter friend. Subsequent hands failed to produce any evidence of chicanery, which led Prescott to reassess his initial reaction; however, being a consummate cynic, he maintained a wary vigilance.

As Prescott continued to indulge his gambling pleasures, his wife's carriage arrived at the entrance of the Academy of Music, located virtually across the street. Although still reeling from an earlier altercation with Alfred, Rebecca wasn't about to miss one of the biggest events of the social season. As she stepped down the stairs of the brougham and caught sight of Delmonico's, she knew full well that her husband was mere yards away; however, the fact hardly fazed her. Recent events, culminating with tonight's heated exchange, had proved to be a catalyst. No longer were Alfred's frequent absences, refusals to participate in social events or cold attitude, gnawing at her soul; and despite his command to stay at home, she once more contacted her brother, who always was able to secure tickets. Perhaps most importantly, she remembered that her newfound, and now forbidden friend, Major Carnahan, had mentioned during their conversation the other evening that he would be attending tonight's concert.

Despite having been schooled in the importance of punctuality by her straightlaced parents, she arrived late. Yet considering the circumstances, including her and her maid's frenzied fussing over her makeup, Rebecca was surprised that the performance had not yet started. As she approached the entrance, she met Powell who confessed his inability to find tickets. Undaunted, she dragged her sibling to the foyer box office in the hope of securing a pair of last minute returns. Frustrated over their attempts with the clerk, they asked to see the manager. Just then, Carnahan came strolling out of the man's office, headed for the corridor leading to the private loges. Upon spotting her, he stepped forward with a bright smile etched across his face, and after hearing of their plight, insisted that they join his party; however, when an excessively diligent usher balked at proceeding without tickets, Finbar quickly won his cooperation via the passage of a three dollar gold piece. Once again impressed by the Major's grace and power, Rebecca lost no time in taking his arm as he led the way.

"The former cavalry officer arrives just in time to save the day! Thank you, Major," she happily giggled.

"How could a gentleman ignore the plight of a desperate lady; especially one so beautiful, and what do they say in music? *Allegretta, lively, vibrant!*"

"Your chivalry and flattery are most welcome, sir. They delight me even more than the prospect of hearing Madame Adini, tonight."

Once inside the box, Rebecca found herself not only impressed by the quality of his guests, but dazzled by the opulent atmosphere of the room. Instead of the usual bare walls and wooden seats, the room was flush with brocade drapery, brass fixtures, Queen Anne style chairs and polished mahogany woodwork. An enameled Chinese wine cart stood off to the side. It contained a variety of European wines, along with an expensive collection of crystal goblets. All this was done at Fingers' expense, in an effort to impress his guests.

Reveling in her element, Rebecca managed to put off, at least for now, her earlier pain and bitterness. Yet as she feasted on the plush surroundings and celebrated the company of the other guests, Finbar could no longer hold back his tongue; for despite Rebecca's attempts to shield the one side of her face, he was able to make out a faint bruise under her makeup. "Please forgive any misplaced familiarity on my part, but are my eyes playing tricks on me, or did you somehow injure yourself on the side of your cheek?"

"Ah… no, your sight is fine, Major," she stumbled, briefly. "Despite my best efforts at concealment, I must admit I bumped into a kitchen cabinet." Feeling the muscles in his forearm contract into a rock-hard rope, she kept up her attempt at subterfuge, "the help failed to close the door, but I must blame myself for being so clumsy."

"I should send over my housekeeper, Madame Woo, she'd straighten things out," he smiled before turning serious. "Still, my dear Missus Prescott, you must promise to be more careful. I hate to see such a lovely and delicate flower marred in any way." Yet as he poured her a glass of vintage Bordeaux, all he could think of was how to deal with Alfred T. Prescott.

XII

The cold wind shook the windows as a November storm swept in from the lake; however, from within Collins' office, it was hard to tell the actual source of the tempest.

"You struck a fellow officer," the captain roared.

"Like I said, he grabbed a lady's chest!"

"First of all, he was following my orders and investigating insurrection. Second, he was apprehending a possible suspect. Besides, what kind of lady is that, being involved with those union anarchists and meeting with all sorts of men not her husband."

"That's enough!"

"What!"

"She's a fine lady, educated, kind. Maybe a bit radical in her ideas, but she's the daughter of Blinky Shea and more important, a friend of mine."

"Don't you dare be insubordinate to me, Doyle! I'll cut her slack as a favor to Blinky—"

"And his powerful friends."

"Watch your insolent tone, boyo! I'll put your ass on leave!"

"With all due respect, sir, we both know that would be a mistake. You need me as much as I need you."

"Don't over play your hand, Sergeant. You're on thin ice and you've been slipping. What kind of beating did you give Toohey? He took the kids and moved to his mother's."

"Your niece should be glad such a terrible man is outta her house."

"And bringing up her name in regards to Sergeant Perry, in front of that Shea girl!"

"Like nobody knows. Besides, Spit 'n Polish shouldn't be so thin-skinned."

"Or be left… with his balls up his throat!" Collins screamed as he trembled with rage.

Danny could barely suppress a snicker as his commander pressed on, "You've got no more chances, Doyle! You'll straighten up, if you know what's good for ya!"

"So what have you got for me, Captain," Brick Fist asked, stone-faced.

Frustrated at his Sergeant's unwillingness to be cowered, but anxious to address a growing problem, Collins replied, "More and more of the factory owners and suppliers are complaining about thefts getting out of hand at their businesses."

"I'm aware of the situation and I'm working on it."

"I need your unique skills on this. The bosses at City Hall are watching, so I'll be there to guide you."

Listening to a man he considered a puffed-up, desk-riding, incompetent, Danny needed all the restraint he could muster to keep from laughing in his face.

"But I have to focus most of my energy and much of the resources of this precinct on this union situation. I wish I could count on you, but there are suspicions that you hold sympathies for the rabble."

"I have one sympathy, and that's me."

"That's not what I heard from Captain Wurtz. He insists that you ignored his order to fire at that union mob during the 'Battle of the Buffalo Creek Bridge'."

"As you may have noticed, I can crack heads better than anybody, but on that day, all them big, bad conductors and porters yelling at us musta froze my trigger finger."

"See! It's that flippant attitude that's gettin' ya in trouble! Now, get outta here before I get really mad! And oh, yeah, before ya go, ya better be votin' Republican tomorrow, and ya better get dealin' with those Foleys. We can't be havin' criminals shootin' at the police."

Smirking not only at the thought of Collins' threats, but at the captain's less than overwhelming concern over his personal safety, Brick Fist got up and left without saying another word. Happy to be done with such a nettlesome gnat, he was anxious to grab Costello and get on with his plans; however, just as he reached the base of the stairs, he ran into Billy Broderick.

"Danny, before ya go headin' off with Hugh, I got some good news for ya. The last couple of days, I had a crew lookin' for the Foleys and then last night they got 'em comin' outta that opium den on Fly Street. Gave 'em a good thrashin' and warned 'em that every man on the force would have 'em in their sights, no questions asked, if anything happened to you. Theil and young Gannon even got nice shiny pistols outta their little meetin', ta boot."

Although never one to wax sentimental, Danny was moved by Billy's constant loyalty and friendship. Moreover, being the pariah of the force was beginning to wear thin; consequently, he couldn't hide his feelings, "While I was itchin' to run into the boys, your bein' the pal that ya are, means a whole lot to me, Billy. And thanks to all the fellas for backin' me up. But enough of all this fartin' roses, I got my work to do; and where's that college-boy cousin of yours."

"He's already waitin' outside. And remember to keep that thick Irish head of yours up. Those Foleys are still dangerous."

After collecting Costello, he lost little time in describing what happened to the Foleys, before going on to explain his objective for this morning. Just as he was about to cross Terrace Street and head into the Canal District, he caught sight of Liam Riley pulling up to a walkway in Prescott's buggy. He was delivering the boss's daughter to Van Cleff's millenary shop a few doors down from the Mercantile Exchange. Watching as the secretary dutifully waited on the chubby young heiress, Danny couldn't help but revel in the thought that it served him right to play the role of a bootlick, given his calculated treatment of Keena.

Anxious to press forward, the policemen marched down to Boiler Street, home to some of the most "infected" dives and bordellos in the District. After slipping behind a newsstand across from the Bosun's Knot Saloon, one of Fingers earliest acquisitions, Danny surveyed the alley next to the closed-up gin mill. As expected, he spied Harpoon Marley standing sentry between a back door and an outside staircase leading to the top floor. The bodyguard's presence confirmed what Danny learned some time earlier; that very Monday morning Carnahan convened a meeting with his principal lieutenants, to go over business operations. Although the bar was not the sort of venue for such a profitable and far-reaching enterprise, Fingers was determined to keep these discussions away from his legitimate businesses. As such, he was unwilling to host such a nefarious crew at his headquarters-residence, where he had begun to entertain some of the city's most influential and respectable citizens.

Satisfied that all was set, Danny was quick to act, "Now, Hugh, I told ya what he'll do when I make my move. Like I said, don't hesitate or we'll both be hurtin'. Okay, get goin'."

Once Costello took off, Brick Fist ambled across the street, where he was stopped by Marley as he approached the staircase. "Stop right there, Doyle. Whad'ya want?"

"I'm just here to pay my respects to the Major."

"You know the rules. He only sees those he sends for."

"It's police business, Georgie."

"Then see a judge, Danny," Marley smirked.

"I don't care about any rules or judges; now get outta the way,"

"We never had a dust-up, Danny, but if ya take another step, I'll be stickin' your head up your arse." With that, Harpoon slipped on a set of brass knuckles and began to circle towards the stairs.

"Talk is cheap, boyo," Brick Fist shot back as he made his move.

"Get on your knees and put up your hands," Costello yelled from behind Marley.

Ignoring Doyle, Harpoon spun towards the young officer, "Why ya little…"

Before Danny had a chance to react, Hugh began to pull out his nightstick, which sent Marley into a fearsome rage. Howling like a demon, he hauled back and sent the billy club spinning off into the distance. Despite Costello's game attempt to grapple with the monster, Harpoon lifted him up by the belt, and smashed him into the building with a force that rattled the windows. By now, Danny was riding the leviathan's back and applying an eye-popping choke hold, but to no avail. Fearing for his young charge's life, he finally grabbed his blackjack and delivered a blow that dropped the charging beast in his tracks.

"Stop it! Stop it now, or I'll shoot!" Fingers bellowed from the top of the landing, as he stood flanked by two of his chiefs.

"Don't even think of it," Doyle glared as he drew his revolver. Satisfied that he made his point, he rushed to his crumpled partner. "Are ya all right, son? Are ya injured?"

Lifting himself to his knees, the young patrolman rasped, "Ohhh …
my back feels like it's been run over by a trolley and I'm still a bit dizzy, but
I'll be fine."

"Well then, for Christ's sake I told ya not to draw a weapon! Are
ya daft, lad! He's left bodies on battlefields and back alleys all over the
world. All I wanted was for ya to do was distract 'im while I got the jump
on 'im. That stick of yours was no more than a feather duster to 'im. Ya
don't go yanking the tail of a bull!"

"Sorry, Danny, I got carried away."

"Well, at least ya got guts but don't ever go defyin' me again.
Now, pick yourself up. We got work to do."

By now, Fingers had made his way down the stairs and was
standing at the door as his henchmen helped Harpoon into the saloon. As he
dusted off his new bowler, Danny walked up to the still-groggy bodyguard,
"Sorry 'bout crackin' ya on the noggin, Georgie, but I was afraid ya were
killin' me young partner."

As Marley responded with a glassy-eyed nod, Fingers spoke up,
"That's three, Sergeant; first Emmon, then your pals beating up Doc and
Mike last night, and now this. What's going' on, Doyle?"

"Like I told Georgie, I just wanted to talk to you."

"You should've arranged for an appointment. I've been quite
busy."

"An appointment! With all due respect, Major, you're not the
bloody pope. Besides, you're not so easy to find."

"I won't bother to ask how you did find me; but let's not waste
time. Come on in and do your talking."

With Costello following on his heels, Brick Fist strolled into the
Saloon that reeked with every conceivable putrid odor. Walking past blood
stained floorboards, broken bottles and a dirty garter draped atop a chair, the

policemen had no trouble imaging the festivities that prevailed the previous night.

"Let's escape this fetid air," Fingers suggested, as he pointed to a room at the side of the bar.

"Hugh, you just sit here and watch for any funny business," Danny ordered, before following his host.

"Well, talk, Sergeant," Fingers snapped, as he took a seat.

"Before we get started, sorry about Georgie; and as for last night, the boys got a little rowdy about me getting shot at last week."

"I heard about the shooting but you're barking up the wrong tree. Listen, you made it clear during our last discussion that you were going to do things your own way. You didn't want to cooperate and come to me with any problems. Still, despite that, I had a little talk with the brothers. They got it and they wouldn't defy me."

"Well, somebody shot at me and I have a funny feeling it was the Foleys. The other coppers feel the same way. I trust you can keep control of your boys, but if not, we'll take care of things."

"Watch it, Danny! Don't go lecturing me. I run a tight ship; so, I hope you're not suggesting the police are going to squeeze me; but just for the record, how many police are on the force?"

"About two-twenty, I reckon."

"Two hundred and eight, to be exact, and I can have twice that number on the street in an hour."

"Don't make me laugh, Major. We both know a mob doesn't make a good army; and you forget our volunteers and the militia, but that's beside the point. I know you got some high-falutin' friends who wouldn't take kindly to that sort of trouble."

"I'm merely suggesting that we both have an interest in not giving each other problems. Your boss, Collins, although an idiot and a weasel, has enough sense to know he doesn't want waves. Bad for business and elections; and make no mistake, he's much more a political hack and business toady that an officer of the law."

"You're dead-on about Collins; but you keep your boys in line and there'll be no problems."

"I do and I will; and if they lie to me they'll be very sorry; but if I believe my workers are being unduly harassed and if it's hurting business, I'll be very unhappy. And that means trouble for everyone," Fingers bellowed as his impatience grew. "Now, is that all?"

"Not quite; the thefts involving the factories and such are getting worse."

"Tell your piece of shit friend, Prescott and his pals to pay their workers a decent wage; and that syphilitic wart better stop accusing me, if he knows what's good for him!"

"Actually, I just want to know if you heard anything."

"As I told you before, I'm in the insurance business, so it's my concern too."

"And sometimes the greater threat of risk leads people to buy more insurance."

For a moment, Fingers sat there, tight-jawed and eyes burning. "Don't ever imply I'm a liar; ever!" After catching himself, he returned to a more amicable tone. "I always liked you, Danny, but you're testing the limits of our friendship. If you got any evidence, see the prosecutor or come back and see me. Otherwise, I have to get back to my responsibilities."

"Sorry, Major, I'm not polished like you. I fumble with my words. I guess I'm just a bog-hopper at heart, but I'm glad we cleared the air."

After a parting exchange of pleasantries, Danny offered to see himself out, while Fingers headed back upstairs to the company of his lieutenants.

"Got a little heated in there, eh, Danny?" Costello observed as they walked out the door.

"Just remindin' 'im he ain't the king

XIII

"Lemme try some of that podada soup, ya got, Tim," the youngster begged as he poked his wooden spoon towards the little bucket.

"Mind your manners, Marty! Me ma made it special for me, got some pork in it; but go ahead. Ya need it, ya half-pint runt, but don't go touchin' the meat!"

"I may be little, but I can whack a ball further than you," the little fellow laughed as he scooped up a juicy wedge of spud.

"That ain't gonna happen! Everybody knows I can hit a ball longer than any kid on Katherine Street."

"Hey, speakin' of hittin' long, I heard the Bisons might be gettin' Big Dan Brouthers," one of the Brady boys interrupted as he wiped his forehead with a dirty rag laying on the bench.

Despite the blustery conditions that prevailed beyond its walls, inside the factory, it was a boiling caldron of heat. As the boys sat in a corner, wolfing down their suppers, they were already sweating through their ragged work-clothes.

Rows of hissing presses that ran the length of the floor, churning out miles of wallpaper every day, generated enough heat, that when combined with outside air created a fine mist that hung over the gas-lit workplace like a ghostly curtain. The heavy scent of naphtha, along with scattered pools of water formed from leaking pipes and leeching walls, only added to a fetid scene better suited to the underworld.

"Say it's true, Seamus," young McCarthy gasped.

"On me mother's grave, it's true. And that ain't all. I heard they're bringin' in Jimmy O'Rourke, too!"

"And what makes you the baseball club expert," the ever-skeptical Duffy Carr piped in.

"Me da heard it down at Blinky's."

"Yeah, I heard Pud Galvin sometimes goes in there; along with Bill Crowley and Jack Rowe," the McCarthy boy added.

"And I suppose the great Pud Galvin just happened to sit your ol' man down and tell 'im all the club's goins' on," Duffy smirked.

"Come on, ya know I don't go flingin' the malarkey," Seamus proclaimed. "No, me da's a big baseball man; played ball down in Scranton, years ago. And he knows some of the fellas who work at the ball park."

"Holy Mother Mary, we're gonna win the National League next year," Cassidy, the paper cutter shouted.

"Those fellas at the ball park, they must know Pud,"

"Sure do; they even got tickets through Pud for me da."

"No way!"

"I swear by all the Saints and Martyrs. He took me up to Riverside Park the year before last. Saw the 'Little Steam Engine' pitch."

"What's the ball park like," someone at the edge of the group asked.

As a chorus of young voices clamored for more details, the Brady boy obliged, "Beautiful green grass and spankin' white uniforms and stands filled with thousands of people. Never seen nothin' like it, way out in the sticks; past all them fancy houses on Delaware Street."

"That's where Mister Prescott lives. What's those houses like?"

"Like gleamin' fairy castles. Could live a hundred people in each one of 'em."

"Someday I'm gonna go to a game," little Marty piped up. "Ya know, I had a dream Pud was my long lost brother, who found us and moved us all uptown and took us to all the games."

"Whad'ya doin,' nippin' your ol' man's poteen," Duffy countered with a shake of his head.

"Hey lads, we better quit yappin' before Caldwell comes back, screamin' like a banshee and crackin' the whip," Tim Hannon groaned, before coaxing along the rest of the boys.

No sooner had the children returned to their posts at the first two press lines, than Hannon, the oldest boy and lead operator, noticed that the troughs holding the varnish and dyes were running low. Summoning the two Brady brothers, he ordered that they grab the barrel cart and hurry to the storage tanks to replenish their supplies. As the minutes slipped by, he maintained a nervous vigil, knowing that any dry run would require the time-consuming and expensive task of shutting down the line—an outcome that would ignite his bosses' ire. While fixing his focus on the printing trays, he failed to notice wisps of smoke drifting from the roller's journal bearing. Just as the Bradys returned and began transferring the liquids into buckets, the great mechanical behemoth let loose a grinding screech that resonated throughout the hall. As the upper cylinder seized to a halt, the onrushing paper quickly jammed; yet the lower roll continued to spin, straining against the blockage. As Hannon and the others wrestled with the equipment in an effort to clear the logjam, the clumped mass began to heat up from friction, until reaching the point of combustion, it ignited in a plume of smoke. Before the workers had a chance to react, the flames spread to the dye trays, which set the entire press ablaze.

Blinded by fear, two of the younger boys flew off in a panic; but not before slamming into the barrel cart, and spilling its volatile contents onto the floor. As the rest of the crew battled to beat back the blaze with their shirts, or anything else at hand, a glowing ember of paper slowly floated down onto the spill. In a flash, the shimmering rivulet of chemicals burst into flames as it raced towards a sealed-off area that held obsolete equipment and other junk. As the blaze streamed under the loading door and danced up the walls of the room, a full-scale conflagration was now at hand. Despite the foreman's command to form a makeshift bucket brigade, the workers knew better, and ran for their lives. Just as the last of the crews made their way to the exit, the storage room exploded, sending a rolling ball of fire across the great hall.

Confident that all twenty had made it out safely, Hannon grabbed one of his friends, exhorting him to warn those below while he would do the same above. With the stairwell beginning to fill with smoke, he wrapped a shop rag across his face and began to grope his way along the steps.

Up on the fourth floor, the union activist, Padrig Tierney was making some adjustments to his blotching machine, when he heard a ruckus down below. No sooner had he left his post to investigate than the floor began to rumble and jets of flame came shooting through the belt holes. Knowing that catastrophe was upon them, he rushed to gather all the boys in an attempt to flee down the stairs.

No sooner had the terrified group arrived at the exit than Hannon stumbled out, choking from the heavy smoke and having barely escaped the searing heat and flames that raced up behind him. Realizing the stairwell was no longer the avenue to safety but had become an instrument for stoking and spreading the fire, the little band beat a quick retreat to the center of the room.

As the hall began to fill with smoke and the heat became more unbearable, one of the boys, the machine polisher Tommy Smith, made a mad dash for the exit; yet as he neared his hopeless goal, he suddenly combusted. Screaming for his mother, he careened about like a runaway firework, before dropping to his knees and collapsing on his face. Helpless to even approach their doomed comrade, a blood curdling sense of panic swept through the ranks of the trapped.

Knowing he had mere moments to act, not only to save his own life but to stave off certain catastrophe for almost twenty children, Tierney stifled his cough and yelled out in a forceful yet calm voice, "Gather 'round, lads. I know a way out. Grab each other's hand and follow me; and stay calm."

But none of his words could hold back the young foreman, Bob Farmer, from resorting to more desperate measures. Pulling himself onto the window shelf, he pleaded, "Better to jump than burn alive like Smitty." Kicking through the glass, he threw himself towards the telegraph lines two stories down; however, rather than break his fall, the wires spun him around and launched him, headfirst, onto the cobblestone pavement, much to the horror of onlookers who had begun to gather outside.

Leaving his place at the end of the line, young Hannon rushed to the window, only to be greeted by the grisly scene below. "Keep goin', lads. Bobby didn't make it; bless his soul." Reeling in shock from all that was happening, the horror-struck children could do little more than follow their leader.

With flaming tongues of belting raining down from above, the ragtag little party cut a twisting path through a growing inferno that moments before was a humming factory. Fighting for every breath and dodging a patchwork of blazing equipment, Tierney prayed that his gamble would pay off. Over the last few weeks, he had been smuggling the union organizer, Raphael Taglieri, into the building in an effort to lobby the workers. Access was gained via a rear door in an obscure utility room at the far end of the shop. The little metal portal led out to the roof of the administration building; but more importantly, one could easily make a one-story jump to the roof of Tifft's Pattern Shop, on the west side of the factory. Tierney figured that such a maneuver would at least buy them time for a rescue. Unfortunately, an unknown snitch had revealed the union's scheme to management, who quickly took steps to remedy the situation, including securing the clandestine passage and even seizing the rope used to pull the organizer up from the adjacent alley.

Almost certainly, their lives now depended on the answers to the fateful questions that Tierney kept turning in his head: to what extent was the door secured and did they have time to crack it open? Still, their perilous trek was worth the chance, since the only other option was a return to the windows that were now beginning to crack from the heat.

Upon reaching the object of salvation, there was little time to waste. The heat was beginning to singe their exposed flesh and the air was almost too thin to breathe, as the fire continued to consume the oxygen in its path. Grabbing a nearby pry bar that was now hot to the touch, Tierney threw open the utility door and rushed forward. Much to his everlasting relief, he discovered that although the latch plate had been newly welded, a pad lock had not yet been attached. Flinging open the portal, he rejoiced at the rush of rejuvenating air; but knowing the hunger of the flames, he realized he had mere seconds left. "Come on, lads; run! And jump down to Tifft's roof on your right."

As Tim Hannon pushed through the last boy, he took a look back for any stragglers. Much to his horror, he spotted two brothers huddled in a corner, paralyzed with fear. Just as he rasped out a plea to follow, a blazing beam came crashing down on the enwrapped pair, spewing out a blizzard of sparkling embers. Helpless to act, he turned away. Yet no sooner had the young hero come bounding out the door, than a blast of flame quickly followed.

Although having escaped the hell that had become the plant, the workers' plight was far from over. Not only was the roof beneath their feet becoming increasingly hot, but smoke and flames were now billowing out from the sides of the pattern shop. After lowering the last of the small boys into the arms of their friends below, Tierney jumped down and began to take stock of the situation. Much to his chagrin, there were no fire crews in sight, despite the steamer house being virtually next door. No doubt they were battling the main source of the blaze at the opposite side of the building. Faced with little time to spare, he and the others would have to take matters into their own hands.

With fear-filled eyes, the band of survivors gathered around their shepherd, looking for guidance. Despite having suffered frightful scars to his face and hands, the result of a ruptured steam line years earlier, Tierney was never the object of repulsion or derision; rather, his fellow workers viewed him with respect and admiration, due to his warm manner and strong and steady hand. As such, the burden of their fate fell onto his shoulders.

Padrig knew that any three-story leap was a last resort and that many, if not most, would resist the call; however, as he scanned the terrain, a vision of hope came in the form of a newly installed telephone wire running from the edge of the administration building to a pole ten yards in the distance. Moving quickly, he gathered a group of the biggest boys, who hoisted him up to where the line met the building. With the help of his pocket knife, he managed to pry the wire from its attachment. Racing to the corner of the roof, his team heaved and tugged until the wire snapped back from the pole.

Time was now of the essence, as flames were shooting high above the entire west side of the pattern shop; however, luck was smiling as the back of the building was free of hazards and more importantly, a vent pipe stood mere feet from the edge of the roof.

After securing the line to the sturdy iron anchor, and stuffing some shirts between the wire and the rim, Hannon was the first one down, so as to steady the line from below. As random flames began to burst through the front end of the roof, Tierney yelled out, "Now ya seen how Tim did it! The young ones with rags go first. If ya don't have a rag, start rippin' up your shirts. You'll be slidin' down and ya don't wanna burn your hands; but no matter what, keep goin'. You're better off burning your hands than dyin' up here!" As each stepped up, he offered words of encouragement and a pat on the back, before helping them over the side.

Satisfied that all were safe, save for some awkward landings and rope burns, it was now Padrig's turn to head down; however, mere feet from the edge, the line finally broke, sending him crashing to the ground.

While the fourth floor workers were busy rigging their escape, the city's newly chartered fire crews were fighting a valiant but increasingly futile battle to contain the fire and save those still trapped inside. In the twenty-five minutes since a boy came running into the nearby station with news of the disaster, the plant had become almost fully engulfed. No doubt, the massive quantities of paper and chemicals housed within the factory walls served to fuel the rapid spread of the fire. Fortunately, the workers on the first three floors were able to flee virtually unharmed; however, those on the two floors above the source, faced far grimmer prospects.

While the fourth floor widows appeared lifeless, belching out smoke and flames, one could still make out the desperate situation through the windows on the fifth floor. Figures, racing about in a panic, cast chilling silhouettes against the orange glow of their blazing prison. At the far end of the building, men were hanging onto the casements, frantically waving their shirts, hoping to grab the rescuers' attention; however unbeknownst to them, not only were the firefighters' ladders too short, but the intensity of the inferno prevented their deployment. Faced with few options, the fire crews had to be content to pour water into the lower floors before making their way to the top. Yet as the minutes ticked by, one of the trapped workers could hold out no longer; and to the horrified screams of the spectators, took flight. His broken, bleeding remains lay untended for some minutes before rescuers could get close enough to retrieve them.

By now, hordes of on lookers had descended onto the surrounding streets, including not only the curiosity seekers intent on witnessing the disastrous spectacle, but also families desperately in search of loved ones employed at the plant. Joining the onrush were two priests from Saint Brigit's. Running with their sacramental stoles flapping in the wind, they turned down Perry Street before stopping dead in their tracks. Greeted by the sight of the towering citadel emblazoned against the night sky, they began to perform the rite of general absolution for the helpless victims trapped inside.

Meanwhile, newly arrived reinforcements from the fifth and eight wards were busy setting up their steamer pumps and unwinding their hoses; however, Liam Riley, who had been working late in the office, was hampering their efforts. After requisitioning a couple of wagons and conscripting a group of escaped workers, he was busy trying to save stock from the loading dock before the fire reached it. Finally, as the flames began to threaten that end of the building, he reluctantly submitted to the fire captain's demands. Afterwards, he retreated with his prize to a street far removed from the danger.

Shortly after the first alarm was sounded, Billy Broderick and a squadron of deputies sped to the scene. Their purpose was to keep order and provide any other assistance to the beleaguered fire crews. He and his men were just in the midst of setting up a line that cordoned off the site from the surging crowds, when he heard the chorus of screams that accompanied the horrifying spectacle of two bodies hurtling to the ground. Quickly grabbing a couple of his charges, he rushed off to the victims; however, upon arriving, it was obvious one was dead, having impaled himself on a cast iron hitching post. The other man, lying like a discarded, twisted doll, had somehow managed to survive the fall and was signaling as much with a feeble wave of his hand.

Braving the hot embers raining down from above, and ignoring the terrifying prospect of additional leapers, Broderick and his men took care in ministering to the pitiful victim; and despite bones sticking out from various places, the man succeeded in choking out the words, "Tell my wife and kids, I love 'em."

Using their coats as a stretcher, the policemen carried him across the street to Geyer's Tavern where a neighborhood doctor had set up a temporary aid station. As they placed him on a makeshift bed formed by two tables, the victim managed to cut through the fog of stupor and identify himself as a block cutter named Connelly. Broderick promised that the police would get word to his family; however, when he turned to Doctor Skelton, the physician signaled his prognosis with a resigned shake of his head.

Although shaken by the enormity of the unfolding events, the lieutenant quickly returned to his post, hoping to help stave off further disaster. After ordering his men to shore up the lines, he passed a livery whose owner was about to close shop, fearing both the growing hordes and the encroaching deluge of sparks generated by the inferno. Billy was already past the stable when he remembered seeing a wagon brimming over with hay. Recognizing the possibilities, he rushed back, and after persuading the reluctant owner with a threat of arrest, commandeered the vehicle.

By now, although barely forty minutes into the catastrophe, virtually every element of the structure was ablaze. Towering jets of flame had burst through the roof and raging fireballs were leaping from the previously spared front entrance. Even Tifft's Pattern Shop, along with other nearby buildings including the fire steamer house, were now ablaze.

In the face of searing heat, fire crews were forced to retreat to a safer distance, and any hope of working their way through the building had gone up in smoke. Still, a trio of workers managed to cling to windows at the rear corner of the top floor, in hope of delaying their fateful decision until the last moment.

Convinced they recognized loved ones among the soot-covered faces, scores of screaming onlookers surged into the police lines. Only the heroic efforts of the officers prevented further disaster.

After soaking down the hay, and covering himself with a wet tarp, Broderick placed his jacket on the horse's face and along with a fresh recruit named, Shaw, led the wagon towards the trapped workers. Fortunately, the area in question was devoid of windows on the lower floors and flames had not yet breached its walls.

Despite the pervasive heat, Broderick managed to position the makeshift cushion as close as possible to the building foundation. Yelling up, he pleaded that jumping was their only chance. For a moment there was no response, before the largest figure grabbed the smallest and threw him out towards the wagon. The screaming pinwheel landed with a resounding thud; but when the sounds of muffled whimpers came drifting out, Billy ordered young Shaw to snatch the child and make for the lines.

Just as the next man was about to leap, a long seething groan filled the air. In an instant, the wall came crashing down with a massive blast, even drowning out the shrieks and cries of the horrified onlookers. Yet as a thick cloud of dust billowed over the devastation, all became quiet, save for the relentless crackle of flames.

XIV

A pungent mix of smoke and chemicals filled the air as Danny picked his way across the smoldering ruin that was once the Prescott Wallpaper Company. Twisted tangles of metal and steaming mounds of brick and mortar were all that remained in a debris field that stretched over two city blocks. Streaming arches of water kept the hot spots at bay, while recovery workers ventured into the abyss in search of bodies; and despite the deadly mayhem that prevailed last night, all was now silent, save for the hollow beat of picks and shovels, and the distant drone of fire pumpers.

Doyle's lack of sleep only added to the surreal sense of seeing an empty landscape that until yesterday was a thriving manufacturing quarter; but nothing could match the desolation of his soul in knowing that Billy Broderick was dead.

He had already been immersed in the pleasures of Big Tits Kate's when he got news of the disaster. After throwing on his clothes and paying the girl, he ran towards the pulsating glow that was lighting up the entire lower end of the city. Upon turning down Perry Street, he was greeted by a scene culled straight from the pages of Dante's reflections on hell. As scores of firefighters were desperately laying rivers of water onto the flame-belching colossus, a surging sea of faces, including those gripped in various stages of suffering, encircled the nightmarish scene. Just as he tried to squeeze his way through the crowd, he heard reference to a certain Lieutenant Broderick falling victim to an earlier collapse.

Seized as if by madness, he shoved aside some hapless bystanders before running along the edge of the blaze, screaming for his friend. As he neared the rear of the building, he came upon a swarm of uniforms feverishly attacking a mountain of rubble in search of their entombed comrade. Flying into the heart of the effort, he began to tear at the steaming debris. A shift in the wind sent the others scrambling, but there was no stopping Brick Fist as he dug on with a manic ferocity, ignoring not only the threat of the flames, but the cuts and burns to his hands. His commander's screams to fall back fell on deaf ears, and only the concerted effort of a squad of police, could wrench him from the smoking pile.

He was there, hours later, when they found Billy, still holding the reins and surprisingly unscathed, save for a gaping wound to the back of his head. Now, as he wandered the shattered landscape, Danny couldn't bring himself to grieve for his friend or to think about the good times that they shared together. Instead, he steeled his will. He had a job to do, and as was his practice, he threw himself into it.

While having long ago come to the belief that there were no happy endings, he nonetheless searched for answers as to what brought on this terrible calamity. He refused to accept that this was some mere accident, or what was often described as a random act of god. In a world so rife with corruption, he was certain that man's hand was somehow involved; and as was always the case, those on the bottom felt the brunt of the blow.

Despite his go-it-alone attitude, he was beginning to realize Keena was right; that the toiling masses needed the protection afforded by a group. As he continued to scour the desolate landscape, he watched as the ghost-like figures of loved ones wandered the roped off fringes of the ruins, hoping for some miracle that he knew would never come. While the heartbreaking scene set aflame his legendary anger, it also spurred his hunger to set things straight. Just as he was about to scale the last remaining outcropping of wall, he heard a shout from behind, "Yo, I think we got something."

Turning, he watched in horror as a team of workers lifted out the charred stumps of two bodies wrapped in a grisly, yet heartbreaking eternal embrace. Although the remains lacked any discernable features, the boss was quick to offer his take, "Sweet Jesus! It must be those two brothers from the fourth floor. I heard they went down together." After signaling for a canvas, he shook his head and grumbled, "Cover 'em up and take 'em over to McComb's Boiler Works. I think that makes ten."

As Danny kept scratching his way through the rubble from the back section of the factory, he stumbled upon the remnants of a doorway. Despite its battered condition, he was able to determine that the lock bolt was still engaged into its splintered frame; and he felt his stomach twist into a knot upon realizing that the doomed workers may have been locked into their burning pyre. Although not all the victims had been accounted for, company crews were already in the process of salvaging whatever they could from the debris. It only reinforced what he had come to know, that profits always came first. Recognizing a fireman from the neighborhood, Doyle pulled him over and asked that he save his discovery by taking it back to his home station. After spending another fruitless hour sifting through the debris, he finally retreated to the fresh air beyond the lines.

By the time he arrived at the corner of the now-barren Indiana Street, he spotted Captain Collins, heading his way.

"What are you doing here, Sergeant? I thought you had the day off?"

"I've been here all night, Captain. Billy was my best mate, and I'm just scratching around to see what happened."

"This is not your case, Sergeant. I've already got you on the important matter of all those burglaries and pilferages plaguing our city's businesses."

"Just the same, I discovered a door that was locked from the outside."

Rather than appearing intrigued by Doyle's find, Collins took on an angry look. "Mister William Scott is convening his coroner's jury. I'm quite sure he has the expertise and resources to arrive at a speedy explanation as to the cause of this unfortunate occurrence." The Captain's reference to an "unfortunate occurrence," left Brick Fist wanting to smash in his face, but more importantly, his alluding to the assumed impartiality and so-called "expertise" of a dishonest businessman and political hack like Scott, only served to inspire Danny's suspicion and loathing. "And I won't have you muddying the waters," Collins bristled. "Do I make myself clear?"

"Yes, sir," Doyle muttered, all the while plotting ways to circumvent the order.

"Very good! Now, I must be on my way. As you can imagine, they need my input on this matter."

Once again, Danny could barely hide his contempt as he watched the man he considered and incompetent weasel grab his bootlick, Sergeant Perry.

Unnerved by his encounter with Collins, and knowing that sleep would elude him, Doyle hoped to find some respite in drink. As such, he hopped aboard a nearby trolley that would take him to Blinky's; however, no sooner had he passed through the tavern doors than he encountered a scene befitting a wake. Scattered throughout the room were clusters of people consoling each other in hushed tones. At the center of this sad tableau, sat the barmaid, Kitty McCoy, surrounded by her family, including Keena and her father.

As Danny waded into this unsettling scene, he ran into one of the bar regulars, Tom Beahan, standing at the rail.

"Don't tell me, Tom, Kitty's boy?"

"Kitty's boys; two of 'em, Danny. Good Lord, Maura Hackett's son; the Brennan's and at least six others; and I just heard about Billy Broderick. There's a lot of bleeding hearts this morning, my friend."

Staggered by the news, Danny couldn't keep his eyes off Kitty as she swung between hysteria and stoic suffering. A steady stream of friends and loved ones offered sympathetic embraces and whatever words they could muster to balm her unstanchable wound; and kneeling at her side was Keena, gently stroking her cousin's hair whenever the horrific reality of her circumstances came crashing down.

After offering her place to Father Morris, Keena headed to the bar where her father had set up a buffet. Spotting Danny, she could no longer hold back her tears as she rushed to his side. "Oh, Danny, ya heard; young Aidan and Jack; oh, my dear, sweet Kitty."

"I got the news from Tom. I'm sorry, Keena," he whispered as he wiped away a tear rolling down her face.

"Father Pat just told us that they found them, but they're not fit to be seen by their parents and brothers. We'll see about that. There'll be no holding back my Kitty."

Grabbing her hand he implored, "Believe me, Keena, he's right. I just came from over there and it will crush her heart even more to see 'em the way they are."

"Oh, can it get any worse, Danny," she cried before burying her face into his shoulder.

Feeling her shake against his chest, he wanted to sweep her in his arms and carry her away from all this horror. She deserved more than all the pain that this world so cruelly offered. She deserved the love and strength of a man who could protect her from life's inevitable suffering. Yet he knew such thoughts were mere mocking illusions; that such musings belied harsh reality. All came to naught and nothing had meaning; and although he found relief in power, money and whores, he believed she deserved to revel in the joy of illusion; unsoiled by the darkness of the world he had come to know.

Catching herself, Keena straightened up and wiped her face before reasserting her resolve. "My darling Kitty needs a strong shoulder at her side. I don't know why this happened, but by the Grace of God and the Holy Mother, we're gonna get her, Charlie and the boys through all this."

"I have no doubt you'll help her, Keena. And while I know there's no God who could let this happen, if the hand of man's involved, I promise you, I'll find him."

"Thank you, dear friend; but I do wish you'd open your heart up to the Lord. It's not weak or pie in the sky; but it's at these times that he leads us to understanding."

"I wish it were so, Keena; but I respect your feelings."

"I always know that, Danny. But right now, I have to fix some plates for Kitty and the others. They'll need all their strength. And I also have to take care of my non-believing but wonderful friend, Sergeant Doyle."

"I suppose I could use some grub, especially coffee."

"You look like you've been up all night."

"A hard night, that's for sure. We lost Billy Broderick."

"Oh, please say no," she pleaded as she grabbed his arm. "He's your best friend, and a good man; with that pretty wife and those red-headed scamps!"

"It's bad, Keena. I'll miss him, greatly," he said before quickly shutting off.

Knowing his way, she merely nodded before pouring his cup and preparing his plate. All remained quiet as she went about her task and he wolfed down his meal.

As the wails of female keeners began to pierce the air, Danny joined Keena in delivering the trays to Kitty and her family. Following her lead, he found himself face-to-face with his shattered friend; and despite having tried all day to bury his feelings, he realized there was no escaping the tragic reality that had come smashing into the world around him.

Seated in a wing-back chair that Blinky pulled from his office, Kitty was dressed in her Sunday best, no doubt in honor of her sons; but the spirited woman long familiar to friends and customers was no longer there. In her place was a limp and confused figure, appearing barely able to comprehend the tumult swirling around her. That she seemed to have aged a decade in the span of a night, only added to this aberrant portrait. With her crippled husband and five remaining sons draped across her feet, she tried her best to acknowledge the comforting words of her many friends. Yet nothing could free her from the anguish of knowing her boys were never coming home.

As Danny approached a scene that mirrored renderings of the suffering Madonna, he focused onto her dark green eyes, swollen by grief and seeming to plead for answers to the unanswerable. Grasping her weathered hands, he was stunned by their feeble feel; as if stripped of all the vitality behind them.

Finally recognizing her longtime friend through the cloud of sorrow, she could do little more than raise her head and offer a wistful lament, "Danny, oh, Danny, my sweet darling boys are gone forever."

"I'm so sorry, dear Kitty."

"I heard from Father Pat that you were there this morning." Reminded of earlier reports from the scene, she sobbed, "my golden haired angels are now burnt sticks."

"They were wrapped in each other's arms; brothers to the end."

"That gives me some peace, knowin' they weren't alone. And that's why I don't care how they look. I'm their ma and I got to touch their bones before we send 'em off."

Knowing her stubborn spirit, he had no doubt she would do it; and his heart flowed out to her. He longed to share his thoughts and feelings; however, given his disposition, he couldn't bring himself to go there. Although knowing that nothing could balm her pain and sorrow, he wanted to convey some sense of condolence. After struggling to find the words, he could only repeat his earlier lament, "I ... ah ... I'm so sorry, sweet girl."

Despite his fumbling, Kitty was moved by his awkward, yet heartfelt expression. Knowing her friend, a look of gratitude swept across her face before she drew him closer and whispered words of thanks. Returning her gesture with a squeeze of the hand, Brick Fist quickly withdrew, ever-protective of the fortress he constructed to separate himself from the rest of world.

XV

All was quiet outside Saint Joseph's Cathedral except for the muffled clap of hoof beats and the sound of blades cutting across a fresh layer of snow. Even the otherwise boisterous teamsters maintained a respectful silence as they repositioned the black-creped sleigh in front of the entrance. Lining up behind the hearse was a long cortege of wagons and sleds, their horses discharging billows of steam, as they waited the return of their grieving passengers. Inside, more than a thousand sat beneath the vaulted ceiling, attending a funeral mass for the Prescott fire victims.

A deathly cold had descended on the city and the frigid conditions served as a perfect complement to a somber sky that stretched out over an equally bleak Lake Erie. Despite the soaring beauty of the French Gothic Cathedral, on this morning its gray limestone hues only added to the mournful atmosphere of the occasion.

Wrapped in a heavy woolen coat and wearing a knit cap pulled down around his ears, Danny stood sentry at the curb, alongside a multitude of others who were unable to cram their way into the church. As he looked about, he was reminded of an earlier time, when a similar cloud of loss and despair engulfed the mourners like a cold fog.

Although loath to find any solace in the religious service, he was nonetheless anxious to show his respect. His presence also served to reinforce his resolve to unearth the truth about the tragedy. After stomping his feet and clapping his arms in an effort to ward off the cold, he watched as the great oaken doors finally swung open and a seemingly endless parade of priests and bishops came filing down the stairs.

Peering through the tiered arches of the entranceway, Danny could see the stained-glass image of the Risen Christ looking down from the rear of the altar as a line of coffins crept along the main aisle. Carried on the shoulders of the victim's young co-workers, the simple pine boxes were greeted with a valedictory blessing as they emerged through the doors.

Struggling not so much with the weight of their cargo, but with swollen eyes and streaks of tears rolling down their cheeks, the still-stricken pall bears carefully placed the remains of their friends onto the deck of the sled for their final journey in this world.

Despite his best efforts to maintain his reserve, Brick Fist couldn't help but be moved by the sight of the loving yet grief-filled families holding on to each other, as if for dear life. Some were dressed in little more than washed and ironed rags, while others had managed to secure more traditional funeral wear. Yet all maintained an air of dignity as they headed to their rides for the trip to Holy Cross Cemetery. There, their loved ones would be buried in a common grave, reflecting not only the sad circumstances of their common end, but the meager means of their survivors. In fact, the purchase of the little plot had been made possible, for the most part, by the generosity of Saint Joseph's parishioners.

As the last of the suffering families climbed onto a wagon that only a day earlier had been hauling animal offal, Danny spied a party from the wallpaper company leaving the church. Led by a strangely distracted looking Alfred Prescott, the group included his wife, daughter Victoria, Liam Riley, Arthur Spenser, the plant manager, and two of his assistants. Watching as they boarded a pair of gleaming carriages, the detective couldn't help but observe that Missus Prescott seemed intent on maintaining a distance between herself and her husband.

With the massive Hook and Hastings organ pumping out the last strains of Mozart's Requiem in the background, Danny spotted Billy's widow, Clare, standing inside the vestibule. Flanked by her mother and aunt, the local superior of the Sisters of Charity, she was talking to a woman he failed to recognize. Not wanting to interrupt, he waited for the woman to leave before rushing inside. No sooner had he exchanged greetings with the two old women, than his heart broke at the sight of tears running down Clare's face.

"Oh, Clare! Just a day after Billy's funeral. This may be askin' too much, dear girl."

"No, no, Danny, these are tears of happiness. That was Nan Gallagher, mother of the boy who landed in the wagon before the wall fell down. She said he made it through the worst last night and he's gonna make it, praise be to Mary and Her Loving Son."

"That would make Billy happy, knowin' what he did," Danny smiled as he fought to keep from choking up.

"It was always about others with my Billy," she added with a determined resolve.

"Don't I know. Not many men like him, Clare."

"The Lord blessed me with a good man, Danny; and I can feel Billy's strength sustaining me through this black time."

"And you're a good woman yourself, Clare Broderick. Billy told me many times how much ya meant to 'im and how you were the rock of the family."

"Thanks, Danny. That means a whole lot hearin' it from his friend."

"And how are the boys holdin' up? They were like brave little soldiers, yesterday."

"They're tryin' to be strong for their ma, but they're takin' it real hard. Billy loved 'em so much and they worshiped him," she sighed, unable to hide the crack in her voice. Yet after reasserting herself, she declared,

"That's why I couldn't put 'em through another funeral. They're back home with me brothers."

"I know they'll be all right. They're lucky lads. They take after their ma and da."

"I'm anxious to get back to 'em. We'll be takin' 'em down to the Beaches. They like it down near the water with the birds an' all. I gotta go callin' on the widow Hackett. The poor thing, lost her boy Cormack, who was the sole support, besides her sellin' her little ribbons and such. Just six months outta the ol' country. First her husband to the fever and now this; left with two little girls, barely three, and livin' in nothin' more than a shack. She needs help and if need be, I'll be bringin' her back home. Billy wouldn't be wantin' me wasting the extra space," she added with a wistful smile.

"I know ya got your kin and Billy's people, but there's nothin' I won't do if ya need me," he insisted as he made a move for his wallet.

"That won't be necessary, Danny," she smiled. "We'll be makin' do; but ya could do us a favor, now. Me ma's got a friend's sled, but Sister James is walkin' over to the Chancellery offices next door. If you could go with her, it's so slippery."

"Of course, but my other offer will always stand, Clare."

After a heartfelt hug, he turned to watch as she assisted her mother into the little sleigh. He was immediately struck by the thought that it was no wonder why she and Billy were such a magnificent couple. They had much in common, most notably a fundamental selflessness; and although such sentiments were long missing from Danny's make up, he could appreciate the unfolding legacy of Billy's goodness. Reflecting on Clare's words, he almost wished he could be like that, but he knew it wasn't in him. He had grown to embrace isolation and was driven by darker impulses; impulses seared into the deep recesses of his heart.

"I remember Billy talking about you on a number of occasions. He was quite fond of you, Sergeant."

The sound of the old nun's voice brought him back to reality. "And I remember Billy saying how much he admired you, Sister; especially when it came to running the infirmary."

"The sisters do a wonderful job ministering to the sick. I just try to assist the efforts as best I can. I mainly sign the paperwork," she added with a wink.

"You're too modest, Sister; but speaking of Saint Mary's, I understand you have a guest who I had to nab for a robbery, Emmon Foley."

"A bad egg from what I heard, but by the Grace of God, hopefully, we can help heal him both physically and spiritually."

"Good luck; that's a tall order about that spiritual thing, Sister; but how's he mending?"

"Poor soul! As you know he had a bad head wound. Then there were a couple of infections. Lately, he's been in and out of delirium. Just last night, he was babbling about Prescott. He must have heard the nurses talking about the fire."

"Maybe just a guilty conscience bubbling out from his madness. Ya musta heard about him rippin' the jewelry off Missus Prescott's neck."

"Ah, that must be it," she mused. "I thought he was going on about larks, you know, the song birds; but he must have been saying locks or lockets."

"Well, if he ever gets his wits about him, I'd appreciate it if you'd contact me at the precinct. There's still some questions that are naggin' me."

"Of course, Sergeant; and I'll keep you in my prayers. Just as I hope you keep Mister Foley in yours."

"Thank you, Sister, but you're talking to the wrong man about such things."

"Such things as compassion are important to all of us, Sergeant. All of God's creatures, no matter who they are or what they did, are deserving of love. Remember, the criminal Dismas is the only person, other than the Holy Mother, that we know is in heaven; and that's because, our Lord promised him while on the cross next to him at Calvary."

As they arrived at the entrance of the diocesan offices, he paused, "I saw such compassion in Billy, but that's not the way I go. Now, you take care, Sister. It was nice talkin' to ya."

"God bless and thank you, Danny; and one last thought. Life has a way of taking us in directions we don't always anticipate," she added with a look that suggested a long history of experience.

After helping her through the door, he headed down to the waterfront for a rendezvous with his protégé, Costello. The young patrolman was anxious to get back to work as a means to somehow balm the loss of his cousin. Brick Fist also sought escape in his work, but unlike the case with Hugh, his job was one of the few things that gave purpose to his life.

As he passed a team of mules pulling a wooden plow down Main Street, and watched as gangs of idled grain scoopers cleared the trolley tracks of snow, he wondered if his young charge would be on time. His worries proved unfounded, after eventually spotting Costello as he waited outside their destination, the Madison Cargo Company. Located just west of the Elk Street Market, it was one of the most successful freight operations in the city.

Hugh was dressed in civilian clothing so as not to attract attention, and absent his uniform, looked even younger than his years. This inspired a hidden chuckle on the part of Danny; nonetheless, the detective was not only beginning to develop respect for his new-found partner, but much to his chagrin, was starting to like him as well. After marching through an opening between the massive wooden doors, they entered a great hall, alive with workers darting about, and brimming with wagons, sleighs and draft horses. Not wanting to waste time, they headed straight to the shipping office at the far end of the building. There, they met the chief dispatcher, Charlie Dwyer, perched atop a draftsman's stool and shuffling through a ream of paper. Peering out from under a weathered visor, he cast a jaundiced eye at the two strangers. "Who are you? It better be important, 'cause I'm buried up to me arse in work. Now, state your business and be quick with it."

Flashing his badge, Brick Fist announced, "I'm Detective Sergeant Doyle and this here is Officer Costello. We'd like to have a word with you, Mister Dwyer, if ya don't mind."

Backpedaling, the man quickly changed his tone, "Ah... of course, Sergeant Doyle, ah... what do ya want? Is there anything wrong?"

After staring into his eyes with a skeptical squint and waiting a moment to ramp up the pressure, Danny finally spoke up, "Is there anything wrong? What are ya, man, daft? All the thievin' and pilferin' goin' on around these parts and you ask that!"

"Ah... ah, that has nothin' to do with me. We just pick up and deliver goods for our customers. We've had no problems."

"Well, I've got a problem! I've been getting a lot of heat over this from my bosses."

"Is there any way I can help, Sergeant?"

"I'm glad you asked, Mister Dwyer, or may I call ya Charlie?" Paying no attention to a nervous nod from the clerk, Danny rolled on, "Naturally, I've been snoopin' around, tryin' to figure out things. Now I heard from a couple of, let's say, friends of mine on the street, that they saw your company's wagons; ya know, with the big yellow letters spellin' out Madison Cargo. They were drivin' around way after midnight, way after the time for pickin' up or deliverin'."

"Oh, they must be wrong, or even lyin'."

Shaking his head with a weary laugh, the detective replied, "Oh, Charlie; come on, you're not stupid! Do I have to paint ya a picture? These friends of mine, due to certain circumstances, are very careful in what they tell me, and they would never ever lie to me."

"Well, I'm no guardian angel. I can't be watching over this place night and day. Things could happen outside of my control."

Taking a more aggressive stance, Danny fired back, "I talked to a bunch of folks and they all tell me that a fella can't scratch 'is arse around here without you knowin' about it. So that makes me think you might have some ideas about what's happenin' around here."

"No, no, I swear!"

"So you swear it's true; you bein' a good Catholic lad an' all."

"Yes! Yes, sir."

"Now I heard from some of your old neighbors down the Ward, neighbors bein' the nosy creatures that they are, that ya bought yourself a cottage up in the Hydraulics. That's a fine place and a fine thing to pull off. Ya musta done some fancy dealin', since I heard you're always short on cash with the neighborhood merchants and landlords."

"Well, I guess I finally got wise with me money." His eyes darted about nervously, before settling on some newspaper clippings tacked to the nearside wall. "And then I made a killing on the Paddy Ryan championship fight against Joe Goss last spring."

"Makes my heart swell with pride; an Irishman, and beatin' an Englishman ta boot! Musta been nice rakin' it in; but between you and me, who was the book? He musta taken a hit, since it was enough to put on a house."

"Oh, Sergeant, I can't go talkin' about a book. He'd send his boys after me."

"Are ya sayin', I got a big mouth; that I can't be trusted with a confidence?"

"No, no, please."

"I know all the books around here. And believe me, I got all sorta ways 'a findin' out."

"Well, I went through a friend."

"Ah, ya did now, and who would that be?"

"He'll get mad, if—"

Before Dwyer could utter another word, Brick Fist grabbed him by the collar and pulled him to within inches of his face. "Lower the shades and lock the door," he ordered Costello before snarling at the clerk, "You heard of me; heaven help the piece of shit who lies to me! I know you know what's goin' on. So you better start tellin' me the truth or I'll beat ya like a rabid dog; and then I'll take up this business of the wagons with your boss."

"I got a wife and kids," he whimpered.

Lifting him off the stool and slamming him against the wall, the detective growled, "Don't ever use your family as a shield." In an instant, he raised his fist and hauled back before catching himself when the man began to sob. Releasing his prey, he returned to a more measured tone, "You're gonna tell me everything ya know about these late-night wagon trips. If it turns out to be true and if I crack the case, you'll stay in one piece and your bosses won't be any wiser. Otherwise of course, it won't be pretty.

Just then there was a knock on the door and a voice rose up, "Are you all right, Charlie? I heard a crash."

"I knocked over some boxes of paper; everything's fine."

"That's good, Charlie! Now, since you're a fine Catholic lad, just pretend I'm hearin' your Confession," the detective smirked, sarcastically.

After hesitating a moment to summon his courage, he came clean, "The three Foley boys and some other fella, I didn't know 'im—looked like a gentleman and stood off to the side—they showed up and made me an offer about using some horses and one or two of the big wagons. Said they'd need 'em every so often, but late at night. The payoff was good but they also warned me. That's why ya gotta protect me, Sergeant! They're animals."

"Don't worry, I already got one of 'em and I'll be takin' care of the other two, soon enough; but gettin' back to business, what were they gonna do and how did this scheme work?"

"They made it plain that what they were up to was none of my business, and I wasn't gonna be stickin' my nose into it. As for the plan, they'd send over a kid with a note in the afternoon tellin' me to meet 'em that night. They'd show up with a couple a' blokes, usually dirty or stinkin' of oil or such, and then they'd return with the wagon a few hours later."

"So did ya recognize any of these pals of theirs?"

"No—wait, except for one time. I think the fella's name is Kennedy or Kenny, and I think he works at one of them foundries down around Illinois and Ohio Streets."

"So how often do they show up?"

"Once, sometimes twice a week over the last couple a' months."

"Any idea when the next one might be?"

"No; they were supposed to show up the night of the fire but I haven't heard anything since."

"You better be lettin' me know the next time you get a note; understand?"

"Ah, yes, yes," he stammered.

"Good! 'Cause if you betray me, or otherwise fuck things up, you'll be prayin' it was the Foleys, rather than me comin' down on ya. And remember, I got my eyes and ears all over the place."

"Don't worry, Sergeant, I don't want no more trouble," the clerk pleaded as his shaking hand pulled out a cigar from his vest.

As he watched the man fumble through his pockets, Danny flipped out a match and lit the stogie before casting a look of warning and turning out the door.

No sooner had they reached the great hall than Costello leaned over and whispered, "You sure put the fear of God in him; but you were only blustering about beating him, right, Danny?"

"While I was tempted to thrash his arse, he's just a snivelin' little man who was cuttin' corners for his kin. So no, I wasn't gonna hurt 'im; but he better mark my words if he knows what's good for 'im."

Yet, as Hugh followed him to the door, he seemed to detect an air of weariness on his friend's part; a weariness born from his efforts to impose a sense of order onto his little slice of the world.

XVI

As Collins rose from his chair, he looked out his office window at a daybreak vista that included the soaring spire of Saint Joseph's Cathedral and the newly constructed clock tower of City Hall. Yet rather than relishing the beauty of the scene, he viewed it as a distracting nuisance and quickly pulled the shade.

"So, I think the Foleys have some sort of stolen equipment scheme going on," Danny reported as he sat facing his boss's desk. "Maybe even Fingers is behind it. We can stake out the freight hauler's place, once I get word from the shipping clerk."

"Very good! I'll have Perry write out some orders and have a couple of our boys keep an eye on the place."

"But I meant me and Costello. I think I can to crack this case."

"Things have changed, Sergeant. My main reason for bringing you here at this hour was to put you on a homicide that just came up."

"But I've done lots of murders. I can handle both, especially now that Costello's helpin' me." Not only was Brick Fist anxious to bring in the Foleys but he was equally intent to remain close to the waterfront, where he could dig around regarding the tragic fire; an investigation that Collins ordered him to stay out of.

"I think I'm a better judge of our manpower needs than you are, Sergeant. Besides, this homicide is both an important and sensitive matter. The victim is the businessman, Robert Van Cleff. I assume you've heard of him."

"Owns a bunch of businesses, including a jewelry store that's big with the rich folks in town; and if I recall, he's known to be a 'nancy'."

"Putting aside his sodomite ways, he is, or should I say, was, a popular man about town, and a big supporter of the Republican Party. He was especially good friends with Mayor Brush and they say that Missus Brush likes to turn the bricks produced in her husband's yard into jewelry from Van Cleff's store. So, as you can see, I want this taken care of as quickly and discretely as possible. And one more thing, he was killed alongside a woman who was not his wife."

"Pesky little detail, eh?"

"Her name was Bonnie Crane and from what we can tell at this point, she was pretty much a nobody from out of town."

"Except for her family, of course." Although he wanted to toss Collins out the window for his cavalier attitude about the woman, Doyle was biding his time. As such, he carried on, "So, when and where did this happen, and what other details do you have?"

"It happened late last night at the Excelsior Arms, where Van Cleff lived. Some neighbors heard shots and saw a couple men running down the hall. When the patrol officer got there, he found both of them dead, each shot once in the head."

"A robbery gone bad?"

"I don't have any more details, other than our man took some statements and is guarding the place until you get there."

"Well, I better get up there before he starts touching stuff and fucking things up. And I'll be needing young Costello on this."

"Fine, it'll be good experience for him; and it's good to see you're not stinking of gin mills or brothels. I was pleasantly surprised that they found you at home."

"Is that all? Danny replied, as he bristled at his boss's none-too-subtle dig.

"Just remember, quickly and discretely!"

As he made his way to the stairs, Danny was steaming. Yet it wasn't so much the crack about the women and booze the set him off. It was the last command concerning the case. If Collins expected him to sweep the matter under the rug, he would be sorely disappointed. For Brick Fist Doyle, there was no compromising when it came to stealing a life; and although there weren't many things sacrosanct in Danny's world, bringing killers to justice was one of them.

By the time he entered the main hall, he ran into Costello reporting to his desk sergeant. Grabbing his young charge by the collar, he announced, "He's goin' with me," before heading out the door.

"McNery isn't gonna like that; and neither are the other commanders for that matter," Hugh remarked with a mischievous grin.

"Fuck 'em; those lazy bastards never get off their fat arses."

After Danny explained what was known about the crime and described Van Cleff's background, they hopped aboard a trolley and headed in the direction of the Excelsior Arms, one of the most exclusive addresses in the city.

As the streetcar paused at a crossing just before Niagara Square, the detective noticed Missus Prescott leaving a nearby residence. After looking about, she stepped into a hackney that trotted off in the direction of the waterfront. While not making much of it, he did wonder if the disaster at the factory had impacted her lifestyle, especially the use of her husband's luxury carriage.

They proceeded a short distance up Delaware before stepping off outside an imposing neoclassical structure that took up half a city block. After passing through an elaborate wrought-iron gate crowned with a gilded *fleur-de-lis,* they came upon a doorman standing alongside the entrance. Wasting no time, Danny immediately identified himself before launching into questions about the events of the previous night.

Dressed in the uniform of an eighteenth century royal footman, the doorman confirmed that he had been on duty since last evening. He went on to insist that although Van Cleff had a standing order to admit anyone citing his name, Miss Crane was the only person, other than the building residents, who had passed through the doors during his watch.

After asking the man to direct them to the delivery entrance in the basement, Danny discovered that the locks had been jimmied. The detective then took his young partner up the back stairs to the fourth floor, where they spotted a young patrolman standing vigil outside the ill-fated apartment. Upon identifying himself, Danny asked Officer Shultz to go over the statements taken from the neighbors. Reading from his notes, the patrolman described how none of them had heard or seen anything unusual, until shortly after midnight, when three shots rang out from inside Van Cleff's apartment. Despite being terrified, an old lady peered out her door, only to catch sight of two shadowy figures racing down the hall. Although unable to point out any discernible features, she did note that one of them wore a military style cap. She was certain of that, since the wearer knocked it off on one of the sconces along the corridor, before retrieving it and flying down the back stairs. Fearing for her life, she waited a number of minutes before venturing to Van Cleff's residence and finding the lifeless bodies of the victims.

After checking the lock on the door, which appeared to be intact, Danny followed the patrolman into the apartment. Once inside, they could instantly grasp the extent of the late businessman's wealth. Passing through the walnut paneled foyer, they were greeted by a spacious parlor awash in shimmering light cast through the floral design of an art-glass skylight.

The room reflected the height of Victorian elegance, featuring an oak parquet floor, Persian carpets, silk drapery, and mahogany chairs and couches upholstered in cream-colored fabric. Paintings of European masters, including those from the new Impressionist School, covered the linen-papered walls, and a host of expensive antiques were scattered throughout the room like so much bric-a-brac. Dominating this stately enclave was a shoulder-high marble fireplace, topped with a seventeenth century mantel clock. Even for someone as aesthetically challenged as Brick Fist, it was an impressive display.

Finally, the patrolman led them into the library off the parlor, where they came upon the grisly sight of two bodies splayed in their chairs, and bathed in pools of dried blood. Turning towards his partner, Danny couldn't help but notice the wide-eyed look on his face. "They never look good when we find 'em."

"Still, it can't hide her obvious beauty," Costello replied with an air of sadness.

"Well, it ain't gonna do her no good anymore." Refocusing his attention on Van Cleff, the detective observed, "Sure looks shocked, don't he?"

"I suppose under the circumstances."

"I've seen a boatload of murdered stiffs, but naw, that ain't it. He wasn't expectin' this."

After being assured that Shultz didn't touch anything in the room, Danny carefully slipped behind the desk where Van Cleff took his last breath, and began to take stock of his surroundings. The walls were lined with row upon row of leather-bound books, along with numerous works of art interspaced among the shelves. The furniture, including the massive desk and matching leather chairs, mirrored the level of luxury as seen in the parlor; and sitting atop the desk were a gold-lettered edition of Dickens's

"Pickwick Papers", and a teak box containing beautifully illustrated decks of cards and alabaster dice. It was obvious, not only to the detective but to any observer, that this was a gentleman's retreat, where its owner could wile away the hours pursuing his passions. The room also served as a residential office, with trade catalogues and appraisal books stacked on the desk, and a number of empty shipping boxes set in a corner and addressed to various jewelry stores around the state. Yet strewn about this otherwise orderly domain were a slew of papers, no doubt coming from a desk drawer that had been pulled open.

After bending down to pick up some papers, Danny spotted a shiny object laying next to Van Cleff's chair. "So, what do we got here! Not quite a friendly little chat."

As the detective lifted up the gun and checked the chamber, Costello observed, "One of those pea-shooter Derringers."

"Yeah, a one-shot pea-shooter that can put ya in the ground."

"Rules out murder-suicide."

"Yeah, the chamber's empty but I got a feelin' that him and the girl weren't firin' away at each other," Danny was quick to add. Turning to Shultz, he asked, "And the neighbors heard three shots, right?"

"That's right, sir," the young patrolman answered dutifully.

"No doubt, a robbery gone bad." Costello declared. "The dirty villains must have rifled the desk before running out."

"Not quite that simple, Hugh. Sure, the locks were jimmied downstairs, but not up here. They didn't want to be seen by the guard. I think Van Cleff knew 'em. He was relaxed; look here at the half-empty brandy snifter on the desk, and what's left of a cigar in the ashtray. The girl wasn't on her guard either. No sign of struggle and they weren't bound or nothin'."

After looking over the papers he grabbed from the floor, Danny mused, "Now this is interesting, a bunch of gamblin' bills and IOU's, all of 'em involvin' Fingers' places. Now the two of ya are gonna pick up the rest of these papers and check 'em; but don't go touchin' nothing else! In the meantime, I gotta keep goin' over this place."

After making notes in his pad, he measured out the number of paces from Van Cleff's body to a settee sitting across from the desk. He then proceeded to sit up and down on the couch, while thrusting out his arm in a firing motion. During the last such maneuver, he looked down and noticed something on the dark carpet. Pulling out a handkerchief and dropping to his knees, he began to dab the surface. "Looks like dried blood, lads. And it looks like some more headin' out to the door.

Still on his knees and following the path of the droplets, he arrived at a small table next to the library entrance. There, behind the table legs and lying against the baseboard, was a pistol, its scrimshaw whalebone handle plainly visible next to the dark wood. Picking it up, Danny announced, "Only one man around these parts carries an iron like this, Harpoon Marley. That could explain the witness seein' a military cap. Harpoon still wears his unit kepi from the War."

"Musta been wounded and dropped the gun while runnin' out," young Shultz anxiously proclaimed.

"Could be." Brick Fist replied while checking the chamber. "Two rounds missin'." Thinking out loud, he mused, "But this ain't Harpoon's way, gunnin' down a nancy and an innocent girl."

"But all the bills and IOU's to Fingers. Maybe he was putting the strong-arm on Van Cleff and something went wrong," Costello chimed in.

"Sure, slippery types like Van Cleff don't like to ante up, but he ain't about to go payin' up with his life. Besides, can't ya see, he's got money comin' outta his arse," Doyle replied.

"People often live beyond their means," Hugh suggested. "And one more point; seeing all this wealth while making his collection, maybe it got Marley thinking about cashing in for himself."

"But that would mean goin' rogue on Fingers and Harpoon's too loyal for that. Just the same, Hugh, check Van Cleff's pockets and the girls purse, while I go through the desk."

Although squeamish about wrestling through the pockets of the bloody, and now fully stiff body of the jeweler, the young copper plunged into his task with a forthright sense of duty; and after performing the sad but far less onerous job of examining the contents of Miss Crane's handbag, he reported on his findings, "Stumps me, Sergeant. Van Cleff's got over two hundred dollars and she had almost fifty."

"And there's a whole box of cash in the second drawer," Danny added. "So it seems to rule out robbery, but—"

"Excuse me, Sergeant," Shultz interrupted, "but I didn't mention that the old neighbor lady reported that Miss Crane was a frequent guest and she was always well dressed and wore a lot of jewelry."

"And there's no jewelry on her body. Well, that could be a stick in the spokes, but I was gonna say that I found a couple of notebooks that are very interestin'. The one lists most of the expensive hotels and private clubs in the city, along with dates and the names of a lot of bigwigs and their losses. We're talkin' serious money, as ya can see. One of the biggest losers is none other than my friend, Alfred Prescott. I heard Van Cleff liked his gamblin' but I didn't realize how he had this thrivin' little sideline."

"See," Costello blurted out "besides collecting on his debts, maybe they were also squeezing him for some of the action, or maybe protection; or maybe blackmailing him with threats of setting the law on them."

"Him and his friends don't worry about the police. Gamblin' laws are for the little guy; but lemme check somethin'." Once more opening the teak box on the desk, Brick Fist began examining its contents. After a few moments he smiled, "Ah, that's it. Come here, lads, I wanna show ya somethin'." Beckoning them to his side, he began to riffle a deck of cards. "See those little white spots between those fancy designs. See how they seem to be dancin' across the surface of the cards when I flip 'em. Them are the markings that tell 'im what the cards are." He then proceeded to snatch a pair of dice from the box and raise them towards the light of the window. Placing two sides of the cubes against each other, he pointed out, "Now look at this. The one side is as flat as a pancake but the other dice has a little bulge to its side. It's called bevelin' and it's less likely the dice comes to rest on this side. Over the long run, more of an advantage goes to the fella who knows it." Shaking his head, he went on to observe, "Seems like our rich little dandy was quite a cheat, fleecing those uptown dupes of their money."

"Going back to what I said before," Costello interjected, "maybe he didn't like being threatened with the exposure of his scheme and pulled a gun."

"If he did, that was a big mistake, as you can see; but I think he was too smart for that."

"And what about that other notebook," the young partner asked.

"Looks like some sorta business record; columns for debits, credits, suppliers, buyers and products. All showin' some pretty hefty dollar amounts. Strange thing though, except for the values, all the entries are just a bunch of 'o's and 'a's. Here, whaddaya make of it?"

Taking the book from Brick Fist, Costello took a moment to peruse the pages before offering, "Looks like some sort of crude accounting ledger, all coded. Now, Danny, didn't you say he owned some liquor stores and tobacco shops? Maybe he had separate books for the taxman and this coded version for himself."

"Or maybe he had some partners and had a second set so he could skim from the top. Whatever it was all about, he was up to no good. As ya can see from his gambling practices, not to mention his demise, he wasn't exactly an upright citizen. It's just too bad he seems to have taken an innocent girl with 'im."

"I know, the poor thing. So beautiful, and all the world to live for. Danny ... er, Sergeant, can I take up that part of it. You know, finding where she lived and the next of kin and all? I'd like to compose the telegraph message; at least to let them know someone cares and is seeking justice."

"Sure 'nuff, Hugh. Ya got a good heart, lad; and ya can call me, Danny, even in front of others. We're a team, now, but I'm still the boss and don't you forget it! So, I want ya to hang onto this book and see what ya can figure out, Mister College Man."

"Sure thing, Danny."

After folding a couple of the IOU's in to his pocket, Danny turned his attention to Shultz, "Now, as for you, Officer, when ya go back to write your report, there'll be no blabbing about what ya saw here. I got eyes and ears everywhere, so ya don't wanna get me mad; right?"

"Yes, sir."

"Now that's what I wanna hear. But before ya go back, I want ya checkin' the area behind the little couch. The killer musta got nicked or whatever, and the bullet coulda ended up in the wall or books. Then I want ya to make sure this place is secured before seeing the neighbors and tellin' 'em to contact the police if anyone tries to get in. Do the same thing with the building custodian and put the fear of God into 'im about lettin' anyone in but me. Ya got that?"

"Yes, sir."

"Good, now in what apartment is the old lady witness?"

"Missus Wilkerson is in the next one down, four, oh, three."

"Good lad; I'll be tellin' your boss what a fine copper you're turning out to be."

"That's Captain Wurtz, sir."

"Oh, that piece of shit! Likes to shoot at strikers. Listen, I'll be givin' a good word about ya to someone else who can help ya."

"Thank you, Sergeant."

After delivering a few knocks to the door and placing his badge close to the peephole, Brick Fist announced, "Police Sergeant Doyle, Missus Wilkerson; we'd like to talk to you."

A moment passed before a faint voice in a clipped Yankee accent responded, "Of course, Sergeant, please come in."

As the door slowly opened, the policemen could hear the delicate strains of a Viennese waltz coming from a nearby music box; and after waiting for their eyes to adjust to the muted light, they were able to see a pencil-thin dowager emerge from the shadows of the hallway.

Despite the passage of over eight decades, Missus Wilkerson still possessed a patrician beauty and an unquenchable sparkle to her light gray eyes. As she invited them to enter, her alabaster features and snow-white bun, stood in stark contrast to her black dress and dark surroundings. Flicking the switch on the porcelain couple in the middle of their dance, she sighed, "It's a sad day indeed, isn't it gentlemen, particularly about Miss Crane. She was such a sweet, pretty thing."

"A true shame, ma'am," Danny replied, as he pulled out his pencil and pad. "Now, can you tell me more about her, what she did, where she lived, any family, that sort of thing?"

Taking a seat in the rose-scented parlor, she paused a moment before answering, "Unlike Mister Van Cleff, who despite his social reputation, kept to himself when here, she was most outgoing. Although I didn't know her well, I did encounter her every so often when she was visiting her friend." Responding to the look on the detective's face, she added, "I had no problem with that, knowing Mister Van Cleff's proclivities and the fact that he was much older; perhaps a family friend. In any case, I could tell she was well bred and educated. I believe she once said she attended Mount Holyoke, back in my part of the country. She was always so well dressed, including having the most lovely and tasteful jewelry. I remember how resplendent she looked last night as she waited for Mister Van Cleff to retrieve something from the apartment before setting out for dinner."

"So, not only did you hear them laughing later in the evening, but in fact, you saw her in the hall earlier last night, and she was wearing jewelry."

"Yes, that's correct. I thought I told that to the young policeman?"

"And the jewelry, you're sure she was wearing jewelry? Including a necklace?"

"Yes, a necklace, as always. I'm certain of that."

"So where did she live?" he asked.

"I believe she said in the Templeton Apartments on Tupper Street."

"Pretty nice address."

"Like I said, there was no doubt she came from good stock."

"And did she work?"

"An appropriate occupation; she was a French tutor to some of the families in town."

"Do you know anything about her family," Costello broke in.

"She came from one of those charming, old Dutch villages upriver from New York, Wappinger Falls; and I believe her father was in the wholesale grocery business."

Returning to the subject of the shots and the fleeing suspects, Danny probed on, "I believe you told officer Shultz that you heard three shots?"

"Yes, absolutely, it woke me up."

"Were the shots in rapid succession?"

"I'm not sure, but I think there was a brief pause before the last one."

As Brick Fist mulled over the implications of the sequence of shots, he began to grow angry at the possibility of the young witness begging for her life before being shot. Regaining his reserve, he refocused on the query, "Now, about these men who ran down the hall, did they have any particular characteristics, you know, height, weight, coloring? Or were they wearing any clothing that stood out?"

"Not really, it all happened so fast."

"Except for that military cap you mentioned last night."

"Oh, yes; hard to describe, short brim, dark. It was similar to the one my nephew brought home from the War."

Hoping to help her along, he made a quick sketch on his note pad before showing it to her. "Is this the type?"

"Yes, yes."

"It's called a kepi and it was a common uniform cap in the War; actually still is."

After once more going over the details of her account, the detective asked that she contact the precinct if anything more came to mind. Satisfied with what he had learned up to this point, he bid his farewell before grabbing Costello and heading to the door.

No sooner had they arrived at the ornate lobby than Doyle spotted the building superintendant and began to instruct him regarding the security of the crime scene. Afterwards, as they stood on the slush-filled walkway, waiting for the trolley, Costello was bursting with anticipation, "Looks like Marley's our man! So, are we going to nab him before he can work on an alibi?"

"Calm down and hold your horses. The pistol grip was good evidence for sure, but this ain't no locked-down case."

Well, what about the IOU's and the kepi?"

"Yeah, the IOU's can help with motive but there's still a lotta kepis floatin' around and besides, little old ladies ain't the best of witnesses; you know, the memory an' all. No, there's still a lotta open questions. So, there's more facts that need to be brought out and examined before we nail this down. In any case, Harpoon's gotta lotta answerin' to do and that'll be a good start."

"Then what's next?"

"We'll be headin' down to Harpoon's favorite places around Canal Street and the waterfront. So, ya better make sure your iron's loaded!"

XVII

Wisps of steam floated above the harbor waters as an arctic cold wave blew in from the north. The ghostly specter only added to the melancholy air that pervaded the waterfront now that the lake shipping season had ground to a halt. The forest of masts that dominated the landscape just weeks earlier was for the most part gone, and the beehive of activity along the docks was now a memory.

From the harbormaster's office in the upper corner of the Central Wharf, Brick Fist Doyle had a sweeping view of the waterfront and the neighboring "Infected District." The detective had secured the room's use in return for a favor granted to its occupant, Carl Meuller. Recently, Danny let him go with a warning after shutting down an opium den that operated out of a hovel he owned in the District. With the wharf building virtually deserted, Meuller's office was the ideal vantage point for observing the comings and goings at the nearby headquarters of Fingers Carnahan.

Up to now, the search for Marley had proven to be fruitless. They had spent much of the previous day either staking out Harpoon's apartment next to the Peking Saloon, or visiting the bordellos and gin mills he so often frequented. Yet not surprisingly, Marley's fellow denizens of Canal Street were reluctant to talk; their silence no doubt owing to both the popularity and fearsome reputations of Fingers and his principal enforcer.

Knowing that at some point Marley would report to his boss, Danny patiently watched the activity outside the crime lord's warehouse lair; however, no sooner had he begun to look for Costello, whom he had sent out earlier on an errand, than his eyes caught sight of a woman and child arrive at the station for a train that crossed a bridge between Buffalo and its Canadian neighbor, Fort Erie. There was little question that the two were mother and daughter, as each brandished auburn hair and a fresh-faced, porcelain complexion. Although bundled up against the cold, they appeared to be wearing their Sunday best, perhaps for a visit to family. Then, just as the mother was about to lead the little one onto the platform, she stopped and began to fuss over the curls spilling out from under her daughter's hat.

Despite the surrounding chill, the scene brought a warm glow to Brick Fist's heart, and despite the distance that separated him from the woman, he could virtually feel the silky thickness of her hair and the tender softness of her cheek. He was poised to call out to her when the sound of a squeaky hinge brought him back to reality.

"Danny, I found Meuller drinking on one of the tugs. He said the spyglass was in the top drawer of the cabinet next to the door."

"Hugh, you're becomin' a fine one at trackin' down suspects," he laughed, "but before ya go pattin' yourself on the back, go get the damn eyepiece."

No sooner had Costello arrived with the telescope, than the detective noticed a figure in the distance, making a fast march down Lloyd Street in the direction of Carnahan's warehouse. Snatching the instrument from his startled partner, he set his sights on a big man sporting a shaved head that shimmered in the morning sunshine. As he narrowed his focus, he was able to make out mutton-chop whiskers and more importantly, an arm in a sling. That's 'im! Follow me, but keep your distance." Barreling down the stairs, he yelled back, "and be ready with your gun!"

Once outside, the detective flew up Main to the corner of Water Street, the site of Finger's headquarters. Looking back, he signaled for Costello to lay low, before slowly peering around the edge of the building. There, approaching the stairs, was Harpoon Marley in all his fearsome glory.

After grabbing his Colt and stepping from the side of the building, Doyle yelled, "Stop right there, Georgie! I wanna talk to ya about the other night."

For an instant, the enforcer froze, appearing to not know what to do. Frantically, he looked about, but found no avenue of escape. Yet just as the warehouse door began to squeeze open, Marley pulled out a gun and began shooting.

Despite hearing a withering gasp and the sound of a body falling, and ignoring the sting of brick chips ricocheting all around him, Danny stood his ground and returned fire.

Somehow avoiding the fusillade and showing a nimbleness of movement at odds with his bulk, Harpoon leapt behind a frozen rain barrel sitting next to the building.

Sensing his adversary was reloading, Danny scrambled for refuge alongside the entrance stoop. Although fearing for Costello, he tried to keep his eyes trained on the rain barrel; however, unable to resist the urge to check on his partner, he turned for a quick look back.

Seeing his opening, Marley raised his pistol and squeezed the trigger. The crisp, cold air seemed to intensify the blast as it rang out between the buildings. Slowly lowering his arm, the legendary gangster stared intently at his target. Yet a quizzical look seemed to cross his face as the great behemoth crumpled to the ground with a resounding bellow. For a moment, all remained still before spurts of blood started pumping out from the gaping hole in the center of his chest.

With Harpoon's legs now kicking out in violent spasms, Danny rushed forward to grab the sling and apply pressure to the wheezing wound; but his frenzied efforts proved futile, as the chest grew still, the twitching stopped and all color drained from the hoodlum's face.

Looking down at the lifeless hulk of his longtime opponent, and occasional drinking companion, Danny felt a mix of sadness and anger, realizing that the sound of a clap splitting the air could fell such a great warrior. Adding to his frustration was the seeming insanity of Harpoon's laying down fire when Danny's intention was to just question the man. Perhaps most of all, he sensed that here was a kindred spirit, barreling his way through a hostile world on the strength of his courage and muscle.

Turning around, he was met by young Costello, ashen as the nearby corpse and holding the pistol that delivered the fatal shot. "I... I... I had no choice, Danny. He was gonna kill ya."

"That's all right, son. Ya did the only thing ya could."

"I know, but forevermore I'll have to live with having taken a man's life," he moaned while trying to hold back tears.

For once, Danny's bravado was absent as he faced his friend's anguish. "Killin's a sad thing, Hugh. Not much worse than that, and I ain't gonna sugar coat it. I know—"

"Da... Doyle... ya... ya bastard," a voice gasped out as it struggled with every syllable.

Suddenly, the policemen realized that the surrounding mayhem was not confined to Marley's shooting.

Leaning against the warehouse doorway was Fingers Carnahan, gripped in pain while his Chinese housekeeper worked on his wound. Caught in Harpoon's crossfire, he had taken a bullet to the shoulder upon opening the door to check on the disturbance outside his office. No stranger to the carnage of the battlefield, if not the street, the crime lord managed to keep his wits while fighting off the crippling effects of his injury. As such, he maintained a steely glare as Brick Fist approached the landing.

"Ya killed my best friend, ya rat," he spit out with a grimace.

"I'm a lawman and he shot first; even after I told 'im I just wanted to talk."

"Ta... ta... talk with your gun drawn!"

"He had a lot of answerin' to do about Van Cleff. We found his gun and his cap there. We ain't fools."

Summoning what was left of his strength after Madame Woo stanched the bleeding, Fingers seethed, "We ain't fools, ya say! Ya dumb… fa… fucking bog hopper. He was set up, and I can prove it!"

Just then a carriage burst out of the warehouse doors, carrying a pair of Finger's henchmen on its sideboards. Scurrying to his bosses' side, the taller of the two blurted out, "She told us what happened, Major. We'll be getting ya to Sister's right quick now."

With that, Madame Woo pointed at Danny, "You, big man; help carry Major to buggy for hospital."

"Don't touch me, Doyle! I don't need a dead man helping me!"

"I ain't the one to be worryin' about the hereafter, Danny shot back, "but if ya do make it, ya better know I'll be askin' ya about your dealin's with Van Cleff."

Ignoring Doyle's remarks, Fingers turned to his protégé with a grimace, "Okay, Roscoe, gimme a hand, lad; and make sure Madame Woo has the boys take Georgie inside."

While watching the gangster's men lift him up, Danny spotted Rebecca Prescott, dressed in a robe and appearing much like a wide-eyed doe caught in the sights, cautiously peering out from behind the door. No sooner had the attendants hustled their leader into the carriage, than she took notice of the detective's attention and pulled the door shut.

"Do you think he was telling the truth about Harpoon, Danny," Costello asked nervously.

"No, I don't. He's a self servin' criminal but there's still a lotta questions that need answerin'."

"Sweet Mother of Jesus, I hope you're right, Danny. It's bad enough killin' a guilty man, but an innocent one…"

"No matter what, he put a lotta men in the grave and his time's been comin'."

"But there's courts and juries for all that."

"Now listen, as I was sayin' before, I wish ya didn't have to take this on, Hugh. I've been there and it hurts; hurts a lot. Ya go home and begin thinkin' how this fella would be with his family and friends if not for your hand; ya go figurin' that he'll never love a woman or lift a pint again; but ya gotta be strong and put it outta your head! Nothing can change Harpoon blazin' away. This ain't no easy job that you and your cousin Billy took on; but the folks of the city trust ya to protect 'em, even if it means goin' the distance. Now I want ya to go home and be with your kin and pals, and knowin' your beliefs, even a priest if ya have a mind to; but keep busy and don't be goin' over this in your head. Take tomorrow off, too. I'll cover for ya; but then I want ya back with me bright and early on Wednesday mornin'. Ya gotta get back on the horse. Gettin' the job done will help put ya right."

"Thanks, Danny. I need your words of advice. They help a lot."

"And thanks for savin' my hide, Hugh. If it wasn't for you, that would be me lying there all stiff and cold. Now get goin', my friend. I gotta get word to the station."

XVIII

It felt good to stretch his legs and work off some of the stress that had been building up these last few weeks. After a restless night, rather than grab a trolley, Danny was anxious to clear his head with a vigorous walk. As he made his way up Main Street, he stopped at a news shanty in front of Prescott Wallpaper's retail store. Before picking out a paper, he watched through the storefront window as a clerk prepared a display of the latest patterns. The scene brought to mind that on the day after the factory fire, the company announced that store operations would continue uninterrupted. The memory of such greedy behavior in the face of tragedy, served to further fuel his disdain for his sometime employer.

Returning to the task at hand, he snatched up a copy of the *Morning Express,* only to read a headline proclaiming that the Van Cleff murders had been solved. Filled with grisly details of the murder scene and subsequent shoot-out with the "notorious brigand and ruffian, George, 'Harpoon' Marley," the article repeatedly referenced and quoted the local precinct captain; consequently, there was no ambiguity on Danny's part as to the source and motivation behind the story—Patrick Collins and his greater glory. Barely able to contain his fury over the potential compromise of his case, Brick Fist slammed down the paper in disgust.

After taking a moment to calm down, he resumed his trek up Main Street. Despite the shadowy cast of the predawn sky, downtown was fully awake and awash with activity. Waves of workers hurried to their offices and shops, while a sea of hackneys, wagons and street cars packed the manure and slush rutted streets. Scores of sidewalk peddlers, including boot blacks and "Street Fakirs," hawking everything from cheap novelties to out-dated clothing, had already staked out prize pieces of real estate along the busy thoroughfare; and a squad of municipal lamplighters, with their long metal hooks poking the air, were busy finishing their early-morning ritual of turning off the gaslights that lined the streets. Yet as he approached the Templeton Apartments, where Bonnie Crane last made her home, he once more confronted the dark underpinnings that lurked just beneath the surface of civilized society. Murder was the ultimate expression of this dark side of life, and despite the onerous nature of the task, Brick Fists's job was to clean it up

Upon entering the foyer, he was both surprised and happy to see his partner standing outside the superintendent's office, awaiting his arrival. "I thought you were taking the day off, Hugh?"

"I took your advice about getting back in the saddle."

Not one to waste time over pleasantries, the detective was quick to move on and introduce himself to the building superintendent, a Mister Thomas, who proceeded to lead the pair to Bonnie's flat.

In keeping with the tony address, the apartment, though small, was first class, with richly appointed floors, ceilings and millwork; however, the furnishings were beyond spare, consisting of a table, chair and tiny bed. Sitting atop the table were a few bottles of toiletries, some odd pieces of china and silverware, along with a notebook and leather-bound copy of *A Tale of Two Cities*. A steamer trunk holding her clothing, jewelry and boxes of candy represented the rest of her worldly possessions.

After making his tour through the rooms, Danny turned his attention to quizzing Thomas. "So, what can you tell me about Miss Crane, you know, how long she's been here, her friends, her habits, where she did her tutoring?"

"She was no tutor," he revealed with a leer. "Out all night; sleepin' all day."

"Christ, are you telling me she was some sort of hooker?"

"Can't say for sure, but I heard the whispers. Sure wasn't workin' at no convent at those hours; especially bein' all dressed up, lookin' all fancy and such when she went out."

"She ever bring men here?"

"No way! Hers wouldn't be the only ass outta here. It'd be mine, too! But no, I had no problem with her; quiet; kept to herself and always paid the rent on time; goin' on over a year now. She was recommended by her friend Van Cleff, who knew the building owner, Mister Lawrence Lee."

"Lawrence Lee, the builder?"

"The very same, Sergeant."

"With her connections, this whole hooker thing doesn't make sense," Brick Fist mused out loud. "Besides, I heard she came from money downstate. You know anything about that?"

"She was polished all right; but a neighbor said she told her that the family money was gone. A no-good brother ran the late father's business into the ground."

"And what about friends?"

"Besides Mister Van Cleff, the only one I know of is a fella who she sometimes met for breakfast over at the Iroquois Hotel restaurant up the street. And that's about all I know about her. Like I said, she was quiet and kept to herself."

"That's fine, Mister Thomas. I appreciate your help, but if you think of anything more, get a hold of me down at the station house. In the meantime, we won't hold you up any longer. We're gonna go over things a little bit here, and then we can let ourselves out."

After bidding farewell to the manager, the policemen began to go through her effects. For Brick Fist, it was a requisite professional exercise he had performed many times before; however, for young Costello, it took on a more personal, melancholy tone the further he went along. Searching through the steamer trunk he lamented, "Not much here for an entire life."

"At least she left somethin'; not like some of those poor beggars in the fire," Danny replied as he searched through the room.

"Folded so neatly, not knowing she would never use them again; they smell so lovely. She must have looked so beautiful in all these things."

"Careful now, remember what I said about bein' strong. I don't want ya bein' lured by some sorta ghost fairy and loosin' touch of the job ya gotta do."

"I know, and don't worry; but I can't help but feeling sad that if it wasn't for her ne'er-do-well brother, she might be back in her little town living in a nice house with her husband and kids instead of doing what Mister Thomas was talking about, and ending up dead."

"It is a sad thing. Ya got a kind soul, Hugh but ya can't forget that life can break your back. That's just the way it is. There's nothin' you or me can do for Miss Crane, other than to bring her justice; and that's why we're here, doin' this rotten business."

Moving past the porcelain teacups with hand-painted scenes of Japanese gardens, Danny grabbed the notebook from the table and began inspecting its contents. "Sweet Jesus, she was a busy girl!"

"You mean prostituting herself, like Mister Thomas said?"

"Sure 'nuff looks that way. All written down nice and thorough: names; dates; amounts; hotels."

Lifting his head up from the jewelry box, Costello was quick to add, "Just like Van Cleff's gambling records, eh?"

"Speakin' of which, did ya make any headway with the coded notebook from Van Cleff's desk?"

"Sorry Danny, with all the goings on with Marley," he briefly paused before continuing on, "I didn't get a chance to examine it at any depth; but I promise I'll get on it tonight and try to figure it out."

"Ah, lookie here, speakin' of the devil. It seems our friend, the late, rich, society boy, Van Cleff, was gettin' a cut of the action. And look at all these names, some of the biggest names in the city: August Miller, William Barley, Simon Bracewell; listed next to dates, hotels and amounts. Like here, Stuart Marvin, Iroquois Hotel, November third, fifteen dollars; and what do we have here, the recently mentioned owner of this fine buildin', Mister L. B. Lee, but she just has a note sayin', 'incredible;' and right next to it is an odd listing, Dirt, Tifft House, November fourth, twenty-five dollars and sparklies."

"And speaking of sparklies," Hugh announced, "she has quite a collection of jewelry, here, like this gold necklace with an engraving on the back of the pendant that says, 'Your faithful slave, November, eighteen-eighty'."

"She certainly seems to have had an effect on that fella," Danny replied "This puts a different light on things. When ya get these society types carrying out this sorta criminal activity, bad things can happen. In that sorta business emotions can run high, not to mention it attracts bad people, whether it be pimps, jealous lovers, or ordinary thieves who hear that some serious money is changin' hands."

"So you think this changes things about the murders?"

"Let's not get ahead of ourselves, son. Like I told ya before, I'll know when I can nail this down. Still, this shows ya that we gotta poke around some more; includin' payin' a visit to Fingers Carnahan over at Sister's Hospital. I wanna check on all his talk about Harpoon bein' set up.

And while I'm doin' that, I want ya to go over to that hotel restaurant up the street and ask about that fella who used to dine with Miss Crane. Try to find out who it is and if he's one of them bigwigs in her book. And before ya head off, go ahead and take some of that candy. I know ya been eyein' it."

"Well, I do have to admit I've got a sweet tooth," Hugh replied with a youthful blush.

After they wrapped things up at the apartment, the pair headed off in separate directions. Eschewing any further benefits of a walk, Danny hopped aboard a trolley for the ride up Main Street.

Sisters of Charity Hospital was the city's oldest medical institution, and its recent move to a larger facility at the corner of Delevan, reflected Buffalo's rising status as a boomtown. Once inside, Danny was quick to identify himself to the nun at the reception desk, who directed him to Carnahan's second floor room. Anxious to question the wounded crime lord, he bound up the stairs before heading down a dimly lit corridor lined with all manner of religious paintings.

Dressed in billowy black habits as they made their rounds between rooms, the nuns seemed to float along the freshly polished floor, carried aloft by their sweeping, white cornette headwear. Adding to the church-like atmosphere was the heavy scent of candles and a pervasive quiet. Only intermittent whiffs of disinfectant and muffled groans breaking the silence, reminded Danny that he was in a hospital. Arriving at room two twenty-four, he delivered a crisp knock on the door, which was followed by the sound of nervous voices and the hurried clink of glasses coming from inside.

"Come in, Sister."

"Sorry, I ain't no healin' angel, Major," Danny answered as he passed through the door.

Surrounded by a trio of henchmen who quickly returned to their drinks, Fingers put down his paper and seethed, "What are you doing here, Doyle?"

"I promised you that we'd talk, Major, and I always keep my promises."

"What makes you think I'd be willing to speak to the man who killed my friend?"

"Because you were at the scene of a killing and I can get an order from a judge."

Gesturing towards the others, Fingers smiled, "Okay, fellas, we'll let Sergeant Doyle play his little game; so if you would go outside and wait, lads."

As his men filed past Danny while casting looks of unvarnished scorn, Fingers nodded towards an empty chair sitting across from his bed. "I see that my boys didn't offer you a drink; but go ahead Sergeant. There's an extra glass. Enjoy it while you can."

"I certainly will!" After taking a nip, he smiled, "Ah, from the ol' country; quite a fine thing! But you're right. I better finish it fast before one of them good sisters come by. Assuming that's what you're talkin' about. Otherwise that could be seen as a threat and threats don't work with me. Ya see, I've killed men who wanted to kill me. But that has nothing to do with a gentleman and officer such as yourself. After all, you know about battles and rules of engagement. You're no street thug wanting to strike back at a lawman defending himself."

"That's a lot to assume, Sergeant. But I believe you wanted to talk."

"Well, the other day, after your unfortunate shooting, you said some things about Harpoon—who I'm sorry about killing and who I've grown to like over the years—you said he was innocent and been set up. But before we get into that, there's some other things I want to get clear on."

"Go ahead, Sergeant, I'm all ears."

"Like I mentioned the other day, Harpoon's gun was found at the site of the Van Cleff murders. In addition, a witness reported that one of the killers wore a military kepi; and I found out one of the killers got shot, with a trail of blood leading out the door. There was also a bunch of Van Cleff's IOU's lying around the murder scene and every one of 'em was made out to some of your gambling joints. Looking at all this, a fella could come to believe that there was some sorta dust up over gambling bills. So what about your dealings with Van Cleff, Major?"

"It looks like a rather effective stage performance, I must admit. Undoubtedly some people out there would like to see this pinned on me. Yet get this straight," Fingers insisted, "I had no dealings with Van Cleff; at least none that I concerned myself with. There was no meeting with Georgie. He was small potatoes. Sure, he owed us money, he usually did; but he always paid up at some point. I heard he lived lavishly and on the edge, even with all his businesses. Cards were another source of his revenue. He regularly fleeced those rich pigeons of his, but he could never get away with that at my places; and listen, I never had to collect from Van Cleff, he wasn't that sort. He was too smart for that. Those IOU's were probably old chits we gave back after he paid them off."

"But that still doesn't explain away the connection to Harpoon: the gun and all. Was he shakin' down the jeweler on his own?"

"Besides being an outstanding soldier during the war, George Marley was my best friend and his loyalty was beyond question. Like I said the day I was shot, he was set up. Set up good, as I can see now."

"What makes ya so sure about that?"

"The night before the murders at Van Cleff's, Georgie was way-laid by a gang of thieves after coming back from a drinking and fucking session at Maggie's Laundry, his favorite whore house. They took off with his gun and wallet before shooting him in the arm; fortunately, clean through, without hitting a bone. He even lost his unit cap which he managed to keep patched together all these years. And although they got the best of him, he put up a good fight, even managing to grab one of the bastards making his escape. He told me that he stabbed the bushwhacker before throwing him into the canal."

"Do ya have any proof of this, Major?"

"Just my word; but since I'm sure that's not enough, Doctor Williamson, who patched him up the next morning, can attest to it, I'm sure."

An uncomfortable silence filled the room before Danny finally spoke up, "Like I said, I'm sorry about Georgie, but I just wanted to question him, before he started firin' away. At the time the evidence seemed just too perfect, and I didn't feel right about Harpoon, knowin' him as I did. I wanted to give 'im a chance to explain some things."

"Georgie probably thought you wanted to bring him in regarding the thief in the canal."

"I've had me doubts and now ya tell me this. Listen, we couldn't find the third bullet fired at Van Cleff's that night; and ya just said that the bushwhacker's shot went straight through Harpoon's arm; right?"

"That is correct, Sergeant."

"Van Cleff was up to some funny business at the time he was killed. Besides marked cards, loaded dice, and records showin' 'im cheatin' those bigwigs, I discovered that the other victim wasn't just an innocent lady friend. Apparently, he was pimpin' her to his rich connections. That can be a nasty business."

"I'm not surprised. He was a shifty little operator. As a matter of fact, I had been hearing rumblings among colleagues in my line of business that this Van Cleff fellow was involved in some crooked dealings, besides the gambling. What is was, I didn't find out, and I don't care, but perhaps it was this prostitution business."

"Well, I'll be looking deeper into that and other things."

"And do you agree Georgie was innocent of these Van Cleff murders?"

"We'll see."

"And if that comes to pass, it would appear that you were set-up, right along with Georgie."

"Believe me, if somebody set me up to kill a man, there'll be god-almighty hell to pay for that villainous son of a bitch."

"And they'll be lucky if you find them before I do."

"I won't be havin' you interferin' with my case, Major! Cause if ya do, I'll be talkin' to my bosses who are just bitin' at the bit to pin this crime on you."

"I'll give you a chance to prove your case, Sergeant; but whatever the outcome, someone's going to pay for Georgie. I'll give my word on that! And oh, yes, despite your noble efforts to shield your partner, a little bird told me that he pulled the trigger on Georgie."

"And I'll give you my word, Major, that I'll be killin' anybody who even thinks of harmin' a hair on that boy's head."

Nothing more was said as Danny turned on his heels. But just as the detective was about to reach the door, Fingers asked, "Before you go, can I trust you'll keep Missus Prescott's name out of things? She has nothing to do with all this."

"I didn't see anything, Major."

"Thank you, Sergeant."

XIX

"On the Blood of the Martyrs, I promise ya I won't be hurtin' nothin' or gettin' in the way, Sergeant."

"Didn't you hear me, woman! This is still a crime scene, and anything could be evidence. Besides, I got a job to do and I don't wanna be worryin' that you're runnin' around and messin' things up."

"But Mister Van Cleff's nephew wants this place kept up."

"So he does, now? Well, you go tell your Mister Van Cleff's nephew that this is my case and so long as I say it's open, I'm callin' the shots around here!"

"Don't go playin' the high and mighty with me, Danny Doyle! That might work with the whores and crooks, or with them politicians ya wanna impress, but not with me. I got work to do to feed those seven hungry mouths of mine. Now, I'm no thief, so I won't be stealin' any of your precious evidence. I'm just gonna be dustin' and polishin'."

"Okay, okay, enough of this! You're keepin' me from my business! Just don't go rearranging things or throwin' anything out."

Realizing the futility of continuing to joust with so formidable an opponent, Brick Fist finally threw in the towel. It wasn't worth drawing the line for a fight that he knew he couldn't win. After all, he was long familiar with her type. Strong and determined women like Missus O'Hara were passionate in tending to the needs of their family, and nothing or no one was going to get in their way. Hard work was the coin of their realm, and no sacrifice was too great in terms of their hearth and home. Although little more than thirty, she looked closer to fifty, given her gray streaked hair and weathered face. The long hours of cleaning the apartments of building residents, along with maintaining a household of nine had taken its toll; nonetheless, she refused to complain. Despite the cramped quarters of a three room basement flat and the meager earnings of her janitor husband, she knew she was better off than most of her brethren. And she was determined to keep it that way. As such, when her husband was busy fixing a gas light fixture in one of the apartments, she was eager to escort the detective to the crime scene and use the opportunity to petition for a chance to make extra money.

As Danny watched her march in triumph towards the pantry supply closet, he couldn't help but admire her tenacious spirit; but his musings were cut short by the sound of heavy pounding on the door. Once at the entrance, he was greeted by the sight of Costello, flushed and out of breath, no doubt the result of having rushed to the scene of their morning appointment. The pink glow of his cheeks and the tasseled look of his hair, only added to the patrolman's youthful appearance.

"Sorry about bein' late, Danny; but I was up all hours. I was—"

"Let's not go wastin' time on excuses. I'll fill ya in on what's goin' on here, but first tell me what ya learned about Miss Crane, talkin' to the folks over at the hotel restaurant."

"I spoke with a number of workers, including the maître'd, and they all knew who she was and confirmed what her building manager said: that she was quiet and kept to herself. She was always well dressed, mannerly and cordial to the staff. Occasionally, she would dine with a young man, but no one knew who he was, or what he did. They said he was ordinary looking, medium build and dressed in business attire. They figured his age as somewhere around the mid to late twenties. When together, the two of them were quite private. One of the waiters said they'd clam up whenever he came over to serve them; however, he went on to add that he believed they were more than friends, sharin' intimacies and such."

"Lovers can turn jealous."

"Well, I asked a number of them about that and they all said they never saw arguing or anything like that."

"I was hopin' for a name, especially if it was one of those rich clients of hers, but I guess we learned something; that she might have had a boyfriend of some sort."

"I suppose so; but I've got better news, Danny. I was about to tell you that the reason I was up all night was that I figured out the code in Van Cleff's notebook."

"Ya don't say," Danny shouted, before grabbing him by the shoulder and breaking into a broad grin.

"Yeah, I'm sure I got it. I'd been looking at it all night, but it was the rhythm of it that kept coming back to my mind. Then it hit me! It was Morse Code! All those 'a's' in the notebook were dashes and all those 'o's' were dots. I remember you telling me that Van Cleff was telegraph operator when he was starting out. And I never told you that I was a telegraph messenger boy on Saturdays when I was going to Saint Joe's. I picked up some of the code from the operators when I would be waiting around the office for a delivery. I still got a copy of the codebook. So, I got right to it and started transcribing."

"I knew ya were a smart lad the minute I laid eyes on ya, Hugh," he gushed before adding, "So, whadya find out?"

"It's interesting and a real eye-opener, and you were right about Van Cleff being up to no good. As I was breaking it down, it soon became clear that he was recording all his dealings as a jewelry fence."

"Ah, a coded ledger for his criminal activities."

"Indeed! In it, he listed dates; items such as necklaces or whatever; the price he sold it for, and the names of buyers, mostly jewelry stores around the state."

"That explains those shippin' cartons in the library that we saw the morning of the murders!" Danny proclaimed.

With that, they rushed back into the room, where they found the boxes, neatly addressed and stacked in the corner. After they took a moment to examine the labels, Costello continued with his revelations, "He also lists the suppliers, who he describes as three brothers, Sikes, Dodger and Bates."

"I don't recognize the names but we'll find 'em and get to the bottom of this."

"Actually, that's the interesting part. He uses pseudonyms for these suppliers."

"Sue... dough... nims? Whadya mean," Brick Fist asked.

"It's sort of a coded alias. You see, that's where it gets interesting. Did you ever hear of a book called *Oliver Twist*?"

"Sure I did; written by an Englishman, named Dickens, I believe."

"That's right. Well Sikes, Dodger and Bates were characters in the book, and they were all members of a gang of pickpockets, Sikes being the most brutal of the bunch. Now just looking around the shelves, confirms to me that Van Cleff was quite fond of Dickens. There's numerous editions of his works: *Great Expectations, A Tale of Two Cities, David Copperfield,* and all the rest of them. In his notes, he refers to the fencing operation as the *Parish Boy's Progress,* which is the subtitle of *Oliver Twist.* He even refers to himself as 'Fagin,' who in the book, was the brains behind the scheme; and he goes on to refer to the apartment as 'Saffron Hill,' which was where the gang's hideout was located. I figure the whole thing was Van Cleff's little joke to himself."

"And the folks he called brothers, one of 'em bein' real bad, I wonder who that could be."

"Yeah, it sure sounds like the Foleys, which brings up one more important thing." Pulling out the ledger, Costello pointed to a hand-scribbled note, underlined and punctuated with an exclamation point, "'Sikes demands more!' It's the last citation in the book."

"That throws a new light on things; and it's a good reason for bringin' in the Foleys and grillin' 'em; but we need more. There's gotta be more around here, like the third bullet. Schultz didn't find it and he swore he looked all over: the walls, the shelves, the furniture, everything; but I don't trust the young pup. I think he missed it."

"And what about your message saying that Fingers told you Harpoon was jumped and shot the night before the murders."

"I talked to Doc Williamson and he backs it up, but remember, there was an accomplice to the killin's."

Just then, a voice came ringing out from the bedroom across the hall, "Mother of Mercy!"

"Dammit! I better get over there and make sure the cleanin' lady ain't fuckin' things up," Brick Fist bristled.

No sooner had they turned the corner than they saw Missus O'Hara desperately trying to contain a blizzard of feathers falling around her.

"Not a word, Sergeant! I was just fluffin' the pillow when all this came flyin' out."

"Outta the way, woman! The back's been blasted straight out!"

After tearing off the bedding, much to Missus O'Hara's horror, Danny yelled in triumph, "There it is, boy! The entrance hole of the bullet!" Now in a full-blown frenzy, the detective grabbed his pocketknife and slid under the bed. "Ah, there's the exit hole right below, and whaddah we got here?" For a moment the room was silent, save for the sound of Danny's grunting and the creaks of metal prying through wood. This was followed by a bellow of glee that filled the air. Upon pulling himself out from beneath the frame, he raised up the small lead trophy while beaming, "The third shot, Hugh! Looks like we got ourselves a whole new ballgame!"

"But what about the blood leading out? Somebody musta been shot," Hugh wondered out loud.

Taking his partner aside, he whispered, "If I'm right, it's probably some sorta animal blood. It's sure beginnin' to look like a set-up to cover somebody's tracks. I don't think the jeweler was target shootin' his pillow. That's why there was a pause before the third shot, like Missus Wilkerson said. After shootin' the victims, the killer walked over and fired into the bed, so that us coppers would think Van Cleff managed to shoot one of 'em. The killer figured whoever came in and cleaned up would think a mouse got into the pillow."

Despite thanking Missus O'Hara for facilitating the discovery of the missing bullet, Brick Fist refused to allow further access to the apartment, in light of the new developments. Yet as he gently tried to ease her out, she resumed her earlier debate. "I can't see how some lousy feathers can lead to ya throwin' me out!"

"I'm sorry, Rita, but with this new evidence I don't want ya touchin' anything else. And more important, I don't want ya hearin' what we're talkin' about."

Digging in her heels as they passed through the library, she fumed, "You're just throwin' your weight around, Danny Doyle! And ya ain't got no heart or respect; like with that," she added while pointing towards an ashtray on Van Cleff's desk. "How could ya been smokin' a stogie while tendin' to those poor victims last week. Ain't ya got no respect for the dead?"

"Whadya mean, woman? I wasn't smokin' that mornin' and neither was Costello or the other copper who was here."

"Don't go lyin' to me, Sergeant. I know Mister Van Cleff didn't smoke and I'm sure pretty Miss Crane wouldn't be firin' up one of them disgustin' cigars."

After thanking her once more, Danny hustled her out the door before quickly returning to his partner. "And Harpoon didn't smoke either; about the only vice he didn't have. Anyway, I think we're lookin' at the cigar of one of the killers, Hugh. Now take your bandana and wrap it up all gentle-like."

Upon picking up the stub, Hugh examined it closely. "Looks like a fancy crest on the band but I can't make it out 'cause it's been mostly burned through."

"Later on, I want ya to take it over to Mister Mathias' cigar store and see if he can make anything outta it. In the meantime, let's give this place another once-over."

The latest search failed to produce any new clues; but as he walked down the hall after locking up, Danny came to an abrupt halt upon nearing one of the gas light fixtures on the wall. "Son of a bitch! How could I have missed this, Hugh? Get over here and stand your arse next to this lamp."

"Sure, Danny; but what's this all about," he asked as he positioned himself alongside the sconce.

"I'll be damned! What are ya, lad, about six feet?" Without waiting for a replay, he continued, "Well this lamp barely reaches your shoulder and yet Harpoon had four or five inches on you. Remember what the old lady said about one of the killers clunkin' his head on the light and knockin' off his kepi. Marley towered over the damn thing! He couldn't hit it with his noggin'. First Fingers and Doc Williamson; and now the bullet, the cigar and this. That's the final nail. Harpoon's off the hook on this one."

Showing no signs of reflecting on the irony of his pronouncement on Marley's acquittal, Brick Fist launched into his plans for proceeding on to Canal Street. He was biting at the bit to grill his usual cast of snitches in hope of gleaning some information on Van Cleff's robbery ring.

Once outside, as they headed up Tupper towards Main, it soon became apparent that Costello was not himself. An air of restlessness and preoccupation seemed to exist just below the surface of his genial demeanor. Noticing the change, Doyle was quick to intervene, "Ya know, Hugh, your cousin Billy would be mighty proud of ya. You're a damn good copper, doin' a fine job, and you're gonna make your mark in this business. I'm lucky to have ya by my side and I'm even luckier to have ya as a friend."

"Thank you, Danny, that means a lot to me; but I've been having second thoughts about continuing as a policeman."

"I hope this Marley business isn't coming' back at ya. Ya did the right thing. He fired first, thinkin' he had to answer for the bushwhacker's killin'; one of many on his soul, I should add."

"I know; but still the man's no more and it's a crying shame he was innocent of this."

"Of course you're gonna question things 'cause of the shootin', but give it time. You'll feel different about it after a while."

"I admit Marley's death got me looking at things real close, but I've been thinking about this for a while now, Danny."

"I know I got my ways and I know I'm tough to deal with, but I hope I haven't soured ya on police work since ya joined up with me."

"Not at all, Danny. In fact, working with you is the best thing that happened to me on the job, since joining the force. And don't get me wrong, I like solving crime and such, not to mention having a steady wage, but in trying to do the job, it's all black and white. Everything is good or bad; crooked or honest; or threatening or peaceful. There's no gray and there's not much room for dealing with the complexities of life. It seems to always boil down to knocking heads, running down thieves, hauling in hustlers, grilling stoolies and as I've come to know, shooting killers."

"Lettin' down your guard and tryin' to figure out the complexities of life, as you put it, can get ya killed in this business."

"And that's another thing that's getting to me, Danny, the ever-looming presence of violence. It's kind of intoxicating at first, you know, the quick solution to problems and all; but there's a price that eventually shows up on your soul, no matter what. It wears you down."

"It can be black as night and mean as hell out there; so ya gotta be tough and willin' to be hard. I can't apologize for that, Hugh."

"No, no, I'm not saying that, Danny. I realize that's how the job may need to be done. I know what folks say about you, Danny, but the fella I know is dedicated and gets the job done for the people around these parts. And I admire him for it. But it's just getting to be too much and I'm beginning to find out the job might not be for me. I think I need something where I can help to fix things for folks; you know, like Keena with the workers, or maybe becoming a lawyer so I can use the law to solve problems and bring justice to people. I'm thinking of going back and reading the law under my Da."

"I can't say I'm not disappointed, Hugh. Like I said, you're good at this. But I understand what you're sayin'. This kinda work demands things most fellas ain't up to, if you're gonna do the job right. And keep your trap shut about this, but I can see how a person would want to use his head and his heart to make things better, assumin' that's possible in such a shit-hole world; but that ain't me and it never will be. You're a good man, Hugh, and whatever ya end up doin', you'll bring credit to it."

"Thanks again, Danny."

"But I'm still hopin' you'll change your mind."

"We'll see."

"In the meantime, you're still a copper and workin' for me, boyo. Now, we got a lotta work to do, so let's quit all this philosophizin'."

As he followed his partner up the street, Hugh's thoughts turned to one of the most complex subjects of his police experience, Sergeant Danny Doyle. Loathed by most of his fellow officers, feared not only by criminals but by many a law abiding citizen and a frequent recipient of "gifts" in return for favors, Doyle was a challenge to the concept of a good cop; nonetheless, he was courageous, tireless, and totally dedicated to bringing his brand of righteous order to what he saw as a dark and tumultuous world. Although the image of Brick Fist Doyle, barreling his way through life, irrespective of the rules, was an accurate one, Costello had discovered there was more to the man than met the eye. Whether it was seeing his outrage over the factory deaths, witnessing his determination to secure justice in the case of Bonnie Crane, or observing some covert and unassuming act of kindness to those down on their luck, Hugh had come to know that there was a moral compass at Brick Fist's core. Why it was so obscured remained a mystery to his young partner; but it didn't dampen his admiration for the department's pariah."

As the policemen approached the portico outside the Iroquois Hotel, a shiny yet dirt splattered carriage came rolling up to the curb. Much to Danny's surprise, as the driver rushed down to adjust the steps and open the door, out popped Liam Riley in the company of Prescott's daughter, Victoria. No doubt they were here to join the throng arriving for lunch at the revamped and increasing popular hotel restaurant; however, as Brick Fist sauntered over and introduced himself, it caught Riley off-guard.

After quickly reining in his testy reaction, the young businessman asked. "Why, ah, Sergeant Doyle, to what do I owe this honor?"

"Just heading back to the precinct house with my partner, here, Costello, when I spotted my friend Liam."

Although put off by Danny's goading emphasis on the Irish name he was so anxious to downplay, Riley quickly collected himself with a cordial introduction. "Forgive me, Miss Prescott, but may I introduce an old acquaintance, Sergeant Doyle and his associate, Officer Costello. Sergeant Doyle has on occasion come under the employ of your father."

"Oh, yes. I do recall Daddy mentioning the name in regards to the capture of the thief who stole my stepmother's necklace.

"One and the same, Miss Prescott, my pleasure, ma'am," Brick Fist replied as he tipped his hat in unison with young Costello.

"And what brings you to this area, Sergeant? Have some business nearby?" Riley asked.

"The usual poking around."

"Ah, no doubt a sensitive investigation."

"No end to police work," Danny quickly responded, unwilling to go any farther.

"Now Officer Costello, wouldn't you agree that this is a lovely neighborhood with its share of beautiful buildings?" Riley inquired.

Just as Costello was poised to extol the virtues of the Templeton Apartments, Brick Fist cast a sharp look of rebuke that inspired a clipped response on the part of the patrolman, "Certainly is, sir."

"And what about you folks; here to enjoy a nice lunch?" Danny interrupted.

"I'm so anxious to try this place," Victoria piped in. "Everyone says the food and atmosphere are wonderful; but I had the hardest time convincing Lee to stop. He's such a fuddy-duddy sometimes."

"Although I've never been here," Riley was quick to assert, "I'm always skeptical of these newly fashionable restaurants, not to mention not liking the crowds and all the noise."

"I keep on telling him he works too hard and should enjoy things more, but that's my Lee. You know, Sergeant, he saved the inventory the night of the unfortunate fire."

The use of the term "unfortunate" in reference the tragedy at the plant, almost lit a fuse under Danny; however, he wisely chose to bite his tongue.

"And he did most of the work in finding our new factory site. We're just coming from there, the old Melodeon plant off Niagara Street."

"An ambitious man he is, Miss Prescott," Danny replied, perhaps a bit too ironically.

"Well on this day he's going to enjoy a relaxing meal." Turning towards Riley, she bubbled, "And you're doing it just for me! And that's all that counts, isn't it, sweetie." With that, she let out a little giggle, before holding out her chubby little hand.

"Yes it is, Victoria," he replied, barely able to conceal his obvious discomfort.

Despite an urge to prolong the man's agony, Danny was anxious to move on, and as such, quickly bid his adieu.

Watching as Riley led her through the portico, Danny couldn't help but notice the man's now petulant mood. It even followed him to the hotel entrance, where he brusquely brushed aside the doorman's attempt to engage.

"So that's the Riley who's the up and comer at Prescott's; but wasn't he courting Miss Shea," Hugh asked.

"Men like that ain't lookin' for love. They go after other things like fat girls with lotsa money."

"The man's a fool."

"No, the man's a rat, but I'm sure the world will treat 'im good."

XX

"It's a cryin' shame, it is!"

"Yeah, it says nothin' about fixin' blame," one of the crowd yelled out.

As he pushed shut the door, which silenced the raging wind outside, Brick Fist was greeted by an animated knot of people huddled around the end of Blinky's bar. At its center sat Kitty McCoy, still dressed in mourning black and surrounded by a group that included Keena, the lawyer, Tom Behan, and Father Morris from Saint Bridget's.

After shaking off the snow that caked his jacket, Danny slowly eased his way around the crowd, whose members seemed transfixed with the matter at hand.

"Ten young souls lost, yet they treat 'em like so much deadwood," Kitty sobbed as Keena and Blinky tried to offer comfort.

As the barkeep, Bobby Kelleher arrived with Danny's usual order of lager, the detective drew him aside and whispered, "What's goin' on here?"

"Didn't ya hear, Danny? The coroner's jury put out its report on the plant fire, today, and it ain't good."

From his warm vantage point across from the potbellied stove, Danny watched as Padrig Tierney angrily waved a copy of the *Courier*. Still hobbling on a pair of crutches since the night of the fire, the union activist began to shout, "Now listen to this! After first mentionin' the stairs and doors and such, they go on to say, and I quote, 'Had it not been for the combustible and flammable nature of the material manufactured, causin' the flames to spread so rapidly that the principal means of escape were cut off, many who perished could otherwise have escaped'. Not a word whether the stairs or elevator or such were adequate. I'm sure my poor dead friends or the rest of us injured workers coulda told those bastards on the jury that the exits weren't enough—if they bothered to ask us survivors!"

"That so-called inquest was pathetic," Tom Behan added with a look of disgust. "They're just a bunch of well-connected fat cats who want to whitewash the whole thing for the sake of one of their own, Alfred Prescott."

"And speaking of combustibles, they didn't even bring up the safety of the manufacturing chemicals, or how they were used or where they were stored," Keena scoffed.

"I can tell ya, it was a sloppy mess," Tierney said with a shake of his head. "Barrels of all sorta dyes and varnishes and the like were all over the place. The boys down on three told me that there were scores of 'em in an old storage room at the end of the building. It's where they would haul off broken down equipment, bales of rags and other rubbish. Them damn drums were even leakin' back there! Tim Hannon, one of the pressmen down on the third, said that's where all hell first broke loose. The room went off like a Chinese candle."

"And if this don't take the cake," Behan roared as he kept jabbing his finger at a copy of the paper. "Let me read from this fine example of a public inquiry," he continued, as he adjusted his spectacles, "'Coroner Scott said he had desired to examine Mister Charles Berrick, the builder, but the gentleman was so busy he was unable to attend. But Mister Scott said that he since talked to him.' Apparently he was quite convincing," the lawyer went on, "because the report does nothing to challenge Berrick's contention that, and I quote, 'the building had been constructed in accordance with the requirements of the city ordinances.' That's your coroner's inquest for you! What a disgrace!"

"And what a rush to judgment; not even two weeks since the tragedy," Father Morris grumbled before adding, "Things would be a lot different if it was ten rich boys at some fancy school or social club!"

After placing his copy of the paper on the bar, Blinky could barely contain the catch in his voice as he looked down at his niece Kitty. "It breaks my heart to see how they said at the end that there should be more safety inspections and fire escapes on the outside of large buildings. Fat chance that'll be happenin', but even if it does, it won't be helpin' our darlin' Kitty and the boys."

"There sure as hell weren't any inspections at Prescott's, only Collin's and his union-bustin' coppers crackin' heads," Tierney spit out with a vengeance.

By now, Keena's cheeks were taking on a crimson glow as she tenderly stroked her cousin's back. Clenching her fist, she stood up and addressed the crowd, "You're right, Da, changes will never come, that is, without pressure. Like Paddy just mentioned, this all ties in with the labor movement. This has to move us to fight even harder for fair wages and worker's rights, especially safe workplaces. And with fair wages, men won't be forced to have their children working beside them in the factories. So, if we commit ourselves to win this battle, Kitty's boys and all the other lads won't have died in vain."

Danny sat back and watched as those in the group cheered in agreement. For her part, Keena blushed in the face of their applause, as she returned to comforting Kitty. Finally, after grabbing a wedge of ham from the bar-top tray and washing it down with his beer, the detective walked over to where they sat. "This here coroner's report, did they mention any locked doors?"

"No, just that there were exits available," Father Morris answered.

"I can tell ya, most of the doors were locked tight to keep us from smugglin' in union organizers," Tierney added. "Still, we were able to slip out by the skin of our teeth, using an outta-the-way utility door off in the back that they didn't get to yet."

"Yeah, I heard that too," Danny nodded before going on. "Now, I see Kevin McBride sittin' over there. Sliding a few seats over, he asked, "You work at the Steamer House don't ya, Kevin?"

"Sure do, Danny, thanks to Mister Shea and Mister Nellaney over at party headquarters."

"Listen, Kevin, they were storin' that locked door and frame that I found in the rubble the day after the fire, weren't they?"

"Yeah, it was sittin' back in the shed, but then Captain Collins came down and had it carted off; said he needed it for his investigation."

"Ah, that's where it went." Drawing Keena aside, Danny whispered, "Investigation, my arse. Probably lying at the bottom of the lake as we speak, but I ain't giving up on this thing yet. Something funny was going on there and I'm going to get to the bottom of it. You can promise Kitty that I won't rest if there was something or somebody behind this fire."

"Thank you, Danny. I know your heart is in the right place, and I know that you're a real bull when it comes to getting answers."

"I don't know what I'll find, but I'll do as best as I can."

After ordering a round of drinks and joining the little circle, Brick Fist couldn't help but watch as Kitty slowly followed her cousin to a nearby table. The once engaging whirlwind of a barmaid had been replaced by a tortured soul struggling to come to grips with the loss of her beloved sons. Already the lack of food and sleep was having the effect of hollowing out her fresh-faced features; nonetheless, it failed to diminish her elemental beauty. On the contrary, it only seemed to imbue an aura of radiant vulnerability.

Despite the lively discussion that swirled around him, Danny sat riveted as Kitty used her pale, thin hand to pull back a renegade curl that had slipped onto her cheek; and as he watched her listen to Keena's comforting words, he couldn't help but notice that her other hand clutched a rosary, as if holding on for dear life.

Perhaps it was the weight of the recent deaths and tragedies that had come crashing into his world; or maybe it was the sight of Kitty's sunken eyes that seemed to be searching for some sign of hope; but whatever it was that struck a chord, Danny was suddenly engulfed by a rush of sympathy for his suffering friend; and despite an oftentimes dark and cynical outlook that long resisted any sentimental urges, he felt compelled to share his feelings with her.

"Beggin' your pardon if I'm interrupting things, Kitty; not that this thick-headed Irishman doesn't bull his way through most everything he does."

His self-deprecating remark brought a smile to her face as she answered, "Don't worry, Danny, it's part of your charm, and ya ain't interruptin'."

"I've wanted to tell you how much your friendship means to me, Kitty. You're always so welcomin' to me, even when some other folks kinda edge away when I show up."

"They just don't know what a good fella ya are, like I do."

"Now enough about this old plow horse. I want to know how you're doin'. I ain't seen you since the funeral; sad day that it was."

"It's been real hard, Danny. I sometimes wonder if I can make it through another day," she stumbled, barely able to get the words out.

Grabbing her hand, he said in a soothing voice, "Kitty, I know. And when I say I know, I mean I know."

"But it's darker than anything you can imagine, Danny."

"Black as ink and wrapping up all around ya, so you can't see nothin' else."

"You're right! That's how I'm feelin', all dead inside."

"It sure ain't easy but folks survive."

"I don't know, Danny," she whispered as she lowered her eyes.

"I want to tell you how I know. None of you folks or nobody around these parts knew me when I showed up in Buffalo after the War. We had a little farm down in Potter County P, A, but I couldn't save it after bein' gone those three years. So me and my wife, who was from down that way; yeah, you heard right, as hard as it is to believe, I was once married."

This new revelation inspired chuckles on the part of the women, and it didn't take long for Keena to add, "Well, I couldn't believe that at some point a gal wouldn't net a looker like you, Danny Doyle."

"Well, I got lucky, I guess. Anyway, after I had a hard time findin' work down there, we packed up the three little ones"—this time he didn't stop to acknowledge their shocked reactions—"and we headed up to the Queen City of the Great Lakes, the land of opportunity; just like my ma and da did after the famine. I figured I'd find work on the docks or the barges, which I did. I worked like a dog but it paid off. After a few years I built a little cottage up in the Hydraulics, on Van Rensselaer Street."

"Ah, over near Saint Patrick's," Keena observed.

"That's right. I wanted Frannie, that was my wife's name, and little Annie, Mary and Henry to have a home of our own; not like me, shot off to the orphan home after my folks died. Anyway, life was good; real good. I had a beautiful and lovin' wife and each of my darlin' children could charm the devil himself. Even in the off-season, I had enough work fixin' things around the neighborhood to take care of all our needs. Then one day when I was repairin' a neighbor's roof before the bad weather set in, Frannie came runnin' down the street screamin' that little Annie had turned deathly sick.

Barely three years old, Annie was the cleverest little scamp ya ever saw, always playin' tricks, but forever gettin' away with it. How could she not, with that mop of curls, mischievous dimples and twinklin' eyes that were bluer than the sky. She owned my heart and I called her my glowworm, 'cause she lit things up wherever she went.

By the time I rushed home, everything was flowin' out of her like a burst dam. I held her to my chest but she kept screamin' from the cramps that were ravagin' her body. There's no words to describe how it tore me to the bottom of my soul. We couldn't get a doctor, but Lucy, the midwife from up the street, told us to keep filling her with liquids. It seemed to help a bit but then she'd start losing it all over again. This kept goin' on til she lost consciousness. Eventually as the hours passed, her little breaths became more and more strained. Just before dawn, she opened her now sunken eyes; yet there was still that wonderful twinkle. Then in a tiny little voice, she goes, 'Daddy,' and made like a kiss with her little tulip lips before dyin' in my arms. Within two days, my sweet and quiet Mary, aged eight and my two-fisted, ragamuffin six-year old, Henry, had followed their sister to the grave. The cholera had taken my children, and changed my life forever.

At first I wanted to hang myself from the nearest tree, but I couldn't because of my lovely Frannie. Frannie, the truest, kindest and most loving mother and wife in the world had died with them. Oh, she breathed and ate and lied down and got up, but her soul was goin' through the motions. Still, on the day she followed their little coffins out the doors of Saint Patrick's, she carried herself with a strength and grace that left me breathless. Over the next weeks, everything was a dark blur. She sat by the fire most of the day with her pictures of the Saints and holding her rosary, as friends and members of her family came to console her. I tried to comfort her as best I could, while at the same time callin' on all my strength to keep myself from goin' mad. Eventually, I had my jobs to fall back on, and yet, that barely worked. My poor Frannie had no such refuge.

At night, we'd hold each other until we managed to make it to the next morning. You see, our love for each other never wavered but it couldn't save us. It was as if we knew what we once had, and it only reminded us what we lost.

I clung to a hope that if we'd just hang on, time could provide some relief and somehow help to set things right. Still, my darlin' Frannie kept losing more and more weight, mind ya, in my eyes she would always be the prettiest girl in the room; but after a few weeks she came down with a fever and within three days, had joined our children. I remember when she slipped into unconsciousness, I kept stroking her beautiful auburn hair and crying for her to fight on; but when I saw that sweet, almost indescribable calm look on her face, I knew she wanted to get back to our children. For the longest time afterward, the only thing that kept me from taking a bullet was the thought that somehow she did.

That was over twelve years ago. Since then, I've managed to survive and make a life for myself. I've gone it alone and for whatever the reason, it seemed to work, and I've carried on. But you're different. You're kind and good and I know you got a lot of people who love and care for ya. Most of all, ya got your five boys. You can survive and be the best mother that ever lived for those wee fellas. Now, I can tell ya that ya still have times of sufferin' ahead, but I know you'll make it."

With tears streaming down her face, Kitty flung her arms around his neck and held him tightly. Not only was her expression a sympathetic response to his long-hidden suffering, but it also reflected a recognition that here was a fellow bearer of unimaginable pain. Yet perhaps at its core, it was a show of thanks for reminding her that there was life beyond the horrors she was now experiencing.

Keena sat back and watched as a hopeful look took bloom upon her cousin's face; however, it was different with Danny. In watching him tell his tragic tale, there was no hint of tears or pain on his part. It was as if any such a show of emotion had been wrung out long ago. Instead, there was just a well-worn look of resignation. Yet, as he returned Kitty's embrace, there was no mistaking the empathy he felt for his old friend.

Although left reeling by Danny's shocking revelations, Keena could not hide the feelings inspired by his thoughtful yet painful effort to help Kitty. As such, she was quick to cast him a heartfelt smile.

Unaware of what had just transpired, others soon joined them, and the conversation took on a lighter tone. For Danny's part, with each successive round of drinks, his stories became funnier and his jokes racier.

The light-hearted revelry continued for another hour before Keena sensed her cousin's growing fatigue. Yet as she prepared to take her home, she pulled Danny aside. "I had no idea, Danny. I wish you told me."

"Talking never changed things."

"But at least I could have told you how sorry I am."

"You're a good woman, Keena, and I know you feel for what happened."

"And I appreciate what you did for Kitty. I know sharing your pain wasn't easy, Danny. Yet, I'm sure it helps her to know she's not alone in living through such a tragedy; and to know that survival is possible. God bless you, my friend."

"I'm glad to help, her. As for God and his blessings, how could he abandon such a darlin' woman as my wife, and our three little angels? No, I don't go there."

"Regardless of your feelings, Danny, I think God looks at you as a good son and loves you."

"And I appreciate your feelins', Keena. So go take joy in your religion. Most good people do; but it just ain't me."

With that, they bid each other a warm farewell. Yet before Keena headed out the door, she turned and watched the detective make his way back to the bar. As he moved through the crowd with a bull-like presence, there was no mistaking his fearsome reputation. Others quickly cleared a path for the department's brick-fisted legend. Still, as she watched him bark out his order for another beer, Keena knew there was another side to the man that most failed to see. Although there was no disputing his shortcomings, most notably, his rigidness, pugnacity and weakness for "gifts," he nonetheless possessed at his core a sense of compassion and a thirst for justice. That, coupled with his stunning revelations about his past, served to cast a new light on Keena's feelings about her longtime friend.

No sooner had the detective begun filling his plate at the bar, than he spotted a slight figure enter through the back door. The man was decked out in all manner of winter regalia, including a woolen scarf that covered his face and a heavy knit cap pulled low around his ears. Judging from the thick layer of snow coating his jacket, it was obvious that he had been outside for some time. After going through the ritual of shaking off the snow, the man grabbed his tool sack and headed to a bench next to the stove. In an effort to warm his feet, he stretched out his over-sized, rag-stuffed brogans in front of the heater.

Once the mystery guest pulled off his headwear, Danny was quick to recognize Kevin Toohey, the hard-luck repairman from the police livery, and onetime object of Collin's wrath.

"For Christ's sake, Toohey, how can ya walk in them boots. They're for a bloke twice your size."

"Sure they're too big but I needed 'em on a cold day like today, workin' on the broken rail of Mister Shea's sleigh. They were me brother Al's, God rest his soul. Got killed last summer while scoopin' at the Erie Elevator. Suffocated to death."

"Ah, now I remember. Well, sorry 'bout your brother, Kevin and I was just pullin' your tail about the boots; but anyway, how are you doin' since I seen ya last."

"I took your advice and moved to me ma's with the kids. The wee lads are doin' just fine."

"Glad to hear it. And stay away from that tart wife of yours."

"I've been doin' real good, but the other day I went to the house to pick up some clothes and I must admit, I couldn't help myself from snoopin' around. And by luck—"

"By luck ya didn't get your arse in a jamb! I coulda been haulin' ya off to jail."

"I know, I know, but when I saw his uniform on the chair and heard 'em both snorin' away, it got me goin'. Fortunately, I got a handle on myself and headed out, but not before comin' on something you might find interestin', Sergeant. I heard ya were askin' around about the fire, and I saw ya talking to Missus McCoy when I was comin' in—"

"So whaddya getting' at, lad? What does your wife and her boyfriend have to do with me, or my investigation about the fire?"

"Well, as I was tiptoein' me way out, I saw his satchel just sittin' there; you know the copper, Perry, Collins' boot lick." Suddenly, Toohey broke off his tale with a nervous look that signaled a fear of having gone too far.

"Don't worry," Danny answered with a wry smile, "I know he's a low-down rat like his master Collins."

"Like I was gonna say, I was lookin' for some evidence like love letters; by the way, I'm gonna divorce her, no matter me soul, and I could use somethin' in writing for the court. Well, after grabbin' the bag and sortin' through it, I didn't find no love letters but I did find a bunch of police orders and such. Well, lo and behold one of 'em caught me fancy, and bein' thankful ya didn't beat me that time at the livery and knowin' how ya been lookin' into the calamity at Prescott's—"

"Just get on with it, lad," Brick Fist snapped, impatiently.

"Right, right. Well, there was this letter, marked as a copy and signed by Collins and addressed to Mister Prescott sayin' how he'd send one of his men down to the factory durin' the night shift to make sure the doors were locked from the outside so that no union fellas could get in and recruit workers. It then says that Collins was gonna send some of his coppers to beat up and harass any organizers. Finally, it goes on to say that, as they agreed, Collins was arrangin' with their friends at City Hall that there'd be no building problems at the plant. I've been carrying these letters with me hopin' that I'd see ya."

As he slapped the little man on the back, Danny shouted, "Ya done good, Kevin! I'm glad I didn't beat ya that time!" Upon making sure Toohey's drinks were taken care of for the night, the detective scooped up the papers and rushed out the door. Ignoring the driving snow, he headed down Louisiana Street towards the home of Tommy Keough, a well connected political hack, who, after a long and rewarding patronage career, found himself in the role of the city's deputy chief building inspector.

After fighting his way through a series of drifts along the street, Danny arrived at Keough's spare yet tidy cottage located in the shadows of the hulking grain elevators. Although small by most standards, the house was a virtual country estate compared to the weather-beaten shacks of the neighborhood. After rapping on the door, he waited a few moments before finally making out a lantern's glow through the window shutters. Despite the howling wind, a cautious voice came floating out from behind the bolted door, "Who's that bangin' away on a night unfit for the devil?"

"It's me, Danny Doyle. Lemme in, Tommy."

Straining against its frozen frame, the door swung open to reveal an elfin figure holding a lamp in one hand and a shillelagh in the other. "Sweet Mother Mary, ya must be daft bein' out there, man!"

"You know me when it comes to business, Tommy."

"So it be your business at this hour?"

"Is everything all right, Mister Keough," a voice rang out from a nearby room that seemed to be the source of potato soup aromas.

"Just one of me political friends, Danny Doyle, Missus Keough." Turning back to Brick Fist, he asked, "So is it a favor ya want with the boys at City Hall, or with your boss and my friend, Patrick Collins?"

"I'm afraid it's not that type of business, Tommy. This is police business."

"Whaddaya mean, Doyle?"

"I mean I got some questions regardin' an investigation I'm doin'."

"Why you! You don't come bargin' into Tommy Keough's house, throwin' your weight around like some sorta big man, and tryin' to—"

"Shut your trap, boyo," Danny snarled before grabbing him by the collar. "Listen good, Keough! I just left a grievin' mother of two dead boys, who's feeling worse now that the coroner's report came out failin' to fix any blame. Now, I've come into possession of some letters describin' how Collins was gonna make sure there were no inspection problems with Prescott's plant. I can promise ya, little man, that I'm gonna get to the bottom of this. Ya hear me!" With that, Brick Fist delivered a crisp slap to the side of Keough's head.

"What's goin' on? Do I have to come out with me spoon and break up an argument like with the little ones?"

"We're just debatin' the next Paddy Ryan fight, Bridie," Danny shouted back with a reassuring chuckle.

"Well just be careful, Danny. You know Tommy and his stick."

Looking down, the detective noticed that the shillelagh was still in Keough's hand; however, a withering glare inspired a quick release of the potential weapon. Once more staring him in eyes, Danny cautioned, "That was a smart move, Tommy; but like I was sayin', I'm gonna find the truth, even if it means crackin' heads. And I don't mean gentle-like crackin'. Now, I know ya cover the north side of town, so ya ain't involved with the Prescott deal; but since ya know everything and everybody up there at City Hall, especially regardin' inspections, I'm gonna start with you!" Twisting the knot that had been the man's collar, he growled, "Now remember, if I catch ya lyin' to me, you're gonna be very sorry and very hurtin', Deputy Inspector!"

With that, Keough proceeded to spill out all he knew about Prescott's bribing of officials to keep the plant off-limits. In addition, Keough revealed that the wallpaper magnate frequently used his contact, Collins, as a go-between with the corrupt officials.

Satisfied that he intimidated the old ward heeler into revealing everything he knew, Danny was content to issue his final order. "And don't go running off to warn your Tammany friends, 'cause every one of 'em is gonna be headin' for cover when the shit I stir up starts flyin' around. But if I hear ya blabbed your mouth, you're gonna find out I'm not so loveable the next time around."

After delivering a menacing smile to his shaken host, Brick Fist stuck his head around the corner to bid farewell to Missus Keough, before returning to the cold dark night.

XXI

As the lilting strains of an Irish reel came floating out the doors, waves of revelers streamed into the basement of Saint Bridget's parish school. Although helped by a January thaw, the enthusiastic turnout was inspired by the worthy nature of the event. Sponsored by the Knights of Labor and the local chapter of the Hibernians, the gathering was a benefit for the families of the Prescott fire victims.

For the next of kin, there had been nothing in terms of formal compensation save for a stipend of ten dollars provided through the beneficence of Alfred J. Prescott. For many, especially money-strapped widows like the mother of the Hackett boy, the loss of a crucial breadwinner spelled disaster for the rest of their families; nonetheless, it was the victim's equally thread-bare friends and neighbors who proved a wellspring of aid and support. Whether it be through churches, neighborhood shops and saloons, or various places of work, all joined in on passing the hat. Tonight's hoolie was the culmination of those efforts to provide much needed relief to the afflicted families.

Danny joined the bustling crowd as it inched its way down the wooden stairs. Upon reaching the landing, he looked out at a sea of faces that transformed the cold, spare hall into a rollicking cauldron of activity. At the far corner of the room, a group of musicians were busy playing their fiddles, tin whistles and concertinas, while a nearby troop of step-dancers were unleashing their feet to the boisterous tunes. Off to his left, a bevy of dignitaries and politicians were already pressing the flesh, and next to them, a number of local *seanachai* had set up benches and were busy spinning tales of heroes and legends. On his right, families of the victims were greeting those arriving, while throughout the hall, clusters of people were engaged in all manner of lively talk. At the same time, some in the crowd were passing along bottles of whiskey or jars of home-brewed poteen.

No sooner had the detective paid his respects to the families, than he came upon a group of organizers in the midst of a spirited discussion with Father Morris.

"Like I told ya, a fella can have a nip of the dew on his time off, and it would be a shame to deny him the pleasure during such a fine event, but I won't be havin' any drunken shenanigans. Do you hear me!"

"Don't worry, Father, our boys are keepin' an eye on things."

"They better be! If monsignor hears of any problems when he comes back from retreat, he'll be shippin' me off to the North Pole; and I wouldn't blame 'im!"

"But it ain't like we're at mass, Father Pat," the youngest of the group interjected, much to the chagrin of the others.

"What are ya, a blockhead, Kelly! Ya may have noticed the statue of our Holy Mother at the top of the stairs when ya walked in; or if ya bothered to show up on Sundays, maybe you'd remember the Consecrated Body of our Lord and Savior is across the yard in the altar tabernacle!"

"Kelly's an idiot, Father, but don't worry we'll keep on top of things," Rory Blake, the leader of the Hibernians was quick to respond.

Stressing the point, the priest shot a finger into his chest, "And remember, I don't want any of our Protestant guests going back home and reportin' it's true that we're a bunch of besotted rabble. Do I make myself clear!"

"Yes, Father," they all dutifully replied before blending into the crowd.

Hoping to avoid the controversy, Danny slipped past the priest before running into Hugh Costello along with his cousin Mick and a young man the detective didn't recognize.

Whaddya doin', leavin' so early!"

"We've been here a while already, Danny," Mickey, the younger brother of Bill Broderick, replied. "Besides, Tim, here, me wife's little brother, has an early day tomorrow and his ma wants 'im home."

"Ah, so this is the young Hannon boy who I heard was a hero the night of the fire?"

Blushing, the youngster tried to play down his role, "Just did what I could; and you're Brick Fist Doyle, ain't ya."

"One and the same; pleased to meet ya, Tim. And you're way too modest, lad. From what I hear, ya did a whole lot to save your friends that night."

"Well, we all pitched in."

"You're a good man, Tim. Not one to go struttin' around, even though ya earned it; but as long as I got ya here, could ya answer me a question. You were on the third where the coroner's jury said the fire started, eh?"

"That's where I was, Sergeant. The coroner said it started with a fire in a machine, which was right, but the real culprit was when the flames hit the back storage room. That's when it went up like one of them volcanoes. They didn't mention that."

"And what was that all about; the room goin' up I mean."

"They had a bunch of old equipment and rags and other junk in the room, but more important they were storin' a lot of barrels of dyes and varnishes and such back there."

"But I heard the supply room was on the first floor."

"That's true, but they kept movin' barrels in and out of that third floor room. I dunno why, but they'd do it on the night shift and always usin' some cartmen from the outside, never fellas from the plant. One of me unfortunate mates, Bobby Schwimmer said he thought one of 'em was a gangster but didn't say who. But that must not have been true, 'cause somebody musta given 'em the run of the place'; allowin' 'em every now and then to load up and take the barrels outta the building."

"Was any of 'em your bosses?"

"Naw, they just didn't bother 'em; musta had orders from up top."

"And speakin' of orders from up top, I heard rumors that the company had the doors locked from the outside to prevent union folks from gettin' in."

"We heard the same thing and it musta been true, 'cause the night of the fire, the back doors were locked or stuck or somethin'. Luckily the stairway in front was clear; and when I got to the fourth, Tierney pointed the way to a little-used utility door that led out onto the roof."

"Is there anything else that sticks out in your mind about it?"

"Ah, nothin' really, other than that the Holy Mother was with us that night. It's the same thing I told Mister Riley when he was talkin' to me about it.

"Well, thanks for the information, Tim; and so, you're back to work now?"

"Yeah, that's why I gotta get goin'. They're workin' us hard, getting' the old melodeon plant fitted with the new presses. That's so we'll be up and runnin' by the end of March."

With that, Danny once more took the opportunity to express his sympathies to his friend's brother, and after observing that Billy's widow must be pleased with the turnout, he leaned over to Costello, "Now before ya go, Hugh, did ya find out anything from Mister Mathias about the cigar band we found at Van Cleff's?"

"Sure did, Danny. I was going to tell you at work. It seems it was an expensive brand, Santiago, from Cuba. Mister Mathias knows them well, since he imports them with the idea of selling them to businessmen, suggesting that they give them as gift to clients. He said a number of bigwig businessmen had done just that; including Mister Van Cleff."

"Like I said, Van Cleff musta known his killer, since there weren't no cigars in the library. He musta given it to 'im at some other time; maybe at one of his stores. We gotta talk to his workers about that. In any case, I don't wanna hold up you and the others any longer. We'll talk more when I see ya at work."

After exchanging farewells, Danny cut a path to the wall, where he was content to lean back and listen to the music. At the same time, he couldn't help but watch as a pair of raven-haired colleens tapped their way to the sounds of a rambunctious jig.

The scene brought him back to another time, when his eyes first caught sight of Frannie Driscoll: Dancing with friends at a barn-raising hoolie outside the city, she was a portrait of sensual beauty. Decked out in a white dress that was growing damp in the evening heat, her lithe figure seemed to float above the floor; and despite a mop of auburn curls that flew about with reckless abandon, her face reflected an air of confident calm as her sparkling blue eyes locked onto his star-struck gaze. At that moment, as surely as he knew the moon caused the tides, he was certain she would someday be his wife.

He could almost smell the scent of lavender perfume when he suddenly realized where he was going. Shaking off the memory, he seized upon a nearby friend who was passing along a bottle. No sooner had he raised the whiskey to his lips than he spotted the glowering figure of Doc Foley through the corner of his eye.

After firing up a stogie, the gangster stood up on a bench to make sure he'd be seen; nonetheless, Danny was undaunted by his intimidating tactics. Instead he took a deep drink of the liquor before hearing a voice over his shoulder.

"Now, I know you can knock off the whole thing, but before ya go shootin' fire outta your arse, save some for me."

Standing before him was his old friend and local chairman of the Knights of Labor, Tommy 'Tip' McCarthy, accompanied by Keena Shea.

"I don't know if I wanna share it with one of these rabble rousin' anarchists," Danny joked before adding, "And besides, the good Father wants any drinkin' to be done on the sly."

"Good luck on that, but he's right ya know. Any kinda row and it's mine and Blake's arses caught in a winch."

"Don't worry, Tip. I think everyone's on their best behavior knowin' the cause; and hats off to you and the rest of your folks on that."

"We take care of our own, Danny," Keena chimed in. "Always go to a poor man if you need help. You sure as hell know those capitalist bastards don't give a damn about workers."

"Ah, ready to go to war, are ya Miss Shea?"

"You're damn right we are, Danny," Tip nodded in agreement.

"Well, I've seen enough warrin' a few years back, my friends."

"But as we all found out, Danny, sometimes ya gotta fight for what's right and good. Now's the time to fight for safe workplaces so we don't have tragedies like this happen again!" Barely stopping to catch his breath, MaCarthy stormed on, "And we're gonna take the battle to the owners for better wages and shorter hours, so the workers who make 'em rich can provide for their families and live fruitful lives!"

"I'm seein' that it's a good thing and ya gotta do it, Tip, but money always wins, and those owners got a lot of it. With who and what they can buy, they can make night look like day, and one and one make three; not to mention hirin' goons to knock in heads."

"They can be beat, once folks wise up and have the guts to band together and demand fair treatment," Keena insisted.

"Good luck on that, gal. Every day I deal with people who cheat and steal, or are willin' to stick a shiv into their neighbor's back to put themselves first."

"It won't be easy," Keena conceded. "It's going to take brave hearts and sacrifice but people are better than you think. I know, because I see it in those workers every day."

"I still don't hold out much of a chance of it happening, but seein' the tears on those mothers' faces, it reminded me … Well, it's a good thing you're trying and I hope you do it."

"Gladdened by Danny's long–sought show of support, Keena grabbed the bottle from his hand and took a victory swig before planting a giggling kiss on his cheek. Yet as she pulled him towards the makeshift stage where they were beginning to assemble a set-dance, a hard voice came booming from the surrounding crowd. "Hey, McCarthy, the folks like to see feats of strength at these here gatherin's. So they're askin' for some wrestlin' matches." Built like a Pit Bull and sporting a tattooed and shaved head done in the Mohawk style, Doc Foley came swaggering over to where they stood. Decked out in a grimy, underwear top that seemed to be straining to contain his muscular shoulders, and wearing patched-over dungarees barely covering the tops of his hobnail boots, the area's most notorious hoodlum projected a ferocious image. The scarred-over knife wounds crisscrossing his massive forearms appeared to confirm this impression, and the perpetual look of suspicion etched across his face only added to the aura that here was a man to be feared and avoided. With arms crossed and standing alongside his criminal cohorts, he waited for an answer.

"I'm sure we can get it done, Doc, but not until later when the women and younger ones are gone," McCarthy explained.

"I ain't much on patience," Foley snorted, before adding in a more genial tone, "besides, me and me lads have to be off to work soon."

Pulling Danny aside, Keena whispered, "I can't believe he's here. I heard at the tavern that they fished out one his cut-throat cousins, Digger Foley, from the canal this afternoon. Even the likes of this thieving dog should have more respect for dead kin."

"Just part of doin' business for him, Keena; besides, if I reckon right, Doc knew about him being dead all along. Now I know it was Digger Foley who Harpoon killed the night he was jumped and wounded."

Not one to be bullied, the union boss held his ground, "Too bad about your workin', Doc, but we got our rules."

Just then, Father Pat showed up, followed by a small crowd lobbying for his attention. "Tip, get Rory over here. They all want to see some wrestling entertainment."

Sensing his opening, Foley spoke up, "That's right, Father. Me and me mates were about to be goin' but folks wanna see a bout between the two toughest blokes in the neighborhood, who just happen to be here tonight; Sergeant Doyle and your humble servant, meself."

Long an aficionado of the fight game, or for that matter, any competition involving feats of strength, the young priest was eager to comply; but knowing Foley's reputation and being wary of the criminal's motives, Father Pat warned, "It better be a good clean match. There'll be no intent to injure or evening any scores or anything like that. Do you hear me?"

After glaring in the direction of his opponent, Foley smirked through a blackened smile dotted with gilded teeth, "You got our word on that, Father; and another thing, with all them folks wantin' to see the bout, they'll all throw in their two bits, which'll bring in more money for the families."

After looking over to Danny, who returned a crisp nod, the priest was quick to grant his approval, but not before issuing one last warning, "Remember, this is Church property, so make sure you act in that spirit; and to make sure everything goes by the rules, a bunch of you big fellas from the plant will be lining the ring." By now the music had stopped and the room was abuzz in anticipation of the contest. Eager to see the epic confrontation between the local titans, the crowd surged to the far end of the building where onlookers were already clearing an area for the bout.

Although having grown weary of this type of fight, the detective could not shrink from the challenge; especially since it involved his archenemy. Yet, no sooner had Brick Fist doffed his jacket and started to wade into the teeming mass, than Keena pulled him aside. A look of fear had already replaced her earlier expression of happiness. "I know better than to try to stop you, Danny, but I beg you to watch yourself. Regardless what that murdering scum told Father Pat, he's an animal, capable of anything!"

Touched by her show of concern, he smiled, "Don't worry, Keena, I've faced worse and never lost yet."

"Just the same, I don't want you getting hurt. So, here, take this." After slipping a ring into his well-calloused hand, she confided, "It's my school ring with an image of the Sacred Heart, and it's been blessed by the Bishop. Now put it in your pocket, I know it will help."

"I promise to bring it back to ya good as new, bonnie lass." With that, he raised up her hand and planted a soft kiss, never taking his sight off her frightened eyes.

As the opponents arrived at the cleared-out circle, now ringed with workers and surrounded by an audience clamoring for action, Foley's henchmen were already celebrating with hoots of triumph while hurling insults aimed at Danny. Reveling in the attention and anxious for the mayhem, Foley stood back, twisting his thick red mustache. For his part the detective was content to sit on a nearby bench, plotting his moves and sizing up his opponent. Suddenly, it dawned on him that Foley was the perfect fit for hitting his head on the sconce outside Van Cleff's apartment. In fact, he was able to make out a freshly stitched scar atop the gangster's forehead; however, just as he was making a mental note, Tip McCarthy tapped him on the shoulder, "Father Pat wants me to referee the match. Now, as ya may know, I was a champ down on the docks, so I know me way around a ring and I'll be callin' a tight bout; but he's a dirty one for sure. I told me lads to jump in if they see any funny stuff. Just the same, watch out for your eyes; they say he a gouger. And don't let 'im get ya in a full nelson, with them big arms of his. I hear that's how he broke another thieves neck in a fight not long ago."

"I got some moves of me own, Tip. Besides, I was division champ durin' the War."

"Now don't go gettin' cocky, boyo. That was a long time ago, so just be careful."

"Don't worry, friend."

Summoning the combatants to the center of the little arena, the hard-nosed union boss barked out his orders, "Okay, lads; like Father Pat said, it's gonna be a good, clean bout, and that means no bitin', scratchin', gougin', or other such nonsense. So, we'll be followin' the Dufur Rules of the Collar and Elbow Style, and the match will be decided on a three point pin with a five count."

After catching sight of Father Pat engaged in a heated discussion with a fellow enthusiast of the pugilistic arts, Foley turned and snarled, "Do fuck the Dufur Rules. Them folks wanna see a nice, wide-open, Catch-as-Catch-Can fight." He then added with a cackle, "Unless your nancy friend, Mister Breakfast, is too scared!"

"Why you no-good bastard!"

"That's all right, Tip," Brick Fist broke in, "I fought me share of Catch-Can matches. And by the way, Foley, I'll do my talkin' in the ring, and then we'll see who's laughin' at the end."

With that, the referee announced the bout would commence with the clap of his hands, before ordering the pair to assume their stances at arm's length. As the fighters now stood face-to-face, Foley kept pounding his fists into his hands, while mouthing the words, "You're a dead man, Doyle." Rather than being cowered, Danny sensed an opportunity. Leaning in so close he could smell his opponent's fetid breath, the detective calmly whispered, "So, how's your brother Emmon doin', Doc?"

The taunt sent the gangster into a fit of rage, which forced McCarthy to step in between, before restoring order. With Foley sneering that Emmon would be faring better than a blind copper, the two combatants resumed their positions. As the crowd held its breath, Tip waited a tantalizing moment before unleashing a frenzy with the clap of his hands. In a flash, Foley flew at Danny with his hands stretched out, going for his face.

Summoning all his strength, Danny grabbed him by the wrists and stopped him dead in his tracks. Inches from his face and glaring straight into the gangster's pestilent eyes, he slowly forced down his hands, before snapping them to the side and nimbly flipping him over his hip.

The crowd roared its approval, not only in recognition of the deft move, but also reflecting its pent-up rage over years of Foley's criminal bullying. Undaunted, if not surprised by the turn of events, the gangster sprang back to his feet. Deciding to take a more deliberate approach, Foley began to slowly circle, much like a predator stalking its prey. After a couple of probing feints, he momentarily relaxed his stance, only to follow up with a leaping kick that caught Danny squarely in the chest and sent him hurtling into the crowd.

After pushing his way out from the swarm, the detective responded with a flying forearm to the head that left both men sprawled on the ground. As Foley struggled to his knees, trying to shake off the fog, Danny came smashing into his back, driving his face into the hard-packed floor. Anxious to put a quick end to the match, he clapped on a withering headlock while wrapping his legs around his trunk. With Foley unable to move, he waited for McNally to start the count; however, the veteran street fighter was far from finished. Twisting and bucking with a manic energy, he somehow managed to free a hand. In an instant, Foley was digging his talons into his captor's throat. Unable to breath, Danny was forced to pry off the suffocating grip. Seizing the opportunity, Foley squirmed out of the hold and kicked his way free.

As Danny bent over to catch his breath, the gangster grabbed him from behind and began to apply his vaunted full nelson. Anticipating the move, the detective dropped to his knees and pulling him forward, sent his attacker tumbling over his head. Once more the crowd went wild; however, as each man stumbled back to his feet, Danny had little time to collect himself. Wild-eyed and sporting a savage grin, Foley seemed revived by his narrow escape. With his henchmen screaming in the background, he lowered his head and charged forward like a runaway locomotive.

Although prepared for the blow, Danny nonetheless found himself flat on his back, and with his wind knocked out, he lay helpless, fighting for breath. Diving in for the kill, Foley grabbed his throat and began pounding his face; however, this time it was the detective's chance to turn the tables.

Calling on what strength he had left, he threw his legs around the gangster's neck and flipped him backwards.

Before Foley could scramble to his feet, Danny lurched forward and delivered a vicious head-butt that opened a wide gash across Doc's brow. Seeing that it also left him reeling, the detective lowered his shoulder and crashed into the slumping gangster's chin. With the audience roaring in the background, Danny leapt onto his opponent and began to apply a cradle hold for the pin. Yet just as McCarthy started to slap out the count, Foley once more managed to free his hand, and using a metal-studded wrist band, tore a slash across the detective's face that narrowly missed his eye.

Enraged at this latest attempt to blind him, Danny broke off the hold and yanked the wounded pit bull up by the collar. Hauling back, he delivered a crippling roundhouse that split open his nose and sent a spray of blood flying across the room. As Foley stood wobbling on gimpy legs, Brick Fist finished the job with a bull rush that left the gangster lying motionless on the floor. Taking no chances, Danny flew onto his opponent and applied the pin.

As the referee yelled out the five count, the hall rocked with cheers. Not waiting for the customary raising of the arm, the detective walked over to where Foley left his coat. After pulling out a cigar from the top pocket, he fired it up before crowing, "Thanks for the stogie, Doc! I know ya won't be wantin' it with your face all busted up."

Unwilling to acknowledge his humiliating defeat as he lay propped up on his elbows, Foley merely motioned for his cohorts to help him out the door.

The musicians had already begun to retake their places when Keena arrived with a washcloth and bucket. Beaming with happiness and relief, she lost little time in getting to work, "Now, sit down and let me clean out those wounds."

"And just as I promised, here's your ring as good as new," he smiled as he slipped it onto her finger.

"See, didn't I tell you it would work!"

"I don't know, but I'm sure you'll keep wearin' me down."

"It's my Christian duty. Just the same, you had my heart in my throat for a while there. Don't you think you might want to start changing your ways, Sergeant Doyle?"

"Foley wants to kill me, Keena. And that beatin' was a good reminder not to push his luck."

"And you want to keep pushing yours," she barked before twisting his face to the side. "Now yank that cigar out of your yap so I can wash that cut on your chin."

As he sheepishly complied with her orders, he looked down and noticed the name on the band was Santiago, the same as the one found at the Van Cleff murder scene. Shooting up, he scanned the room for Foley. Yet as Keena scolded him, he retook his seat, but not before snuffing out the cigar and slipping it into his pocket.

"That's better. You know, I'm beginning to hear that smoking is bad for people."

For a moment her words failed to connect as thoughts about the murder raced through his head. "Oh... ah... yeah, well, that's craziness. For God's sake, if women had their way, there'd be no fun left."

Just then, a clamor of voices began to rise from the area near the entrance. As Danny turned to check on the commotion, he spotted Fingers Carnahan descending the stairs.

Dressed to the nines and wearing a sling, he waded through the crowd like a conquering hero; and as was the case with the chieftains of old, a phalanx of guards stood close to his side. While some in the audience no doubt viewed him as a criminal pariah, most were not only willing to turn a blind eye to his reputation, but were eager to embrace him for his service in the war and for his generous and ardent support of the local Irish community. Most of all, he was seen as a neighborhood boy who made good, not an easy accomplishment given the climate of the times and the prevailing attitudes of established society.

After greeting the families and various dignitaries at the base of the stairs, he flashed a luminous smile while stepping atop a box of schoolbooks and addressing the crowd, "It's a terrible loss your friends have endured. Their loved ones were all fine lads, who will be sorely missed. But tonight's gathering is a great tribute not only to the boys and their families, but also to you, their neighbors. It shows the goodness and loyalty, not just of the sons and daughters of Erin, but of all the hard-working men and women who live along these streets and labor among the nearby docks and factories." Holding up a thick wad of bills, he shouted, "In support of your noble efforts, I'll be matching every penny raised here tonight!"

As families engulfed him and politicians scrambled to grab his hand, wild applause and shouts of "Finger's our boy," and "Carnahan for Mayor," filled the air. Escaping from the cascade of hugs, and waving off the cries of support, he proclaimed, "No, no, it won't be me, but soon enough, one of us is going to be sitting up there in City Hall!" Once more, the room erupted in cheers before he began to pay his respects to the family survivors.

No sooner had he stopped to speak with Father Morris and the event organizers, than he spotted Danny standing with Keena in the middle of the crowd. After taking time to press the flesh and exchange small talk, he cut a path through the throng in Danny's direction. Upon arriving, he was quick to offer greetings to Keena before excusing himself and taking the detective off to the side. "They tell me you just delivered a beating to Doc Foley."

"I told ya before, Major, it has nothin' to do with you."

"Don't worry, I sacked him and his brother the other day. They've been working on the side against my orders and besides, my spies tell me they could be planning to make a move against me. But most of all, I heard some rumors that they may have been involved in framing Georgie."

"They fished Digger Foley outta the canal today."

Suddenly a cold, brutal look descended on his face as he sneered, "Something tells me he was stabbed, and something tells me the police better come up with answers before all hell breaks loose."

"The law's the law and it's my case, so there won't be anybody goin' off on their own, Major. You know that's how it works with me. Do I make myself clear?"

"I'll hold off; but the clock's ticking, Sergeant."

"I get things done, Major; maybe it's the luck of the Irish, like with you. You're lookin' all fit after getting shot."

"I've received loving care, which reminds me, Sergeant, thank you for maintaining your discretion regarding Missus Prescott's presence at my home that morning."

"I don't make judgments and I don't talk, Major."

"Since you've been so forthright in respecting my confidence, I want to share some things with you. I know what people think, Sergeant, but I can assure you, Missus Prescott is of the highest repute. She is a lovely, intelligent woman with a good heart; a person with a good heart who has been too long exposed to the biases of her class, but who now sees the light. She has long suffered the emotional abandonment and physical abuse of her husband. She's finally had enough, yet her reward is desertion by not only her friends but even her family. She's changed me; helped me to see things in a different light. I'm even moving up plans to get out of the, let's say, less savory side of my business interests, and concentrate on my more traditional commercial enterprises. It's the least I can do after seeing her sacrifice; such as having her name smeared by so-called proper society, especially that no-good husband of hers!" Unable to contain his mounting anger, he boiled over, "Believe me, I'm not done with that piece of shit yet!" Suddenly catching himself, he added in a more measured tone, "Well, you won't be butting heads with me any longer, Danny. My longtime associates, Bones Murphy and Roscoe Walton will be buying me out."

Now anxious to be on his way, Fingers quickly bid his adieus before gathering his men and heading for the door; however, given his popularity among those in attendance, his exit proved much slower than expected.

Already feeling the effects of his showdown with Foley, Danny was quick to follow suit. Yet after paying his respects to Father Pat and the others, he was surprised when Keena asked if he would walk her home.

After weaving a serpentine path through the crowd, they finally made their way through the doors, now flung open in response to the sweltering heat downstairs. Once outside, they saw Finger's carriage parked alongside the curb. Despite the side curtains being fully drawn, Danny was able to make out Rebecca Prescott casting a nervous glance through the edge of the window. Judging from the look on her face, she was anxious for Carnahan's return. It was also obvious, as she clung to the side of the housekeeper, Madame Woo, that the working-class world outside the carriage doors was as alien to her as another planet.

As they left the fading strains of a jig in their wake, they turned down Louisiana Street in the direction of Blinky's tavern. Feeling rejuvenated by the crisp air, Keena turned and smiled, "You know, Danny, after all these years, I'm starting to feel that I know who you really are."

"So ya say?" he asked with a curious look etched across his face, before adding, "I don't believe I'm much of a puzzle. I just do my work, enjoy a beer and try to line my pockets with some money."

"Did you forget the whores?"

"I still got a bit of a gentleman in me, but since you're not pussyfootin' around, I'll just say that a man sometimes got his urges, you know."

"Please, I hear that all the time at the bar. But I don't think it's as simple as that with you, Danny. It seems to me that you were once a one-woman man, filled with love for his family."

"That was a long time ago, Keena."

"Even after your unspeakable loss and pain, that kind of a heart is always there; even if it's hidden. Like when you wouldn't shoot at the strikers in seventy-seven, or when you protect people or fight for victim's justice. The courage that you show in doing what you think is right, well, a fella doesn't put himself on the line like that just for the money."

"I don't think high falutin' thoughts when I'm just doing my job. I ain't looking for anything special. The sun rises the next day no matter what."

"But there's great meaning in what you do. Despite your being so calloused over with hurt, you can find great joy in life again. You're a good and courageous man, Danny. I'd like to see you remind yourself of that."

"Thank you, girl," he said, moved by her kindness. "I've seen a lot lately, and while I don't go blatherin' on about my feelings, I give weight to your words, because you're a fine woman, Keena. I know I tease you about your radical ways and all, but I admire your strength and your wanting to help others."

"That means a lot to me, Danny," she smiled as she placed her hand upon his cheek.

Long unaccustomed to such a tender gesture, he returned an awkward smile; and for the first time in ages, he could feel himself opening up.

Resuming their trek, they kept up a lively banter, while at the same time enjoying the beauty of the clear, still night. Bathed in the glow of a radiant moon, the surrounding landscape took on a snug, charming air as hundreds of little cottages, locked tight for the night, released shimmering ribbons of smoke into the crystalline sky.

In the midst of picking their way across the muddy ruts of O'Connell Street, Keena stopped and asked, "Isn't this where you have your place?"

"Yeah, two doors down on the right."

"Ah, a white picket fence. Now, I can see I was right about you."

"It ain't much, but I take pride in it."

Walking towards the little cottage, she spun around with a sly grin creeping across her face, "Aren't you going to ask me in?"

"Ah ... I'd love to, assumin' ya think it's proper," he stumbled, surprised at her question.

"Proper, ah, malarkey; I'm my own woman, Danny. I'm confident in what I do and don't care what others say."

Taking her by the hand, Danny led her inside, where, after fumbling with the lamp, he welcomed her into a neat and well-appointed setting that was much at odds with his rough-hewn image. Anxious to make her comfortable, he walked her to the parlor, where he wasted no time in preparing the fireplace; and after grabbing glasses and a long neglected bottle of wine from a nearby cabinet, he joined her as she settled onto the carpet facing the fire.

At first, they sat back, enjoying the wine and warming themselves in front of the blazing hearth. Yet after sharing some light-hearted moments, their talk soon took on a more intimate tone. Not long afterwards, they set off on a rapturous journey of making love. It was the first time in many years that Brick Fist Doyle felt the sublime joy of true emotion.

XXII

As Danny crossed Franklin Street, once the site of the town's surrender to the British in eighteen thirteen, he was dwarfed by the looming presence of City Hall. Dominating the downtown skyline, its soaring, Gothic clock tower was topped by a quartet of statues representing, Justice, Agriculture, Manufacturing and Commerce. Fittingly, the building's western façade looked out towards Lake Erie, the source and lynchpin of the city's success. Recently constructed of granite cleaved from the quarries of coastal Maine, its fortress-like walls housed a myriad of offices that served a population that had exploded twofold over the last twenty years. This phenomenal growth was in no small part fueled by the ever-increasing labor demands of the economic juggernaut that was Buffalo. For its citizens, City Hall was a proud symbol of Buffalo's emergence as a commercial powerhouse, and its status as one of the country's premier cities. Yet in the eyes of some, if not many, it was also a monument to the spoils of the insidious political machinery of both parties.

As he made his way through the heavy bronze doors and into the ornate lobby, he marveled at a landscape of gleaming marble and brass. The centerpiece of this rich tableau was a massive staircase and matching balustrade that wound its way up to the second floor. Scanning the terrain, he was quick to spy the object of his search standing before the tobacco stall near the base of the stairs. Anxious to confront his longtime nemesis, Danny had discovered that Captain Collins was scheduled to meet with party officials in the office of the police commissioner later that morning. Collins was to report on his precinct's crime-fighting efforts relative to the harborside business community; however, the main purpose of the meeting was to discuss the level of campaign contributions and ward heeling activities of the men under his command.

At the moment, the police captain was embroiled in a heated argument with a charwoman who was in the process of mopping up the muck tracked in from outside. Hoping to surprise his prey before he could make his escape, Danny edged his way close to the action. With Collins showing no signs of knowing his approach, the detective was able to catch wind of the quarrel.

"Your family, especially your two brothers under my command, feeds quite well from the public trough. So they better pony up if they know what's good for 'em, and that goes for you too, sister!"

"I do good work and I always get out the vote for the party, just like Eddie and Dave do; but I can't be payin' up when I got me little ones and with me husband not findin' work."

The sight of Danny hovering over Collins' shoulder gave pause to Missus Cleary's spirited defense. Taking note of her reaction, Collins turned to observe what was happening behind him. When confronted with the detective's presence, he moved quickly to dismiss the woman, but not before issuing one last charge, "And remember, no more warnings. My patience is wearing thin!" Upon refocusing his attention on Danny, he made no effort to hide his displeasure. "Don't go sneaking up on me like that, Doyle! I won't have you intruding on my private conversations; understand! But more importantly, what are you doing here? You're supposed to be out on the street."

Biting his tongue, Danny was intent to placate his boss in an effort to bide his time. "Sorry, Captain, I didn't want to interrupt your important business," Danny smiled, hoping to yank Collins' tail before continuing.

"But I wanted to fill you in on what's been happening, in case you thought the Commissioner should know."

"It better be good, Sergeant. My time is valuable. I have to meet with important people here," he snapped back with an unmistakably caustic edge.

After waiting for a bevy of political supplicants to pass by, the detective affected a subservient tone as he continued to play with his prey, "Of course, sir."

"Well, get with it, man, and quit your dithering!"

Calling upon every ounce of his self-restraint, Danny squeezed out the words, "Of course sir, but some of it is quite sensitive, so maybe we could just go over to that little room next to the stairs."

Although angered by this untimely intrusion, and anxious to get on with his business, Collins reluctantly complied. Still chaffing as he followed Danny to where the cleaning staff stored their supplies, he was fully prepared to deliver a dressing-down if Doyle proved to be wasting his time. Once inside, after assuming his usual condescending air, he announced, "This better be about solving those factory thefts. And I won't be hearing any more nonsense about the Van Cleff murder. It's closed, and you'll be staying out of it!"

"Oh, that's too bad, Paddy, 'cause I'm gonna be doin' that and other things that I don't think you'll fancy."

Seconds passed as Collins' porcelain features blossomed into a teeming firestorm of red. Finally, unable to contain his anger, he exploded, "I'm finished with your impudence! This time you're..." Having been grabbed by the throat and slammed against the wall, Collins was unable to finish his sentence. Instead, he stared out in apoplectic shock as he was raised up to within inches of Brick Fist's seething face.

"No, this time you're finished, boyo," Danny screamed, sending a plume of spittle into his bosses' face.

With the indignation of his little shower being the least of his worries, the little man tried his best to mouth out the words, "You're fired."

Taking his free hand and squeezing his captive's mouth, Danny calmly asked, "Whadya say? Did I hear ya say, I'm fired?" Casting a quizzical look towards his gasping prey, he asked, "How can that be? You ain't me boss no more, with you resignin' and all."

As Collins stared back incredulously, the detective pressed on, "I bet you're wonderin' how I know this. Maybe you're thinkin' I'm like that English Swami down in the District, foretellin' the future and all. But that ain't it. Ya see, I found out some real bad things about ya, Captain."

By now, the look on Collins' face had turned from shock to sheer panic. Taking stock of the situation, Brick Fist drew back, "Jesus, there ya go turnin' blue on me. Now I'm gonna let ya down, but no misbehavin'."

Collins was quick to nod his assent, but no sooner had Danny eased his grip than the Captain let out an abortive cry for help, its feeble resonance no doubt affected by the now shaky condition of his throat.

In an instant, Danny let fly a slap that sent his bosses' spectacles spinning, while his body went crashing down. After slamming his knee into his back and pushing his face onto the rough grain of the wooden floor, Danny leaned down and whispered, "Ah, the shame; not quite a man of your word, are ya. Well, I'd suggest ya not try that again, unless ya want your face used as a rasp on this here floor!"

As his captive mumbled out some barely decipherable words of affirmation, Danny resumed his treatise, "As I was just sayin', I've come upon some incriminatin' evidence like a signed order from you, directin' coppers to go around makin' sure that the doors at the Prescott plant were locked from the outside. There's also a letter from you to Prescott, sayin' you'll take care of safety inspection problems. And then there's a fella at the Inspections Department, who'll testify that you were the go-between for bribin' inspectors to look the other way at the factory. Finally one of the firemen at the steamer house says ya took away the locked door I found at the scene of the fire. It never showed up at the inquest. This all ain't good, Paddy."

Spitting out the words as best he could with his face pressed tight against the floor, Collins countered, "They'll never let you get away with it."

"If ya mean your bosses upstairs, I wouldn't count on it. They'll all be scrambling for cover once the newspapers get hold of this. Most of all, the good folks out there, who were heartbroken over what happened, will be screamin' for justice; and I'm sure Big Steve Cleveland and the Democrats will be leadin' the charge."

"Think of yourself, Doyle. You're as dirty as anyone."

"I'm no good, alright, but I haven't forgot where I came from, or my people. Sure I take money for leanin' on gamblers or protectin' whorehouses and such, but I still look out for the little fellas who got nothin' but what passes as the law protectin' 'em. Corrupt owners like Prescott got their money protectin' 'em, but they still want more, usin' what they got to wring out what they can from those poor souls toilin' under 'em. Still, they couldn't pull it off without traitors like you doin' their dirty work and helpin' keep their heels on the necks of little folk. You then go fightin' for the scraps they throw out there. You wanna join the likes of Prescott but they wouldn't piss on ya. They wouldn't give a shit if you or yours lives or dies, any more than they care about that dead mule lyin' out on the street when I came in here."

"Ya sure like money greasing your palms," Collins argued.

"For years, I've been thinkin' money could give me control over things, but that's like one of them mirages. Look where it got you; and Prescott's gonna find out soon enough."

Ain't you a Saint; and mind you, your brother officers will be finished with you for ratting on your own."

"Christ, they hate you a lot more than they hate me. But I know better than to try an' appeal to your better angels; and I ain't floatin' on some pipe dream. Bigwig bastards like Prescott usually win, but sometimes even a squirt can pull off a fight; like this time. So I'll spell it out for ya. I got the goods on you, Paddy, so I'll be takin' it to my friends at the prosecutor's. I'll be goin' to the newspapers too, just to make sure everything's on the up 'n up. Now, like I said before, you're on your own on this. You'll be needin' a big gun, expensive lawyer, but I betcha you'll be headin' off to jail anyway. I don't think you'll be likin' that, with all them fellas ya used to slap around when they were all manacled up, wantin' to say hello when ya arrive at the gates. But ya might just avoid that if ya listen to what I say."

Finally confronting the harsh reality of his circumstances, Collin's arrogance and institutionally protected bravado were stripped away. In their place, a frightened little man began to emerge. "Oh, but it wasn't my intent, Sergeant. Prescott made it clear it was my job to protect business, and all the other city and party leaders let it be known, business came first. I don't deserve blame, Daniel."

Grabbing his face and twisting it in his direction, Brick Fist snarled, "That's horse shit, Collins. You were takin' big money and you liked bein' on the top of the heap, lordin' over your neighbors strugglin' in the muck; not to mention pushin' around workers. So shut your gob and just do what I say if ya wanna keep your ass outta prison. I got bigger fish to fry than you. So, if ya help with Prescott, I think I can get ya off the hook on jail. But first, we're gonna sit here and you're gonna tell me all ya know."

"But I'm expected upstairs."

"What do you care? You'll be resignin' today, so that ya can wile away your retirement years without worryin' about havin' cocks shoved up your ass in jail; even though ya so dearly deserve it!" As Collins let out a little whimper, the detective refused to pull back, "Now little man, what happened with the door?"

"It's sitting at the bottom of the Commercial slip."

"Just as I figured, dunked."

After Danny lifted him up by the collar, and allowed the now-sobbing Collins to dust off his once-pristine uniform, the pair spent the better part of an hour going over the details of efforts to seal the plant and circumvent safety inspections. In addition, the police captain went on to describe tactics used to harass workers, and provide incriminating information on payoffs used to secure the coroner's exoneration of Prescott.

As the ashen-faced Collins sat shaking, while reflecting on his professional demise, Brick Fist issued a last set of orders. "You'll be givin' no reason for why ya resigned, and if ya try to cut a deal to save your skin or if ya start talkin' to anybody about what's goin' on, well, let's just say you'll be hopin' to go to jail, rather than dealin' with me. You know what I can do, so I ain't gotta say no more."

Collins merely nodded his head while staring down at the floor. With that, Danny rose up and opened the door, "You're free to go; but one more thing, I want ya to take a couple of those ill-gotten dollars in your pocket and give 'em to that charwoman you were leanin' on earlier. That way, she can keep them fine party bosses of yours off her hard workin' ass."

As he watched the former police power dutifully follow his orders, he was reminded of how easily bullies cave in when called to task. Ever disdainful of his former boss, Danny always took pride in his ability to handle the man and ignore his commands. Yet he wondered as to why victims of the likes of Collins were reluctant to take them on; even in the face of their own abuse. Turning on his heels, he simply ascribed it to a frustrating lack of guts.

Satisfied that he had taken care of Collins and secured the information he was seeking, Danny glided out the door and into the crisp winter air. No sooner had he stepped onto the granite stairs leading to the street, than he spotted the pair of street urchins tending to their dogcart filled with cans of ashes. As he looked closer, he was able to see that they were engaged in a heated squabble with a much bigger boy. Recognizing the older youth as a member of the Rat Kickers street gang, he took but an instant to assess the nature of the situation. Rushing over, he put a quick end to the shakedown with a punch to the face and a warning to stay away from the children.

After handing the tow-headed brothers a couple of bits, he headed back to the precinct, but as he walked along the wind-swept street, he was reminded that the poor and vulnerable always needed help as they struggled with the unrelenting toils of their lives.

XXIII

"Get that disease-spewin' beast outta my face before I send it flyin'."

"Beggin' your pardon, Danny. It seems he likes ya and just wants to lick your face," the little man beamed as he cradled his terrier outside the doors of the Packet Stop Saloon. Having just emerged from the basement rat pit of the notorious gin mill, Bobby Porter was awash with happiness over the evening's success. Joe, his pride and joy and principal source of income, had just set the house record for dispatching fifteen wharf rats in the span of three minutes; nonetheless, the joy of counting his winnings and accepting the accolades of his fellow patrons proved short lived.

"Fuckin' lickin' me face! I'd rather have a pig's arse rubbed on me snout," the detective bellowed before calming down. "And as long as I got ya here, I'm gonna check. So put down the mangy creature and open your coat." After shaking his jacket and patting down his pockets, Brick Fist cast a quick nod of approval before adding, "Glad to see you're behavin', Bobby."

Not that that had always been the case. Long a pickpocket and petty thief, Porter finally met his Waterloo when Danny caught him supplying vials of laudanum to the knockout artists who prowled the dives in search of hapless victims. After a memorable beating, and in return for a reduced sentence, Bobby became a reasonably law-abiding snitch and reliable source of information on street crime.

"No more trouble from me, Sergeant. Now would ya like to join me and me friend here, Pete Kenny, for a victory drink celebratin' Joe's championship."

"Kenny? Kenny?"

"You musta heard of Pete. He helps me train Joe. He cages the best damn rats in the city; right outta the grain elevators, big as ponies!"

"Interestin' line of work," Danny mused before adding. "But catchin' rats can't be the only thing ya do?"

"I'm a foundry man by day."

"And which one would that be, Pete?"

"Brown and McCutcheon's down on Ohio Street."

Remembering the remarks of the freight dispatcher, Dwyer, regarding an Ohio Street foundry worker named Kenny or Kennedy who helped with the theft ring, he turned to Porter and said, "Thanks for the offer of a drink, Bobby, but I got other plans. Still, if you'd excuse me, I'd like to have a private word with Pete." Wasting no time, he grabbed the red-haired stranger by the arm and led him to an adjacent alley. "What's this I hear about you bein' part of that ring stealing from the factories and other businesses around these parts," Danny barked.

"I... ah... don't know what you're—"

"Quit your lyin'," Brick Fist snapped. Ya been seen down at Madison Freight pickin' up the wagons for haulin' the loot. "Ya know about the beatin' and jail time Bobby's got, so start talkin'."

"But they'll kill me; even with me bein' their cousin."

"Ah, so you're kin of the Foleys; but don't worry, I'll be takin' care of them. They're finished, so it's me ya better worry about."

"I suppose ya can whip me good, but I ain't goin' to no jail. I trap rats to support me wife and kids, so I didn't have no problem stealin' from those rich bastards who pay us shit."

Confronting Kenny's motive and show of grit, Danny suddenly viewed him in a different light. He was forced to ask himself if he'd act any differently if faced with similar circumstances. Consequently, he adopted a more tempered tone before replying, "There's other ways to skin a cat when it comes to money, man; but don't be frettin' jail. Just tell me who's involved."

"A bunch of the family and Doc's usual pals."

"And who's callin' the shots with Doc. We both know he ain't smart enough to pull it off on his own."

"I know Doc works for Fingers and I know he's got an insider at one of them big companies like Jewett or Prescott or such; but I can't say for sure who else is callin' the shots."

"This insider fella, he got a name?"

"No idea who he is but he must cover his tracks good. Only one fella I know saw 'im, and he only saw his back."

"Okay, Kenny, ya can go back to your rat pit, but remember, I'm playin' nice with ya now; so don't go screwin' me or shootin' off your gob."

"Please, Sergeant, I got enough on me hands takin' care of me family. No more problems, I promise."

With Kenny's release, Danny headed up the street to his destination, the Covent Gardens. As the most notorious, if not most popular concert saloon in the city, it had little in common with the famous English theater from which it took its name. The scene of boisterous musical shows of uneven quality at best, including a particularly ribald version of that scandalous French import known as the Cancan, the Garden hosted a riotous blend of dancing, drinking and all forms of debauchery. Sitting in the heart of the canal district, it was the destination of choice for those unbound by the rules of propriety.

While no self-respecting woman would be caught dead in the place, there were no such qualms on the part of the countless women of easy virtue who plied the streets of the District. Although many were in search of a good time or money, more often than not, these ladies of the street were the exploited victims of abandonment, duress or sheer desperation. For the most part, they sprang from the ranks of orphans or unsuspecting girls from the country and recent arrivals to this country's shores. On the other hand, all classes and stripes of men eagerly passed through its doors. In fact, on any given night, no small sampling of the city's elite mingled among its teeming crowds. The fashionable cut of their clothes quickly set them apart; along with a cordon of bodyguards, whose brooding presence was a persuasive catalyst for discouraging any criminal impulses on the part of the many predators lurking within the Garden's shadows.

Although musical entertainment was the springboard of the Garden's popularity, other more libertine pursuits usually took the lead in attracting customers. Yet on this occasion things were different, as tonight marked the Garden debut of a local singing sensation, Chauncey Olcott. His lilting tenor had already attracted a huge following, especially among his fellow Irish. This was in stark evidence as long lines of concertgoers filled the street.

Not one to suffer the mad crush at the box office, Danny strolled over to a side entrance where he met a long-familiar bouncer who quickly ushered him in. The smell of cigar smoke and cheap perfume hung thick in the air as he swept his way through a threadbare lobby covered with faded posters of past acts.

Passing through the mezzanine doors, he entered into a cavernous hall already awash with a sea of faces. Behind his shoulder, a rickety wooden bar stretched the width of the building, manned by a score of bartenders busily dispensing every kind of drink. Off to his left, a band of street toughs stood before a miniature theater, bellowing with laughter as the Punch and Judy puppets mercilessly swatted each other.

Ringing the sides of the hall were two tiers of boxes, crammed with well-dressed men merrily embracing all manner of depravity while entertaining their lady friends. Down on the floor, a legion of notorious "waiter girls" wound their way through the tables, not only delivering orders, but also soliciting watered-down drinks from lust-struck patrons.

By now, the working class masses were beginning to take their places along the walls and behind the tables, content to drink their nickel beers and await the arrival of young Olcott; all the time wary of the ever-present thieves.

At the center of this lively tableau stood the Garden's main stage, its garishly painted backdrop depicting an Elizabethan street scene. At the moment, a bawdy troupe of dancers were high kicking their way across the boards, bathed in the glow from a bank of lime lights. Seated in the cramped orchestra pit was a ragtag collection of musicians performing Offenbach's famous "Can-Can."

Grabbing one of the last tables at the rear of the hall, Brick Fist sat and watched the action as he waited for his partner to show-up. Despite a lifestyle steeped in brothels and saloons, tonight's visit was strictly professional. Knowing the popularity of the evening's event, he was on the lookout for some of his snitches and any of the Foleys. As such, he hoped to nail more information on the theft ring and Van Cleff murders, and if need be, bring in the Foleys for questioning; nonetheless, as he scanned the room, he was surprised to find no trace of the brothers. The hoodlums' absence was noteworthy, given that Doc was a well-known admirer of Olcott, having vainly attempted to secure the singer's services for one of his infamous gangster parties. In addition to all this, Danny was anxious to bring Costello up-to-date on all that was happening. He was just beginning to survey the upper boxes when a tap on the shoulder interrupted his thoughts.

"Sorry for being late, Danny but the crowds are amazing. Finally, your name got me through," Costello remarked as he grabbed a nearby chair.

"Don't worry, I was late too."

"Will miracles ever cease?"

"Well, the truth be told, I had a dinner engagement with a lady friend," Danny replied with an uncharacteristic youthful blush.

"That explains the fancy duds, but then what are ya doing here, Danny? Have ya gone daft, man?"

"I got some important stuff here and she understands; but just between you and me, dependin' how things go here, I'm fixin' to toss some pebbles against her window tonight," he smiled sheepishly. After pulling his seat closer, the detective began to explain, "So let's get down to business. First of all, we won't be takin' orders from that idiot Collins no more." He went on to describe the case against the former captain, relative to the Prescott fire. Just then, one of the waiter girls came sauntering over. Before she could speak, he barked, "Don't bother with the sweet talk, sister. I'll be havin' a lager and one for my mate, too."

"Please, none for me, Danny."

After sending off the girl with a look at his badge and a warning about knockout drops, he returned to Hugh, "What's that all about, lad?" Ya should have a little fun tonight."

"I'm holding off the drinking for a while. Now don't get mad, but I was drinking too much after Harpoon's shooting."

"That's all right, Hugh, but as I told ya before, ya shouldn't have no guilt. Still, you're doin' right. Drink ain't no good for balmin' feelins'. But we're gonna do good for ya by findin' the real murderers of Miss Crane and Van Cleff."

"I'd like that a lot, Danny. And when the girl comes back, I'm buying you the beer. In the meantime, I'll just occupy myself with this candy that you let me take from Miss Crane's place. Which reminds me, I got a bunch in my pocket. Here's some to take to your lady friend when you're tossin' your pebbles at her window tonight."

"Thanks, Hugh. I'm sure she'll like 'em. But I can't help lookin'at these pretty wrappings without thinkin' of that girl and how she ended up like she did, whorin' and gettin' murdered and all."

"I know, poor thing, but she was trying, Danny. And it could have been worse, other than getting killed of course. She was doing what she could to keep herself fed and clothed, and in a nice place like she had. She could have been like these poor souls, drunk or drugged; living in filthy hovels; fucking and lord knows what else all night; getting spit on and beat up. Good lord what a world!"

"No, the District ain't pretty, Hugh. We ain't nuns or do-gooders, but at least we can act on beatin's and such; and try to scare the newcomers." The detective then proceeded to report on the progress of the Van Cleff case, including his belief that Doc hit the hallway sconce at the murder scene and his discovery that Foley was carrying the jeweler's complimentary cigars the night of their fight. In addition, he described Kenny's link to the theft ring, before summing up the status of the investigation. "So, besides thinkin' I got enough to nail Prescott, I think I'm pretty close to baggin' the Foleys; but there's still some loose ends naggin' at me. I figure Van Cleff was fencin' Foleys' stolen jewelry and they had a fallin' out; but who was fencing the factory supplies? Couldn't have been the jeweler; that ain't his deal."

"Same thieves, different Fagins," Hugh suggested.

"Well put; they had to have another contact."

"And what about Fingers' possible involvement with the thefts?" Costello asked before adding, "He employed the Foleys at the time, and he certainly has contacts."

"It's possible 'cause it's money. Unlike what he says, it might not hurt his business. Maybe it could justify his protection. Ya know, a couple o' scapegoats eventually end up dead and the thievin' stops. It shows he gets the job done. In any case, there's more I wanna check out at Foley's place down at the beaches before I grill 'em."

"Still, there's no getting around the fact that they probably framed Fingers' best friend."

"I know and I agree; but I still gotta eliminate all the possibilities."

By now the waiter girl had returned with his order, along with another beer, compliments of the house. After sending her off with a generous tip, Danny began outlining plans to keep watch for the Foleys, along with going over a list of snitches to look out for tonight. Just then, he spotted Big Tits Kate approaching his table. As was always the case when out-on–the-town, she was dressed elegantly; enough so, that she could easily compete with the fashion elite of the city. Accompanied by a couple of her girls and her "assistant," "Dandy Jack" Bristol, she was quick to voice her frustration, "I finally get here and all the tables are taken. Can we join you, Danny?"

"Sure ya can, Kate; and what a pleasant surprise! So let me get ya drinks, ya seem upset."

"Can't your fellow coppers keep the streets clear? What's a business woman like me payin' taxes for?"

"It's 'cause the best of the lot, Hugh, here, and meself have the night off."

"I wish I could say the same, but while I have a great fondness for young Olcott's voice, we're here to scout out some of the young ladies for openings at the Boarding House."

"It's always all work for you, eh, Kate," Danny observed.

"You're right on that, lad; always a step ahead. There'll never be the poor house for me."

After introducing herself and her party to Costello, and engaging in some genial give-and-take with Danny, the famous madam settled into watching the rest of the spectacle onstage. As the detective occupied himself with a passing waitress who was once Mike Foley's girlfriend, Kate snatched a pad from her purse and began scribbling notes. Yet, no sooner had the dancers capped their act by raising their skirts and baring their bottoms to the wildly cheering crowd, than Kate was already pointing out perspective recruits to Dandy Jack.

In the meantime, satisfied that the waiter girl was unable to provide any useful information on the Foleys, Danny pulled the madam aside, "I've been meanin' to talk to you, Kate. What do ya know of this Crane girl who was killed with Van Cleff a few weeks back?"

"This ain't no investigation of me, is it, Danny?"

"No way, gal. I'd stake me life on that. Besides, I can't see her hurtin' your business. So what can ya tell me, Kate?"

"A lot. There's few secrets in this business. So, how did you get wind of her work?"

"I got hold of her notebook after she was killed; interestin' line of work. I wanna find out if her professional activities could be tied to her tragic death."

"Workin' on her own like that, even with her clientele and Van Cleff lookin' out for her, always has its risks. Still, I never heard of anybody bein' out to get her, or threatenin' her, or anything like that."

"Lookin' at her records, she got big money from some big names; people with a lot to lose. You hear anything about blackmail or that sorta thing?"

"No, but from what I heard, there was reason some of 'em would wanna keep a lid on things. With that, Kate gestured for one of her girls, Jewel, to move over from the end of the table. "Danny, here, is tryin' to find the killer of that Crane girl. Tell 'em what ya told me."

Looking back at Kate, who returned a reassuring nod, the young prostitute proceeded with her story. "I first met her a few months ago when my friend Goldie introduced us. Goldie was doin' some work on the side for her, which is against Missus Eagan's strict rules—"

"I don't expect my girls to rat and snitch," Kate broke in. Smiling, she went on, "So, Jewel, here, is still my top whore."

"Thank you, ma'am. Actually, that's why we're here, tryin' to find Goldie's replacement, since Missus Egan got wind of her activities a while back. Anyway, Miss Crane tried to recruit me too, but I'd have none of it, no matter how much money."

"So ya like workin' for my friend too much," Danny smiled.

"Yes ... but no," the doe-eyed brunette stumbled. "I mean, Bonnie had a few clients who wanted filthy, dirty things that I can't even say; and I ain't no convent girl. Unnatural, disgustin' things that I couldn't face people, knowin' I did 'em." she noted as she began to sob.

"That's all right, Jewel," Danny soothed. "You're a good gal tellin' me this. It helps with the case."

"It's just that I felt sorry for her then, and even more so now that she's dead and gone. I know those goody-goody citizens out there think us whores are no-good trash, but she was nice. She seemed acceptin' of her work, sayin' it was just business and that she made good money that kept her in the kinda life she always knew, like with a nice home, pretty clothes and fancy schools; but I could tell she didn't really want this way of livin'. Still, she was tough; ya know, just grit your teeth and do it. She even bragged about her fella; called 'im 'Lover Boy;' he was a real romantic, givin' her fancy candies and such."

"Do ya know 'im; and was he the fella who used to meet her down at the Iroquois Hotel for breakfast?"

"Never met 'im and don't know his name; but she said he was an up-and-comer. And yeah, she once said he'd meet her for breakfast at some hotel."

"Maybe he was the rich fella who gave her the gold necklace with the inscription, 'your devoted slave'?"

"Oh, no, that wasn't 'im. I heard of that one. He was the worst and most disgustin' of the lot. She called him 'Dirt'."

"Oh yeah, I saw the name, 'Dirt' in her book; and there was another name right next to it."

"We don't discuss names in our business, Danny," Kate interrupted.

"Even when it involves a whore's murder?"

"All right, Danny. You're my friend and I trust ya, if ya say it's important."

"Like I was sayin', could it be Lawrence Lee?"

Suddenly, the serious discussion was punctured by howls of laughter on the part of the two women. "Oh, Danny," Big Tits exclaimed as she began to regain her composure. "Ya don't know him, do ya, lad. He's been a lovely patron of my place for years now."

"Limpy Larry," Jewel added, "he's a sweet, befuddled old gent. He comes in once a week and sits and watches one of us carry on, touchin' ourselves. He's harmless; comes and goes without a problem, and leaves a nice stack of coins on the dresser. Nobody would call him Dirt."

"Scratch off his name," the detective chuckled. "But before ya get back to your work," he noted as he pulled out a pad from his pocket, "could ya take a look at this list of upstanding citizens, I got here? I know you fine professionals will respect their privacy even though they don't deserve to hide in the shadows doin' their nasty deeds. Just the same, I'd appreciate it if ya would tell me if any of 'em may have been in your place and had problems with the girls or if one of 'em could be this mysterious 'Dirt' fella?"

The two women slowly went over the list, every so often raising their eyebrows in a look of surprise, before handing it back with a shake of their heads.

After asking that they contact him if anything came up, the detective shared a few minutes making small talk and finishing his drink. As Danny and his partner began to say their good-byes before getting up to mingle within the crowd, Kate grabbed her purse, but as she was about to slip him an envelope, he waved her off.

Nodding towards Hugh, who was several feet ahead, she whispered, "He won't know."

"But I'll know that he don't know," Danny answered with an ironic smile. "Things are changin' for me, Kate, but I'll always look out for ya, darlin' gal."

By now, the house manager, dressed in a patchwork tailcoat, had strolled onto the stage. Brandishing a megaphone half his size, he began to introduce the night's star attraction.

As Costello circled the periphery of the audience, searching for a prominent snitch, Danny headed towards the crowd at the bar. Yet upon reaching the balcony pillars, he turned back and watched as Chauncey Olcott strode out to the deafening cheers of his adoring fans.

Dressed in the garb of an Irish country squire, the handsome young tenor cut an imposing figure. After thanking the crowd and proclaiming his joy at being back in Buffalo, he launched into a classic Irish ballad, *The Last Rose of Summer*.

It was his wife's favorite song, and it stopped Danny dead in his tracks. Suddenly, those beautiful yet painful memories came rushing through his heart like a torrent; and as he listened to the words of the closing lyrics, he could barely hold his form.

> *"When true hearts lie withered*
> *And fond ones are flown,*
> *Oh, who would inhibit*
> *This bleak world alone,"*

The thunder of applause echoing throughout the hall woke him from his thoughts. Shaking off his melancholy, he reminded himself that he had a job to do and resumed his trek.

Despite making the rounds and buttonholing a couple of reliable sources, Danny was frustrated over his failure to glean any useful information; especially as to the whereabouts of the Foleys. After catching up with Costello, who reported a similar lack of success, the detective decided to call it a night. No doubt, much of this willingness to leave stemmed from an anxious desire to rendezvous with Keena. Still, as Olcott left the stage for a brief intermission, Danny took time to go over his investigative plans with his partner. "Tomorrow, I'm gonna track down the Foleys and bring 'em in for a grillin'. They're a slippery lot. so, it will take some time. At some point I'll be checking their place down at the Beaches. There's probably some last pieces of the puzzle down there. If I need your help in bringin' 'em in, or whatever, I'll send for ya, using one of my squad of street urchins to run a note over to the precinct. So, check back there when you're on your rounds.

Now, I got a hunch about who's Foley's partner in the theft ring. So, while I'm lookin' for Doc, I want ya to pay a visit to Dwyer over at the freight haulers. That dumb bog hopper doesn't know anybody. So, I want ya to take that picture from behind Blinky's bar; ya know, the one showing all us micks at the Hibernian picnic last summer. See if Dwyer can identify the fella he saw with Foley that night at the haulers. If Blinky gives ya a hard time about the picture, tell 'im it's for me and I'll explain why later on.

When we get that all taken care of, I'm gonna stop over at Prescott's and confront 'im on the fire. I want that no-good son of a bitch most of all. And one more thing, I don't want ya tellin' your ma where ya been tonight. I know that woman and she'll be comin' after me with a rollin' pin if she thinks I've been corruptin' her boy. Now, ya got all that, lad?"

"Sure do, Sergeant, especially about my mother," the young officer smiled.

"You're a good friend and partner, Hugh. God bless ya, lad. Jesus! God bless ya? Did ya hear that? Ya must be rubbin' off on me!"

"I'll take that as a wonderful compliment, Danny; but I think it's much more of you rubbing off on me. You're a great copper and a good fella, Sergeant." He was about to add how proud he was in seeing him reject Big Tit's envelope, but he quickly thought the better.

"Ah, the blarney's in your blood, son," the detective laughed as he slapped the youngster on the back. Yet, as they made their way towards the exit, Danny took one last scan of the private boxes along the wall. Suddenly, his eyes turned cold as steel and his hands curled into rock-hard fists, as his gaze settled onto an upper corner. "Oh, no you don't," Danny shouted as he barreled his way towards the entrance to the boxes.

Startled, Hugh looked up and saw Alfred Prescott seated behind his companion, slowly loosening the ribbon around her hair. Although dressed in the tawdry attire of a streetwalker, the girl was no more than eleven or twelve years old. Spitting out an expletive, Costello took off in Danny's wake.

Tossing an attendant aside, the detective flew through the door to the boxes. With Hugh following behind, he flashed his badge to the stunned doorman. Once inside, Brick Fist ran up against a cohort of guards standing before an empty staircase. Led by "Pig Eye" Muldoon, once the most famous brawler on the docks, they weren't about to let anyone through. Yet, in an instant, Danny had Pig Eye by the throat, with his Colt pressed firmly against the sentry's cheek. "Tell your boys to bring down the girl," Doyle growled.

With his eyes filled with fear and rage, the hoodlum somehow managed to express his consent through clenched teeth.

As his captive's henchman reluctantly mounted the stairs, Danny shouted, "Don't test me, boyo; and tell Prescott if there's any funny business or if ya come back empty-handed, I'll be goin' up, and ya know what that means."

A moment of uneasy silence prevailed until the sound of rushing footsteps announced the girl's arrival. Seething, the chastised thug growled as he pushed the girl forward, "He told me to tell ya he won't be forgettin' this."

"And neither will I," Brick Fist hissed as he grabbed the girl and headed to the door. Yet with his partner covering his back and after taking a few steps forward, the detective turned and pointed in the gangsters' direction, "And if I ever find this child on the street again, I'll be fixin' blame on all of ya."

As a cascade of applause proclaimed the resumption of Olcott's show, the little party cut a quick path to the exit. Once outside, as Doyle stooped down to speak to the girl, he detected the unmistakable odor of alcohol. "What's your name young lady, "he gently asked.

Appearing to take a moment to digest his word, she replied in slurred and broken English, "Chrish… Christina, Christina Rolish…

Rolinski."

As Danny looked up in his direction, Hugh suggested, "Must be one of those Polacks or Hunkies, not long off the boat. A bunch of them live on the east side, down by the rail yards not far from Germantown."

"Where's your ma and pa or other kin?" Danny asked while looking into her big blue eyes, now dilated and dancing.

"Dead," she softly cried, as her eyes began to well.

"But where do ya live?" He softly reached out, his heart breaking. Once again she appeared to hesitate before he added, "House, eat, sleep?"

"Mishsus Carter... Cable Streesh," she stumbled. "Ma worked there... died."

"Who gave you the drink?" he asked while pantomiming the sipping of a cup.

"Missus Carter... and man back there," she sniffled, with an empty, disassociated look locked upon her face.

"Christina, I'm a policeman," Danny whispered, while showing her his badge and trying to control the catch in his voice. Patting her blond curly tresses, he promised, "I'm taking ya to a safe place, little one."

Turning to Costello, he announced, "I'm taking her to the convent at Saint Bridget's, and I want you to find that Carter woman on Cable Street. I'm trustin' you'll have a little talk."

"Don't worry, Danny. I know what to do. This is never going to happen again!"

XXIV

The gentle touch of a kiss settling upon his lips finally stirred him from his sleep. Opening his eyes, he reveled in the sight of Keena's face bathed in the glow of moonlight streaming through the lace curtains.

As he slowly began to caress her body, they shared a look of contentment, reflecting the happiness of a couple fresh from having made love. And for the moment, neither one seemed willing to break the spell of gazing into each other's eyes.

Finally, after tenderly pushing back a wayward lock that had slipped onto his brow, she whispered, "I tried not to wake you, but I had to kiss that beautiful mouth. For a big, tough fella such as yourself, you were looking as sweet as a baby in blissful sleep."

"I feel blissful being with you, Keena, and I'm glad you woke me, 'cause I can keep looking at your lovely face and feeling your spirited soul."

"Such a good and handsome lad; and now I'm finding out he's a poet to boot," she giggled before adding in a serious tone, "I feel so good with you, Danny."

Wrapping his arms around her, he confessed, "You moved me the first time I laid eyes on ya, sweet girl. It's like I'm living a dream."

Gently rolling on top of him, she breathed into his ear, "It's my dream, too." With her ample bosom pressing down upon his chest, she smiled, "I don't know how much more I can take, but I want to find out." Yet as he made a move to resume their coupling, she playfully scolded, "But not now, sweet boy! I'm dying to stay here all day, but its four o'clock and my da will be getting up, downstairs."

Despite wishing to further savor feelings that had laid dormant for so many years, he understood the awkward nature of their circumstances. "I suppose you're right. We nearly caught it earlier. I was a wee bit anxious; nearly blastin' a hole in the wall with my pebbles."

"It was a close call. Still, my heart leapt when I heard it," she answered with a mischievous grin.

"I thought I was gonna catch a load of your da's buckshot when I saw that lantern light up. Still, I figured it would've been worth it if I did."

"Well, if we don't want to be plucking pellets from that handsome bottom of yours, we better get moving," she sighed before tousling his hair and planting a warm kiss on his lips. After peeling off the covers, she stepped off to the side of the bed, exposing the full extent of her sumptuous body; and as she brushed back her thick mop of untamed hair, now freed from the constraints of a French bun, she cut an unassuming yet wanton pose.

This didn't escape the attention of her lover, who made one last attempt to reel her back. Instead, she delivered a no-nonsense reply, "You can stay here and deal with da, but I'm off to the Elk Street Market to buy provisions for the tavern. I got my haggling plan all set." With that, she lit a nearby lamp, and after shooting him a quick wink, headed to the washbasin on top of her dresser.

Recognizing the inevitable, he got up and stoked the stove before slipping into his trousers. He then joined Keena at the sink where he helped her with her robe, relishing its sweet scent as he did so. It had been a long time since he had experienced such feminine touches, whether it was the fancy doilies, floral quilts or fragrant linens; and for whatever reason, he felt compelled to drink it in.

He returned to the moment as he felt her snuggle up in his arms.

"Thank you for the flowers last night," she whispered while gazing at the nearby vase. "They're so pretty."

"I'll buy you enough to fill this room."

"You don't have to buy me anything. This is what's important, Danny."

"So I'm learning, darlin' girl. Over the years, I'd come to think that you had to take all you could get, in order to keep safe all that ya love. Well, all the money in the world can't guarantee you anything, and it sure can corrupt. But most of all, it can't buy you what we had this night."

"Not only are you strong and handsome, but you're becoming a wise man, Danny." As she felt his arms wrap more tightly around her, she whispered, "So what's my brave centurion going to do today?"

"I'm bringing in the Foleys on the Van Cleff murders."

"The dirty dogs, it's about time."

"And then I'm gonna crack the case on the fire."

In an instant, she shot straight up and spun around. "Sweet Mother Mary!"

Ignoring the looming specter of Blinky Shea, Danny went on to describe his theory on the circumstances behind the tragedy and the testimony he gathered from the likes of young Hannon, Collins, Toohey and Keogh, the City Hall insider. He then proceeded to go over details of the evidence, such as the locked door pulled from the smoking ruins, before finally announcing, "So I'm going right after Prescott and damn the torpedoes."

Stunned, yet heartened by his revelations, she cradled his face and whispered, "You're doing God's work in bringing justice to those poor souls; and it will surely bring some peace to their suffering families."

For once, he felt no need to dismiss her religious beliefs. On the contrary, he was anxious to help fulfill her faith; nonetheless, he was quick to advise caution, "But you can't go tellin' 'em anything; not until I book the dirty villains and even then, no mention of the inside stuff I told ya."

"You know you have my word, Danny. Prescott's arrest' will be music to our ears; oh, my darling Kitty and the boys! You know, after I get back from the market, I'll be driving her out to Holy Cross, where they'll be dedicating a monument to the victims. Our kind and generous Mister Prescott donated it, and he's making a big to-do about it. I was out there last week, praying with Kitty, when I saw the inscription. I can't forget its words, 'In memory of the faithful employees who in performance of their honest labor fell victim to the fire which destroyed their factory.' It stuck in my craw; making like they had some stake in the company; like they weren't just kindling used to fire the company's moneymaking engine; like they weren't little boy victims of Prescott's greed. If it weren't for Kitty, I would've spit on that cold, heartless slab of rock.

"It'll be a tough road ahead, but Prescott will be bustin' rocks, if I have me way!"

Fighting back tears as she embraced him, Keena cried, "I'm so proud of you, my good man."

By now, the rumblings of movement downstairs forced the couple to hurry their parting. Although already yearning for the next chance to see her, Danny threw on the rest of his clothes, and after lingering over a passionate kiss, deftly sneaked down the back stairs, just in time to avoid meeting Blinky as he emerged from the lower apartment. Quickly putting distance between himself and the tavern keeper, he made his way through the dark streets and towards the still-slumbering Infected District.

Fortified by a hearty breakfast at a boarding-house tavern along the river, Danny began searching the usual haunts of the Foleys; however, whether it be the opium dens on Fly Street, the nickel flop they owned near the wharves, or the little house off Fulton that Doc shared with his girlfriend, the notorious Queenie Pike, the detective met frustration at every turn. Despite threats, bribes or friendly cajoling, none of his snitches or other sources had any clues as to the gangster's whereabouts. Finally, after hours of beating the bushes, Danny decided to push on to the brothers' longtime lair in the Beaches. It was there that he found the youngest brother, Emmon, before their fateful chase last fall.

After hiking across the narrow strip of that made up the Beaches, he came upon the sweet smell of flour wafting from the nearby National Mill. Otherwise, it was a forlorn scene, with makeshift cottages shuttered tight against the relentless winds that swept across the lake. As he marched along the frozen path, all appeared quiet, as most of the squatters had taken their dogsleds onto the frozen lake, to engage in their wintertime task of ice fishing.

Scaling the ancient seawall, next to which many of the shanties stood, he spotted the object of his search, the Foleys' cottage. Although showing no signs of life, there appeared to be fresh tracks in the snow outside its door. Careful not to be seen, he made a wide arc around the back of the shack. Edging his ear close to the front shutter, he failed to hear any noise; and after peering through one of the slats, he was confident there was no one inside.

Raising his Colt, he kicked in the door, only to be met by the crystallized stare of Doc Foley, as he sat frozen stiff on a wooden chair. A tidy hole at the center of his forehead bore witness to the cause of his demise. Yet he did not die alone, for within feet, his nattily clad brother, Mike, lay face down in a iced-over pool of blood.

Despite knowing the extent to which the brothers were immersed in lives of crime and violence, their sudden dispatch came as a thunderous shock to the veteran detective. Given the breadth of their villainous footprint, their deaths would have a monumental impact on the city's criminal landscape. Yet the apparent ease to which they met their fates seemed to defy his sense of logic. Men like this did not go quietly, especially in the case of Doc, unbound and looking quite relaxed. A quick check of their pockets produced thick wads of cash, eliminating the possibility of robbery.

Already, Danny's mind was racing as he began to survey the crime scene. His initial suspicion that Fingers may have finally exacted his revenge, seemed to be born out when he spotted Harpoon Marley's regimental cap dangling from a nearby hook. Lending credence to the possibility of Carnahan's involvement, was the presence of surplus army rifles stacked neatly in a corner. Perhaps the guns were intended for the Foley's rumored move against their former boss. Such plans would not likely have escaped the attention of the crime lord, who in response, may have launched a preemptive strike. Yet the lack of signs pointing to a struggle raised doubts. Surely, the appearance of Carnahan's men would have resulted in a far more chaotic death scene.

Slowly picking his way through the ramshackle cottage, so as not to disturb any evidence, his eyes caught sight of a small bottle sitting atop a nearby shelf. It appeared empty, save for the remnants of dried liquid coating its walls; and after raising the flask to his nose, Danny detected the unmistakable odor of blood. Immediately, he realized that this could be the source of bloodstains used to frame Marley for the Van Cleff murders.

Convinced he was surrounded by a mother lode of evidence, he resumed his search with increased fervor. He rushed over to a broken-down desk leaning against the wall, excited by the prospect of what lay inside. His hope bore fruit when upon pulling open the drawer, he discovered a pair of metal boxes. Wasting no time, he used his switchblade to pop open the first container, revealing a stack of bills stuffed into an envelope. An accompanying letter was addressed to the "Artful Dodgers." It contained a list of transactions along with a compilation of "funds owed for services rendered;" furthermore, it bore the signature of "Fagin," and no doubt represented the Foleys' share of revenues accrued from Van Cleff's efforts to fence stolen jewelry.

Danny quickly moved on to the other box which likewise surrendered its contents to the twist of his knife. Inside was a collection of gleaming baubles. Upon lifting out the most prominent piece, a gold necklace holding an opal pendant, his blood ran cold as he read the inscription, "To Mistress Bonnie, from your piece of dirt slave, A.P." The detective immediately realized that the piece must have been taken from Bonnie's neck on the night of her murder.

Knowing Bonnie's professional proclivities and the make up of her clientele, along with having witnessed the wallpaper tycoon's dissolute actions the night before, Danny was certain that "A.P." was none other than Alfred Prescott. In light of this revelation, he now wondered if Prescott was linked to the Van Cleff murders.

Suddenly, a slew of questions began to rush through his thoughts. Given the potential for scandal, was blackmail involved? Did Prescott somehow secure the services of such notorious gangster as the Foleys, who knew the victims, in this case the blackmailers? Did the killers in turn have to be silenced? Yet how does an esteemed businessman come to associate with the murderous likes of Doc and Mike? Just then he remembered last night's incident with Pig Eye Muldoon, and the answer became embarrassingly clear: When it came to abject self-interest, the powerful always find a way. As such, the detective's reckoning with his former boss, planned later for that day, would now include the matter of Bonnie Crane.

Danny's mind was racing as he continued with his quest. Forcing his way through a door that led into the back room, he was buffeted by the sight of a miniature warehouse crammed with all manner of industrial supplies and equipment. It seemed obvious that this was some of the booty stolen by the theft ring. Cutting a path through the piles of boxes, he came upon one containing a set of expensive gauges and clearly marked with the delivery address of Prescott Wallpaper. Besides recognizing the potential worth of the cache, he was struck by the irony behind this particular piece. He also wondered if this was how the brothers planned to finance their grand entrance onto the criminal center stage.

After finishing a thorough search of the crime scene, the detective repaired to the tiny kitchen. Hoping to find a moment to relax amid all the murderous chaos and corresponding questions, his eyes settled upon a box of cigars sitting atop a nearby table. Its cover was emblazed with the gilded crest, *"Santiago Cigarros de la Habana."* As he reached over to retrieve a welcome tobacco prize, he assumed the box was part of Van Cleff's order from Mister Mathias; however, slapped onto the inside lid was a label announcing "Compliments of Prescott Wallpaper." This newest discovery seemed to explain the source of the cigar in Doc's pocket the night of their fight, in addition to providing a tangible link between the gangster and Prescott.

While still wrestling with all the crime scene repercussions, Brick Fist sat back to enjoy the smoke. Yet he still had to address one more matter before heading back to the precinct to report on the murders. Stepping out into the blustery cold, he started to survey the grounds outside the cottage. Just then, his eyes seized on a spot near the door, where the snow was packed down under a hodgepodge of footprints. It looked as if someone had been biding their time before entering the shanty.

After nearly stumbling over a snow-covered pile of refuse left by one of the storm surges that plagued the area, he looked down and noticed a shimmering object caught in a shrub beneath the window. After snatching up and stretching out the crumpled piece of foil, he was able to make out an emblem embossed onto its surface. For a moment he stared down, studying the golden wrapper. Suddenly, his head shot up in a flash of insight. Tossing aside the half-spent cigar, he rushed back towards the mainland.

XXV

As the shoeshine boy snapped a tattered rag across the tip of his boot, Danny kept a watchful eye on the building across the street. By now, hordes of office workers, shoppers and store clerks were streaming up and down Main Street, anxious to escape the cold and make their way back home.

Continuing his surveillance of Prescott's store, he managed to scribble out a note before stuffing it into one of the envelopes he kept in his coat pocket. Already, he was growing impatient, waiting for the workers to close up shop, so he could confront Prescott, alone in his office at the rear of the store. In an effort to relieve the tension, he pulled out a cigar; however, he soon found himself fumbling for a light. Spotting a street urchin who was working the crowd with her bootblack brother, he called over, "Peggy, sweetheart, I'll be needin' some of them matches you're sellin'."

Dressed in a moth-eaten coat and plodding along in over-sized boots stuffed with paper and rags, she cut a heartrending figure. Yet the newsboy cap covered over with a greasy shawl could not obscure her lively eyes and darling smile. "Mister Brick Fist, I'll give ya five for a penny or ten for two cents," the six-year-old mischievously giggled.

"How could I pass up a deal for ten," He smiled as he bent down and handed her two bits.

She briefly hesitated before piping up, "Ya must notta heard me right, Sergeant Danny. It was only two cents."

"Ah, what an honest angel! Not enough folks like you out here, so keep the reward."

With her dimples spreading almost as wide as her eyes, she quickly thanked him before plunging into her threadbare sack and slowly counting out his purchase.

For the moment, his attention to the job at hand had wavered. Instead, he wanted to sweep up the charming little bundle, take her home, and raise her as his own. It wasn't just that his heart broke at her pitiful circumstances—an all-too familiar tale of a father killed in an industrial accident, leaving behind a wife and house-load of kids; but it was also her uncanny resemblance to his precious Annie, that aroused his paternal feelings. Still, he knew nothing could replace the love of a family, no matter how desperate their circumstances. After lifting his foot from her brother's shoeshine box, he knelt down and whispered, "How's your ma, Eva, doin'?"

In an instant, her eyes began to well as she stammered, "Sh... sh... she's still in bed, but Missus Carroll, the herb lady, says she's doin' a little better."

"Them kinda problems take time, Peg. But to make your ma feel better, here's a few greenbacks. Now, you and Johnny go down to Mister Sawyer's grocery and get the makin's of a fine meal. Then use the rest to give to Doc Skelton to see your ma."

As she grabbed the money with her skinny little fingers, she let out a happy squeal and engulfed him in a hug. Yet remembering the incident with the child last night, and the recent snatching of a street flower girl, he added, before letting her go, "Now ya may have heard, there's some evil ladies out there grabbing little girls to do bad things. So don't let nobody lure ya away, and if they try, start screamin' my name and yelling they're in big trouble. Ya got that," he smiled, hiding the fact he'd tear apart anyone who even thought of hurting her.

"On me word, Danny," she promised as she clutched the bills against her chest before cautiously looking about and stuffing them into her pocket.

Returning to her brother, he declared, "That's a real good job, Johnny! With them shiny boots, I could march right into the Mayor's office like one of them bigwigs! But before ya go headin' home with your sis, I want ya to take this envelope down to the precinct for Officer Costello. Now it's very important, so don't go losin' it or tryin' to peek inside."

As a member of Brick Fist's brigade of street hawker, messenger boys, Johnny O'Toole was more than willing to take on the task, especially in light of his friend's generosity when it came to tips.

After paying the boy and watching the pair scamper off, basking in the glow of their bonanza, he went back to his job. Taking up a spot removed from the light of a nearby street lamp, he resumed his solitary vigil.

Despite the torrent of people rushing about him, he felt isolated and removed from their world. It was a feeling that had become all too familiar over the years. Perhaps operating for so long within the fringes of society, where corruption, brutality and exploitation were so common, had left him disconnected, oftentimes unable to relate to the normal flow of life. Yet it also made him impervious, and an effective tool of the law.

As he continued to train his eyes on the target, he caught sight of the newly installed telephone lines leading into Prescott's office. Such groundbreaking innovations represented the power and influence that the tycoon could command as one of the industrial giants of the city. Suddenly, he was confronted with the daunting prospect of bringing such a man to justice. Moments passed as he cautiously waited for his opening. Yet just as he was feeling overwhelmed by the challenge of his quest, he was engulfed by a sense of comforting warmth. Soon memories of Frannie began to fill his thoughts, and he could once more feel the strength and inspiration of sharing her love. Just then, he noticed the store lights dimming while a throng of workers came filing out the door. A moment later, he spotted Liam Riley driving a new buggy out from the alley next to the building. Wasting no time, he hurried across the street, dodging traffic while trying to keep Prescott's office window clearly in view. Confident that all the employees were gone, he made his way to the rear entrance; however, once inside, he ran straight into the old gatekeeper from the plant, Mister Krueger, standing sentry behind a desk at the base of the stairs. "Oh... ah... Sergeant Doyle, I'm sorry but the shop's closed and Mister Prescott will be leaving in a minute."

Poised to confront his nemesis and unwilling to tolerate any interference to his plans, the detective brushed him aside, "This is police business, so get outta my way and leave!"

When the pensioned soldier made a sheepish, yet misguided attempt to block his path, Brick Fist fumed as he thrust a finger into his chest, "Don't even think it! I'll be slappin' the cuffs on ya if ya don't get goin'!" The old man quickly hobbled out the door.

Flying up the stairs and bursting through the door, he was met by Prescott, who shot up from his desk and screamed, "What's the meaning of this, you Irish thug!"

Ignoring his call, Danny rushed forward and sent the tycoon flying back into his chair. Spinning it around, he leaned down to within inches of the frightened man's face and snarled, "Police business, Mister Prescott."

"I'll have your job for this," he raged.

As Brick Fist pushed aside some papers and sat his bottom squarely on the desk, he smiled, "Well, it ain't gonna be Collins doin' it. He'll be testifyin' against you for trappin' the workers in the plant the night of the fire." As a look of shock replaced Prescott's usual air of superiority, the detective continued, "I got good evidence and testimony from a number of sources about how ya locked 'em in."

"I... I... I had a right to keep out those union criminals who were threatening my business," he stammered. "And no court in the land would disagree."

"And what about bribin' public officials, includin' buildin' inspectors," Danny shot back, almost tempted to reveal Keogh's admissions.

"That doesn't matter," Prescott replied as he regained some of the confidence that had deserted him, "Anyone with an ounce of sense got out. As for the half-wits who didn't, they'd probably succumb to drink or end up at the end of a rope someday. Besides, they were stealing me blind. I have a right to protect my property. I would have shot them, if I could've caught them. Anyway, who cares? They have no respect for life."

Enraged at his callous attitude and glib dismissal of the horrors of that night, Danny let loose a vicious slap that sent the tycoon's head snapping backwards. "Those were my people and mostly children to boot, ya heartless bastard!" As he summoned all his strength to keep from unleashing a hail of blows, his thoughts turned to other children; little Henry, Mary and Annie; and memories of their alabaster bodies lying atop his kitchen table. Returning to the moment, the detective barked, "And don't go playin' the tough fella with me. Ya hire somebody else to do your dirty deeds, so ya can keep your prissy hands clean; like ya did with the Foleys, in order to take care of Van Cleff who was blackmailin' ya. And just for the record, it was them who was stealin' your precious supplies, and not the workers. I know that for a fact."

"Van Cleff, I barely knew him from card games I attended; and as for the Foleys, what would I be doing with that scum after they robbed and assaulted my wife?"

"Cause your wife's fuckin' Fingers Carnahan and the brothers want to topple 'im. It's a perfect match of motives; so that little stageplay involvin' Harpoon Marley didn't fool me."

"Fingers can have her, now. I wouldn't soil my hand with any of that Iri... er, criminal trash."

"But ya didn't mind dealin' with the likes of Pig Eye Muldoon, last night, ya dirty little pervert." Recognizing the box of cigars on Prescott's desk, he added, "I suppose ya gave Pig Eye some stogies like ya did with the Foleys; but I ain't so dumb as to not know that ya got somebody helpin' ya to arrange things with these fine citizens; and once I'm finished with you, I'll be payin' a visit to that one."

By now, a bright stream of blood was trickling from the tycoon's swollen nose. Although reeling not only from Danny's violent tactics but from his revelations, the tycoon managed to compose himself before asking, "Do you mind if I tend to this wound?"

No sooner had the detective nodded his approval and leaned over to grab a cigar than Prescott reached into his coat pocket and pulled out a nickel-plated derringer. Finding refuge at the far end of the desk, he tried to steady his hand as he pointed the weapon at Doyle. "Back to the natural order of things" he smirked. "Superiority always triumphs.

"Superior to what," Danny laughed. "All I can see is a sniveling little slave who gives necklaces to his mistress so she can beat and piss on him or whatever."

As beads of sweat began to slide down his back, Prescott tried to look calm. "Apparently you're more effective than I thought; but you'll be taking that to the grave with you. Let's see, corrupt copper squeezing an esteemed businessman, who is forced to defend himself. The authorities and public will understand."

"Ya ain't got the guts, ya sissy!" Although poised to jump, Danny gambled, hoping to increase the pressure.

While still trying to subdue his nerves, the tycoon was unable to resist the urge to crow, "I'm sure that blackmailing sodomite thought the same before the Foleys had their little talk."

"It's a lot different when ya gotta pull the trigger yourself," Brick Fist sneered as he watched a tic torment Prescott's face. Inching his way forward, the policeman slowly slid his hand towards the gun in his holster.

Panicking in the face of Brick Fist's challenge, Prescott struggled to take aim but was distracted by the sound of creaking floorboards coming from the hallway.

The resonating blasts of gunfire amplified by the narrow confines of the room, were followed by an eerie quiet as smoke billowed beneath the gaslight fixture. An incredulous, if not indignant look crossed Prescott's face before he crashed headfirst onto his desk, sending its contents cascading to the floor.

At the same time, Danny felt a hammer-blow to his arm, which brought him to his knees. Without turning, and after pushing aside a fractured model of Prescott's beloved yacht, the "Triumph," he gritted his teeth and barked, "Ya killed the Foleys, didn't ya!"

After walking over and pulling the Colt from the stricken detective's holster, the gunman, smiled, "Is that any way to greet the man who just shot the fella who wanted to kill you?"

"Ya mean the murderin' scum who assassinated his partners after lettin' 'em kill his girlfriend who he liked givin' fancy candy to? Eh, Mister Lover Boy."

"Scum? After ridding the world of the Foleys? Please! And no, Bonnie wasn't part of the plan. She wasn't supposed to be there, but the Foleys just had to satisfy their bloodlust. That's one of the reasons they had to go; along with their being stupid and a certainty for eventually being caught. But most of all, they were threatening to blackmail me."

"I'm sure poor Miss Crane rests in peace knowin' she wasn't part of the plan."

"Let's not dwell on those sad things. Instead let me compliment you on a job well done; but I'm curious, how did you link me to all of this?"

Knowing his captor had no intention of letting him live, he was loath to divulge anything; nonetheless, he realized the killer wanted to cover his tracks, so in an effort to buy time, he was willing to throw out some bait. "A lottta things, but the fancy candy wrapper outside Foleys' place nailed it."

"Ah, betrayed by a sweet tooth, how ironic."

Trying to rally his strength as the blood kept flowing from his wound, Danny leaned against the desk and asked, "And what about you, Riley? I saw ya leave here."

"Would you believe that gimpy old fool, Krueger, managed to hop up to where I parked the buggy. Fortunately, I was in the middle of trying to seduce that beautiful flower girl over on the next corner, but don't worry, I plan to be fucking her later on. Anyway, I told him I'd take care of it and sent him home. It was too good to be true," he beamed before going on. "I was pretty sure you had Prescott figured out, and I knew he'd fuck it up. You know, for being a big gun, he was an idiot. I had to show him everything, whether it be fixing him up with Bonnie and her friends, arranging for the Foleys to take care of business with Van Cleff—he was an evil little nancy, you know—or even buying off the building inspectors."

Seeing that Riley was on a roll patting himself on the back, Danny interrupted, "And I figured you musta come up with the plan to pin Van Cleff on Harpoon and Fingers. Doc and Mike didn't have the brains and Prescott wanted others to do his dirty work."

"Indeed, but actually Alfie-boy, or 'Dirt,' as Bonnie used to call him, was as dumb as the Foleys; and even though he couldn't deliver the bacon and was brutal to his young wife—imagine wasting a luscious piece of ass like Rebecca—anyway, he was obsessed with getting even with Fingers for making him look bad. Also, he wanted to make things worse for Rebecca. So his ever-resourceful assistant, yours truly, designed the scheme. I'm amazed you got it right; but as I was saying before, you got Alfie on the fire, didn't ya." Somehow attempting to assuage his guilt, he added, "You know of course, I didn't have anything to do with that. That dimwit over there was obsessed with the union. He wouldn't take my advice that you could deal with the leaders more effectively by buying them off. Anyway, it was all Collins' plan to bully them, and lock things up. That certainly worked well."

Realizing he had to move fast as his strength was beginning to fade, Danny scanned the immediate terrain, trying to figure out his next move. Hoping to antagonize his captor and create an opening, he scoffed, "Who are you tryin' to shit, Riley! It was them barrels of varnishes and such that you were hidin' in the back before stealin' 'em, that sent the place up like fireworks!"

"Just bad luck, Sergeant. Still, we made a fortune on that industrial theft ring," Riley crowed, unable to contain his ego. "I used all my contacts in the trade to fence the goods at nice prices. See, the Foleys did prove useful after all! Imagine, me and them. Funny how strange bedfellows can link up when traveling along the underbelly of life. But listen, speaking of luck, Miss Prescott and I are secretly engaged," he reported as his eyes lit up. "I thought my position with Prescott and my revenues from the ring were a windfall, but now that poor Miss Vicky is an orphan, I'm really sitting pretty. That's why the Foleys' debacle at Van Cleff's boils my ass. Bonnie would have been the perfect mistress after I'd marry that cow, Victoria. Yet such is the price of marrying into money," he smiled. "That's why this is so perfect. Despite his reliance on me, Prescott would never have let an Irishman marry his daughter." After pausing a moment to chew on the thought, he hissed, "I've always been paying for those godforsaken people!" Returning to a more genial mood, he beamed, "But that's all changed, now that I killed that useless dolt. I'm gonna be on the top rung. Still, just to make sure everything goes smoothly, tell me what you have as evidence and who you've been sharing your findings with. If you do, I'll go get help, but unfortunately, I will have to testify that you shot Mister Prescott."

Feeling light-headed, Danny still managed to blurt out, "Go fuck yourself, ya ball-lickin' upstart. You'll be getting' yours."

"Not by you! Of course, I wasn't going to save you. Besides, nobody's going to touch me no matter what you've got. Who are they going to believe, the hero who shot a corrupt copper, squeezing an admired businessman who was valiantly trying to resist; or the lies of a dead thug who'd been trying to set things up; fat chance, on getting me, Danny."

"Watch and see, but first suck my cock, Liam."

Pulling out his revolver and bending down face-to-face with the barely breathing detective, Riley whispered, "Still a crude, sarcastic bastard right to the end, eh, Doyle? Too bad, just when you were beginning to enjoy Keena's luscious fruits; but don't worry, once things settle down, I just might go back and start slipp—" Riley's boast was cut short by a blood-curdling scream as Danny plunged a nearby pen into his eye.

As the sound of gunfire filled the air, his eyes began to lose focus. Yet as the pain that racked his body was replaced by a soothing warmth, the scene before him became clearer. Soon, he was able to make out figures emerging from the sun-lit meadow beside the house.

Fresh as spring and wearing the crisp white dress she wore the night they met, her eyes danced with love and excitement as she came closer.

Laughing and chirping as they skipped behind her—the little girls' ribbon-tied curls bouncing up and down, while the little boy's yelps filled the air—the children finally scampered forward, squealing with delight as they recognized their da.

Casting a reassuring smile, she knelt down and cradled his face before drawing the children to his side. With his heart bursting with joy, he wrapped them in his arms and cried, "Henry! Mary! Little Annie! Frannie, my sweet, darlin' girl…"

XXVI

As the sun-drenched day began to draw to a close, even the notorious Infected District had a fresh feel to its air. Everything was teeming with life and although the calendar read mid-March, the weather was more in line with a June afternoon. As such, the summer-like temperatures of the past few days were a welcome relief to the city's winter-weary residents.

Business around the harbor was beginning to awaken after the long, arctic slumber. Supply wagons were already restocking warehouse ship's-stores in anticipation of an early break up of the Great Lakes' ice. At a dry dock along the harbor, shipwrights had stripped to their union-suit tops, while they caulked a weather-beaten hull in preparation for the upcoming season. Even as some early revelers were descending onto the grimy network of canalside streets, there seemed to be a collective bounce to their steps, as if in celebration of the arrival of spring.

For the pensive young man huddled in a corner next to the Avalon Billiard Parlor, there was no such cheery air, just a steely determination to address the matter before him. On the other hand, the well-dressed figure marching up Commercial Street was awash with confidence and dash, certain in the knowledge that he could put this last nettlesome distraction to rest. It wasn't always this way. Seven weeks ago, he was stretched out in a hospital bed nursing an infection from the loss of his eye. Yet, his recovery was hastened as news spread of his swift and courageous action in foiling the criminal who murdered his boss. Now hailed as a hero, Lee Riley wore his eye patch as a badge of distinction. More importantly, it added a swagger to his step, since he soon discovered the buccaneer emblem was a useful tool in seducing women.

It seemed nothing could stand in the way of his ascent to the upper reaches of the American Dream. He was now President and General Manager of Prescott Wallpaper, thanks in part to his yeoman efforts after the fire, and his recent notoriety; nonetheless, it was mostly due to the insistence of his betrothed, Victoria Prescott, the chief stockholder in her late father's company. Shading his eye as he searched for his objective, he finally found success upon seeing an old man fiddling with his pool cue outside the building.

As he approached the appointed rendezvous site near the corner of Canal Street and Maiden Lane, he went over one last review of his plan. Having become quite adept at this sort of situation, he showed no hesitation in following the man with a satchel into the alley beside the pool hall.

As they proceeded down the dank corridor, Riley was tempted to dispatch his host and leave it at that; but curiosity and a healthy measure of caution prevailed as he abandoned the thought and continued on. Their meeting place at the rear of the alley was obscured by a keg-shack jutting out from the side of the tavern next door. But just before they settled in behind the little shed, the young man with the satchel cast a nervous look towards a carriage that had pulled up across from the alley entrance. Satisfied all was safe and in order, he gave a quick nod to his guest before announcing, "I got the stuff I wrote you about."

"Ah, I should have known, the lawyer's kid who worked with Doyle. You look like your ol' man, who I know from Blinky's," Riley fawned, trying to foster a genial, if not unguarded air. "He's a good fella," he added, while failing to mention his disdain for a man he viewed as a dreamy-eyed fool who wasted his time defending the neighborhood rabble.

For his part, Hugh Costello was having difficulty restraining the slight quiver to his hand, resulting from the knowledge of what was at stake. It had been weeks since Danny was killed, yet he steadfastly refused to accept the official determination of what happened that night. He was quick to dismiss Riley's story that after being flagged down by the security guard, he rushed back to the office just in time to witness Danny shoot the helpless Prescott. In the ensuing struggle, the loyal assistant lost an eye before managing to kill the corrupt policeman.

Knowing his friend, Hugh was certain that Danny would never shoot a man in cold blood; nor was there any chance that Riley could prevail in a fight with Brick Fist Doyle. In addition, having heard Danny's take on the crimes in question, and being familiar with all the evidence, Costello was convinced that Riley's version of events was a self-serving fable designed to mask his own guilt. Most of all, he had Danny's last message, that outlined Riley's role in the crimes.

While newspapers were quick to proclaim Riley a hero, and despite being in the throes of grief over his friend's death, the young patrolman lost little time in badgering his superiors to allow him to take his case to the District Attorney. Once granted permission, he proceeded to describe Danny's findings in regards to the fire, the theft ring and the Van Cleff murders. He then carefully reviewed the evidence gathered, such as Bonnie's notebook, the survivors' testimony about the barrels in the third floor store room, and Collins' letter in regards to locking the factory doors. Finally, after going over what was discovered at the Foleys' murder site, including the candy wrapper found outside the door, he revealed the contents of Danny's last message.

Despite conceding that more needed to be done, the young patrolman was unprepared for the response he received. After stating that in light of Prescott's death, the matter of the fire was now moot, the prosecutor rejected the theories linking Riley to the crimes; nor was he willing to assign him any guilt in regards to Danny's death. Citing insufficient evidence, he declared the case closed and ordered Hugh to refrain from any further investigation.

Costello walked away convinced that Prescott's family and friends had the power and influence to see that the matter was quietly put to rest; nonetheless, he remained steadfast. It was this unwillingness to accept the verdict on his friend that brought him here, to this unpredictable situation.

Continuing on with his attempts to parry and probe, the budding tycoon asked, "So why would this nice lawyer's son and partner of Danny Doyle be so accommodating to me?"

"Because I need to feather my nest. I've had enough of all this stuff and I want out."

"Ah, a man not unlike myself, who knows the value of things." Although conceding that he may have misjudged the youngster, and while feeling a new, if begrudging respect for a possible kindred spirit, he remained cautious. "So what do you have, Officer Costello?"

"I've got all sorts of criminal evidence about fires, theft rings and murders and such in this bag, here."

"The grand jury exonerated me on everything, and I'm sure you showed the District Attorney all that you had."

"Maybe I did or maybe I didn't; but do you want to take the chance? By the way, this wrapper you left outside Foley's hideout is for the same type of French candy you kept at your desk and gave to Bonnie. I must add that it tasted good. Which reminds me, you wouldn't want this material, including Miss Crane's diary making its way to your fiancé, would ya, Mister Loverboy?" Although not one to lie, Hugh felt no such constraints in delivering the made-up tale of Bonnie's diary.

"How untidy of me," he mused as he took a candy from his coat and popped it into his mouth. "But not this time." After taking a moment to fashion an object from the shiny wrapper, he slid it into his breast pocket. "Looks like a boutonniere, doesn't it," he smiled before returning to a serious tone. "So, I believe you mentioned five hundred dollars in your letter?"

"No, a thousand; after all, you're a bigwig, now."

"And I have every intention to keep it that way," he said, as he made a move for the pocket inside his jacket; however, rather than retrieving a wad of bills, he came out with a pearl-handled derringer. "I know a little bit about blackmailers. After all, I showed Prescott how to take care of that blackmailing little nancy, Van Cleff. And then of course, there were the Foleys, threatening to play that card. Now, toss that bag over to me and raise your arms."

Hugh somehow managed to keep his cool while doing as he was told.

"Now, what should I do with this deluded friend of the criminal Doyle, who was seeking his revenge?" Riley asked while feigning a sense of indecision; however, regaining his verve, he was quick to boast, "Although you killed once, take my word, it's much easier the second time around; or is it the third or fourth? I lost count!" he laughed devilishly. "The best one was that arrogant stooge, Prescott. You should've seen the look on his face when I fired away. Anyway, I'm sorry, but ..." he sighed as he began to raise his arm.

"Wait! Please! I've got something more to say," Hugh pleaded, before his captor stopped and lowered his weapon. "I'm sorry for misleading you like this. It's probably a sin even though I prayed."

A confused yet irritated look crossed Riley's face, before preparing to once more take aim. Just then, a dark figure burst through the door of the keg-room, and slapped a cord around the murderer's neck. As Carnahan twisted the knot tighter, Riley dropped the gun as he vainly tried to pull off the noose. "This is for Georgie, ya bastard," the crime lord thundered as his victim fell to his knees.

Horrified as he watched Riley's eye bulge out and his gasping mouth emit a deathly rattle, Hugh leapt forward and screamed, "You're killin' 'im; that ain't the plan!"

Loosening his hold, Fingers shot back, "Are ya daft, lad! Doyle was your friend and those blue blood bastards ain't gonna let this case be exposed and go to trial!"

"Danny was a lawman and we ain't gonna be vigilantes!"

As Costello made a move to approach, the crime lord shoved him back with a force that sent him backpedalling on his heels.

Rallying his senses, the emancipated Riley moved quickly to seize the opportunity. As he watched the unfolding confrontation, he carefully slid his hand toward the extra gun tucked inside his belt. Before Fingers could turn back towards him, the former captive was already leveling his weapon. He was about to cock the hammer when a deafening blast echoed throughout the narrow confines of the alley.

Having slipped out of the shed where she had been hiding, Keena stood holding the smoking derringer that Riley had dropped moments before. She began to violently shake as plumes of blood started to gush out from the gaping hole in the center of her former boyfriend's chest.

As Carnahan stood over the stricken killer, Hugh rushed to Keena's side, shielding her eyes and pulling her inside. By now, a couple of henchmen who Fingers had stationed in his carriage on Canal Street came running toward the source of the gunfire. The larger of the two, Bobby, "Heels" Barry, his nickname reflecting a penchant for using the boot to collect on debts, was quick to join his boss at the wounded man's side.

Unfortunately for Riley, any question of assistance proved pointless, as Fingers turned and pronounced him dead. Keena was already awash in tears and racked with sobbing as Costello held her in his arms and tried to offer words of comfort.

Not one to embrace sentimentality, Carnahan wasted no time in dealing with the situation at hand. "Take 'im inside, boys. You know what to do."

"Leave 'im right there, fellas," Costello fired back. "Ya ain't gonna go flushin' 'im down the chute, makin' it look like a Shanghai! This is a police scene"

"Oh, so now ya want this innocent girl to be answerin' for this! Weren't ya listenin' before. Those folks who run things around here and who didn't want things dredged up, ain't gonna take kindly to this turn of events."

"I'll say I shot 'im," Costello was quick to answer.

"Don't be ridiculous! You'll sing like a canary once they start squeezin' ya. This is my bailiwick and I'll be callin' the shots! I'm not gonna be dragged into this; and for what?"

"For the law! Danny worked for that, and I'm gonna make sure things go that way," Hugh yelled back, as he opened his coat, exposing his pistol.

"I like ya, Hugh, but don't go playin' the copper with me on this!"

"Stop it," Keena screamed as she pulled away from Costello. "Hugh's right, so you'll have to kill me too, Major! Despite his crimes, Liam was a child of God, deservin' of respect and not to be dumped off like trash. Everyone knows I once loved 'im, but I'll stand by my actions tonight! Besides, people need to know the truth about what was behind the fire that took those innocent children; and we got to clear Danny's name and show how he fought to bring justice to the boys and Miss Crane, and even to those criminals who died at Liam's hand."

"I see it isn't going to do me any good trying to take you on, Miss Shea," Fingers conceded, while shaking his head. "So, I guess you're in charge, here, Officer Costello. Georgie's avenged, and I'm finally done with all this business." Turning towards Keena, the retiring crime boss added, "You're a good woman, Miss Shea. Sergeant Doyle was a lucky man to know you; and I want you to know that I always thought that Danny was a good fella. Despite some of his shortcomings, he was a man deserving of respect."

Unwilling to stand by for the arrival of the inevitable bevy of investigators, Fingers bid his farewells; but before leading his men into his bar next door, he reminded Keena of his carriage waiting on the street. For Keena, it was a welcome retreat from the horrors of the moment.

As Costello was about to escort his still trembling friend through the debris-strewn alley, Alfie Dwyer, the freight dispatcher, timidly poked his head around the corner; having finally roused the courage to see what happened. His presence was not by accident. After Dwyer had failed to point out any of the faces in the picnic photograph from Blinky's Tavern, Hugh decided to place him at the front of the pool hall, in the hope that he'd identify Riley as the mysterious partner of Doc Foley.

"Sweet Mother Mary," the little man squealed as he came upon the mayhem. "He's the fella who was followin' ya. What happened? He's dead!"

"He was about to shoot, but ended up gettin' the worst of it. But before I cover up his face with this handkerchief, take a close look and tell me if he's the fella we've been talking about?"

Cautiously edging over, he bent down and scrutinized the corpse. "I can't say for sure, but he looks a lot like that gent with Foley the night they took the wagons."

Taking notes, Hugh continued, "Now look again, Alfie, and see if you can be sure."

Shaking his head, the dispatcher declared, "He had his collar up and derby down low that night, and like I said, he looks a lot like 'im but I can't say for sure."

After thanking him, and allowing him to go next door for some barley relief, Hugh once more turned his attention towards Keena. Anxious to leave the bloody scene and await the arrival of the police from the refuge of the carriage, she grabbed his arm as he led the way. Both were lost in thought as they made their way to Canal Street. Yet no sooner had they climbed into the cabin than Hugh finally broke the silence. "I didn't have the chance to tell you at the funeral how sorry I was about Danny. I know how close you two had become. I also know that beneath his occasional bluster, he admired your work and ideals."

"Your words mean a lot, Hugh. I was blessed to finally recognize and discover a good and loving man. Our being together, no matter how brief, brought us both great joy; but I sensed that I only had a part of him and maybe only for a short time. He was always a husband and father, even though they were gone. And he was never really home anywhere else. That's why for so long he cut himself off from most everything, and lost himself in his work. I had a feeling he'd eventually seek that shelter again. But now, it all doesn't matter, because he's back at home with his Frannie and the kids."

For a moment, the policeman sat in silence, trying to capture his own feelings. "I still can't believe he's gone. Danny always seemed indestructible: like Samson in the Bible. And like the mighty warrior, his last act was bringing down the powerful and corrupt, and serving justice. Even though I only knew him for a short time, he had a great effect on me and I'll always miss him. I was going to leave the force and read the law, but now I think I'll stay and try to follow his spirit and serve the folks around here.

"He left me like that, too, Hugh. Just before that terrible night, he told me about an immigrant Polish girl from the streets...'

"I know. I was there that night at Covent Gardens when he saved her from Prescott."

"I was moved by Danny's paternal feelings and by the girl's story. So, I paid a visit to the convent where she was staying. Christina is so sweet. I fell so in love with her. After spending more time with her these last weeks and after reflecting on everything, her and I have decided that she will come live with me and I'll raise her as my child. It's a new and wonderful beginning for both of us, and a testimony to Danny's legacy."

After celebrating the news, and once more comforting her about the shooting, Hugh took care to reassure her about the police probe. He promised that before reporting to the station, he would stop at the office of her friend and lawyer, Tom Beahan, and send him down. After an emotional farewell, he climbed out of the carriage and made his way up Canal Street.

By now, the falling temperature had stirred a stiff breeze that lifted the candy-wrapper boutonniere from Riley's pocket and sent it over the fence and into the canal down below. As the shiny little object bobbed in the water beneath a nearby bridge, a couple of young bootblacks were seated on the rail, taking a break and enjoying the late afternoon sun. As the older of the two spotted Costello turning into an adjacent office, he piped up, "There's Danny's partner who's gonna take his place. He's supposed to be a good fella."

"We'll see. They say he was a crook, but Danny took care of all us workin' kids; and it's a damn shame he's dead."

"Yeah, and he was the toughest fella that ever was. He had fists as hard as bricks!"

"And was a good man, ta boot."

Special thanks to Patsy, Nancy, Murph, Mark, Paul, Isabelle, Jack and other friends for their help and support.

Made in the USA
Lexington, KY
07 January 2014